9-2021

K STREET KILLING

A WASHINGTON WHODUNIT

K STREET KILLING

COLLEEN J. SHOGAN

WHEELER PUBLISHING
A part of Gale, a Cengage Company

GALE
A Cengage Company

LIBRARY OF CONGRESS CIP DATA ON FILE.
CATALOGUING IN PUBLICATION FOR THIS BOOK
IS AVAILABLE FROM THE LIBRARY OF CONGRESS.

ISBN-13: 978-1-4328-8922-7 (softcover alk. paper)

Published in 2021 by arrangement with Camel Press, an imprint of Epicenter Press Inc.

Printed in Mexico
Print Number: 01   Print Year: 2021

ACKNOWLEDGMENTS

Thank you again to everyone who helps make these books possible, particularly my agent Dawn Dowdle, Phil Garrett and Jennifer McCord from Camel Press, and publicity liaison Annie Dwyer. Catherine Treadgold helped grow a mystery novel into the Washington Whodunit series. Special thanks to my family for their continued encouragement, including my husband, brother, sister-in-law, father, aunts, uncles, in-laws, nieces, and numerous cousins. My friends, colleagues at the Library of Congress, and fellow Sisters in Crime are great supporters of the series. A week doesn't go by that someone doesn't offer me a suggestion about how a victim should die in an upcoming Washington Whodunit mystery. Such enthusiasm, while undoubtedly a telling commentary on living in our nation's capital at this moment in time, does guarantee Kit

Marshall will be around for more adventures!

DEAR READER

"Truth is stranger than fiction, but it is because fiction is obliged to stick to possibilities; truth isn't." Mark Twain's quote seems appropriate for contemporary Washington. The line between fiction and real life politics has grown from blurry to indistinguishable. But in reality, Capitol Hill has always been delightfully theatrical. There's an endless supply of entertaining characters, each playing a pivotal role within the unfolding dramedy. As soon as one plot line resolves itself, another conflict presents itself. The action never stops, and the cast is always changing.

Lobbyists are a key part of the story. They provide information to Members of Congress and staff, arguing positions on behalf of opinionated companies, interest groups, concerned citizens, universities, towns and cities, and even the disadvantaged. Their job is singular in nature: to persuade policymakers into action. Money matters, but at the end of the day, personal relationships determine who gets access and when. Lobbyists often get a bad rap in the popular press, but their contributions are neither uniformly evil or virtuous. I decided Kit Marshall should tussle with the morally ambiguous, complex world of K Street in the fourth book of the Washington Whodunit series.

I also wanted to write about the unique pressures felt by a congressional office when its elected Member was engaged in a tight reelection race. As a staffer, I lived through a breathtaking Senate campaign in 2006. Tensions ran high and pressure mounted. Staff felt powerless in Washington as their boss fought a tough race back in the home state. Hill jobs are uniquely stressful because the employer can be fired every other year. In short, election season provides a perfect setting for murder. The combination of campaigns and lobbyists was too tantalizing to resist. I hope readers of the series agree.

CHAPTER ONE

"If I see Maeve Dixon listed one more time as a sponsor for that darn bill, someone isn't going to live to see tomorrow."

My voice echoed inside a corner office suite of the Cannon House Office Building. The staff, packed tighter inside our workplace than Metro commuters during rush hour, knew I meant business. After all, threatening bloody murder wasn't my preferred management style.

Representative Dixon's legislative director Meg Peters, who also doubled as my best friend, cleared her throat. As the head of our policy operation, she was responsible for Dixon's endorsement of pending bills.

"Kit, don't worry. I spoke to Congressman Russell's legislative assistant who's shepherding it through floor consideration tonight. He knows we need to remove Dixon's name as a supporter." Meg sighed deeply and added, "For political reasons."

Six frustrated pairs of eyes bored into me like lasers. Unfortunately, such an excuse had powerful cache these days inside the world of Congresswoman Maeve Dixon. As the chief of staff, I often had to tell our employees why they had to make sure our boss supported certain legislation while she ran away from others. It was a matter of political survival, and it was my job to make sure Maeve didn't suffer a long, painful death on election day.

In my most ebullient voice, I rallied our staff for what felt like the hundredth time this month. "Listen, team. I don't need to go through the drill again. We all need to remember who the enemy is here, right?"

Our press intern Brock Metcalf yelled, "Mack Hackensack!" He thrust his fist in the air for added emphasis.

"She was asking a rhetorical question," said Meg wryly.

Like all of us, Meg appreciated Brock's enthusiasm — to a point. We all had our limits, and Maeve Dixon's nail biter campaign had tested them. To add insult to injury, the election wasn't just around the corner. There were still six excruciating weeks to go before the first Tuesday in November. Rhetorical question or not, Brock was right on. *He-who-shall-not-be-*

named had a real name in our office, and it was Mack "Coach" Hackensack.

"It's worth repeating again. We need to keep our eyes on the prize." I pointed to a dark alcove of the office, where someone had hung a large poster depicting Maeve's congressional opponent with a photo-shopped Ghostbusters "no" symbol super-imposed over his face.

Mack Hackensack was not an attractive man, even on a good day. He looked like a cross between the Pillsbury doughboy and Billy Bob Thornton. In this particularly unflattering photo, he was sweating pro-fusely with his mouth wide open, ostensibly barking a command to an unfortunate underling. A beauty contest didn't matter to the people of North Carolina. Coach Hack-ensack would remain in their minds forever as the man who brought the NCAA men's basketball title to the state. Chapel Hill wasn't even in our district. That geographic factoid also made no difference. Devoted Tar Heel alums lived all over the precious state, including the seventh congressional district. We weren't running against a politi-cal opponent; we were running against a bona fide sports legend.

Brock, whose well-meaning devotion reminded me of a golden retriever puppy,

11

shouted, "Have you seen the latest campaign commercial he's running?"

"What's he doing now?" asked Meg feebly. Like me, Meg had been around Capitol Hill for several years. We'd worked for a United States senator who'd been murdered and knew how difficult it was to find a new job when the boss departed — electorally or permanently. If Maeve Dixon didn't rally against Mack Hackensack, once again we'd have to hustle to find new staff jobs. Privately, I was beginning to wonder whether continuing to run on the hamster wheel called Capitol Hill made sense. Close campaigns were hell, and our boss was trapped inside the inner circle of Dante's Inferno. Maeve's party controlled the House of Representatives, but if too many Democratic members lost their races, we'd lose the majority. That meant even fewer jobs might be available after the election. Would anyone want to hire a chief of staff who'd failed to get her boss reelected?

"Come over and watch," said Brock.

We squeezed around his computer as he pressed "play" on the YouTube video. The title of the video was "Personal Foul." Not a good start. I braced myself.

Mack Hackensack's face appeared on screen. Standing in the middle of a basketball court, he sported a UNC "Champions" polo shirt and wore a whistle around his beefy neck. An image of the American flag with an embroidered "USA" decorated his baseball hat. My politically astute brain churned. Without saying a word, the image conveyed "winner" and "patriot" in a single swoop.

But Coach didn't stay silent for long. "I've always played by the rules. Work hard, play hard. Those are my values. I'm not afraid of making the tough calls or staying late for practice." Then he walked toward center court, where the national championship trophy rested on a table.

He put his hand on the trophy before speaking again. "When my players do something wrong on the court, the referee calls a personal foul."

Then the camera shot tightened. "The voters of the seventh district in North Carolina are the referees. Watch closely how my opponent, Maeve Dixon, plays the game."

The image flashed to a still image of Maeve, standing in front of the Great Wall of China. His voice continued in the background. "While the people of North Carolina were struggling with the economic recession, where was Maeve Dixon? Traveling the world with her liberal colleagues."

The next photo showed our boss in front of Big Ben. She was smiling for the camera, her brown hair whipping in the wind. "You deserve better than being represented by a member of Congress who treats her job like a vacation," said the Coach.

"We shouldn't have tweeted out pictures from her trip to London," I muttered.

Meg put her hand on my arm. "It's not your fault, Kit. She was only there for a two-day parliamentary exchange program."

"Besides, she looks great in the photo," said Brock cheerfully.

Meg and I glared at our intern but said nothing.

The ad returned to Coach Hackensack next to the trophy. "Voters, there's only one smart choice." He pointed to the camera and blew his whistle. "Call a personal foul on Maeve Dixon. Elect me as your next Congressman!"

After putting my head in my hands, I could only manage two words. "Game over."

CHAPTER TWO

Despite the heartburn the latest Coach Hackensack ad had given us, there was no rest for the weary. Hill staffers involved in toss-up congressional races lived inside a perennial pressure cooker, but the last day of congressional session before the election doubled the heat. The Speaker of the House was understandably worried about maintaining the majority, so he abruptly halted legislating in the third week of September. The government had been funded — at least for another five months — and there was no need to keep sitting members of Congress caged inside the claustrophobic walls of the District of Columbia. During campaign season, politicians locked in tight races were restless tigers. They yearned for their natural habitat, where they could roam free and eat their prey. That meant sending every elected representative back to his or her district. Yes, partisanship reigned the day, but so did the roar of incumbency.

I was sitting at my desk, contemplating whether I could somehow persuade House leadership to promote a bill canceling college basketball season this fall. Out of sight, out of mind, right? Just as I was drafting bill language in my mind, Maeve Dixon's voice interrupted me.

"Kit, can you tell me when we're going to leave for the event this evening?"

My office was so tiny, there was barely room for me to swivel around. I almost knocked over my plastic cup of Dunkin' Donuts coffee, leftover hours earlier from breakfast.

Representative Maeve Dixon certainly didn't look like she was in a massive political fight. Her shoulder-length brown hair turned up slightly at the ends, the product of a professional blowout earlier this morning. Her trim, athletic figure was highlighted by a fitted black dress and a shapely blazer. A stylist silver chain necklace and small hoop earrings completed the professional look. Maeve was no Maxim model, but by Washington standards, she was damn attractive.

"Yes, absolutely. The event sheet is right on my desk here. One moment." I proceeded to rifle through a pile of papers. No luck. I moved onto the next mound. Still nothing.

"Having some trouble?" asked Maeve. I could tell by her voice she was slightly annoyed, but mostly amused.

"No, it's here. I read it earlier today. There's a lot going on today since the House is gaveling out tonight until after the election." I sighed in frustration.

"Perhaps you should use the upcoming congressional recess to devise a filing system."

"I'll make sure that's a priority." I grinned. "Right after defeating Mack Hackensack."

My boss laughed. "I suppose if we don't take care of Coach, there won't be any need for filing."

That wasn't a joking matter. "Actually, closing a congressional office is a real pain in the neck. I did it once in the Senate, and I don't plan on doing it anytime soon in the House."

"Don't worry, Kit. I don't plan on it, either."

After grabbing a piece of paper from the fourth stack, I said, "Eureka! I found it." I scanned the sheet and then clicked on an e-mail. "Here's the situation for tonight. Drinks and dinner at Charlie Palmer's, starting at six. But final votes are on for eight."

Maeve nodded. "Plenty of time."

"Absolutely. Remember, the Majority Leader and Chairman Edwards are hosting the event for you," I said.

"How could I forget? They remind me about it every time I see them." The Majority Leader was the second most powerful member of the House of Representatives, and Edwards ran the Transportation Committee.

"That's because tonight is the biggest fundraising evening in Washington, and they can only hit one or two select events. They both chose your campaign as a priority."

Maeve ran her fingers through her hair. "I know, I know. I should be grateful. I also feel after I win this election, I'm going to owe a lot of favors around here."

"That's how it works," I said.

"When will I ever get off this merry-go-round?" she asked.

I wasn't sure if she wanted an answer, but I offered one. "Once more voting Democrats move to your district."

While forcing a smile, she said wistfully, "In the meantime, the name of the game is raising money to fund the campaign. Lots of it."

As Maeve's chief of staff, I was allowed to liaise with my boss about her reelection. Even so, there were many restrictions preventing myself and others on staff from performing campaign duties as government employees. I often attended fundraisers with her and was privy to her donation record. Of course, I kept a separate iPhone for political matters. Becoming ambidextrous had been an unintended consequence of the close race. Oftentimes, I could be seen double-fisted walking down the hallway, and it had nothing to do with happy hour drinks.

"You've done well with K Street. Even some lobbyists who normally stick with Republicans opened their pocketbooks for you," I reminded her.

"God only knows what I'll have to do for them when this is all over," she muttered.

I really didn't have time for an existential conversation about whether our current campaign finance system made running for Congress worth the effort. The phone on my desk rang, and I glanced at the caller ID. Saved by the bell.

"It's my husband," I announced.

We'd been married almost four months, but I was still getting used to the "H" word. At least I didn't stammer anymore.

Maeve waved her hand. "Take it. But I'll

need a quick briefing before Charlie Palmer's."

I grabbed the receiver and silently mouthed, "Got it."

"Hey, I'm here," I said into the receiver.

"Kit, is that you?" asked Doug.

"Who else would be answering my phone? Last time I checked, I don't have an assistant."

"Good point. I wasn't sure. Do you answer all your phone calls like that?"

"Only the ones from my spouse."

"Hopefully that's just me." He chuckled briefly.

"I'm definitely not into polygamy. One husband is enough," I said.

"You seem grumpier than usual. Is something the matter?"

"Nothing's wrong, but this is the last day Congress is in session, and we have a big fundraiser scheduled for tonight. It's mayhem around here."

"So, it's business as usual." The disappointment in his voice was clearer than the springtime view from the top of the Washington Monument.

"Unfortunately. We didn't have plans this evening, right?"

"No, but I want to talk to you about something that's come up, and I thought maybe we could go out to dinner."

Shoot. It didn't matter I hadn't been to church in several years. The Catholic guilt came on strong. Maybe Doug could join us tonight.

"I could call our fundraiser and see if we could comp you at the event. Given all the extra time I've put in after hours, it's the least the Maeve Dixon campaign could do," I said.

"Nah." Doug sighed. "You'll be running around, catering to donors and making sure the Congresswoman has everything she needs. It's not the right time."

"Tomorrow? Because I'm likely to ship out to North Carolina to help on her campaign once I'm not needed here in the office."

"Are you really going to do that?" Doug didn't relish the prospect of being stuck at home alone with Clarence, our slightly overweight beagle mutt, for almost six weeks.

"Listen, if she doesn't win this race, there's no job for me to come home to, right?" Doug had lived in Washington, D.C. longer than me. He knew about the vicious revolving door on Capitol Hill. Now that I was a chief of staff, it would be harder to find a replacement job since I was at the top of the food chain. Besides wanting to avoid another job search, I also didn't want Maeve Dixon to lose. She had her flaws like anyone, but she was a damn good member of Congress. She deserved reelection, and I intended to make sure the voters of the seventh district of North Carolina knew it.

"Well, there's always me and Clarence here at home," said Doug.

"Of course, I didn't mean it that way." I rubbed my temples.

"I know. We can talk later. Just wanted to put it on your radar."

"Sounds like a plan. See you later tonight after it's all over."

"Good-bye, Kit. And watch out for those lobbyists at the fundraiser. That's a deadly crowd."

Doug, as always, was right on target.

CHAPTER THREE

The afternoon sped along as our entire staff banded together to support our boss. There were press releases to write, vote decisions to discuss, and last-minute negotiations on legislation to orchestrate. The craziness of the day aside, I tried to savor the moment. I stood inside the doorway of my tiny office and stared at the bustling office suite. Our D.C. staff finally functioned like a well-oiled machine. I'd only been in charge for six months, yet in that short time, the team had come together. We had a great member of Congress who called the shots, and I enjoyed a modest sense of satisfaction that I'd helped create a dynamo staff. If Maeve Dixon didn't win reelection, this would be the last time I'd see these folks in action. I seriously hoped North Carolina voters would give us another chance.

Meg must have noticed my pensive expression. "What's wrong with you?" she asked.

"You look like you just saw a ghost."

"Hopefully not. I'm just trying to remember what it all looks like in case . . ." My voice trailed off.

"In case what? There's no way Maeve Dixon is going to lose this election." Meg put her hands on her hips. "Especially after you convinced me to leave a stable committee job to come work for you." As if I needed another reason to worry about the election. I'd persuaded Meg to join Team Dixon earlier this year. My job wasn't the only one on the line.

I glanced at my watch. It was half past five, which meant we had to leave soon for the fundraiser. "Are you coming to Charlie Palmer's tonight for the fundraiser?"

"Of course. Dash is going to be there. I even bought a new dress. Didn't you notice?" Meg pointed to her floral printed sheath dress. "End of the summer sale at Lord and Taylor."

"You bought a new dress to attend Maeve's fundraiser tonight?" I don't know why I was surprised. My best friend needed no excuse to buy an outfit. I liked to think she was stylish enough for both of us. Since I became chief of staff, I'd tried to put more effort into my clothes. Today was a minor success. I wore one of my standard black suits, but I'd added a scarf, which I considered a major fashion victory.

"Not really for the fundraiser, Kit. Because I knew Dash was going to be there," Meg said coyly.

"You've been dating the guy for three months and you're still dressing to impress? This must be serious." At this point in most of Meg's relationships, she usually became antsy and looked for excuses to end it.

Meg smoothed her blonde bob. "It could be. After all, the *Washingtonian* did name him to the top Forty under Forty list."

"I'm aware," I said, trying to hide the exasperation in my voice. If I had a vote for every time I'd heard this tidbit about Dash Dugal, Maeve Dixon wouldn't need to attend tonight's dinner because she'd be crushing Coach Hackensack in fundraising.

"And he's devastatingly handsome," said Meg, giggling.

"Terrific. That's very important in a long-term relationship." I didn't bother to hide the sarcasm this time.

"Seriously, Kit. Since you got married, you're no fun. I'm joking, of course." Meg blinked her long eyelashes in a feigned attempt to appear as though her feelings had been hurt.

"Handsome or not, I'm glad he forked

over the money to attend the fundraiser," I said. "Can you find Maeve so we can head over there?"

"Sure thing." Meg took a few steps toward Dixon's office and turned around to finish our conversation. "I was kidding about what's important in a relationship, you know. I'm not a total idiot."

"Meg, I believe you."

"But I wasn't kidding about Dash. He is really hot," she said matter-of-factly.

I shook my head and smiled. Sometimes, conceding a point was much easier than the alternative. I went back inside my office and gathered the information about this evening's event. As the chief of staff, I was allowed to coordinate limited functions between the campaign and the congressional office. Of course, no campaigning could take place inside a House of Representatives office building, and our staff didn't raise money for Representative Dixon during regular work hours. I kept e-mails about donations and associated events separate from my congressional correspondence and only assisted with fundraisers when they took place in the morning before work or during evening hours. I wanted Maeve Dixon to win, but I wasn't going to break any ethics rules or laws along the way.

Thankfully, we had a resourceful Washington, D.C. associate who managed Maeve's fundraisers in town. We'd been lucky to land Clarissa Smythe, who'd helped run several successful House campaigns in previous election cycles. She had a winning track record and vowed to bring home the bacon. One of her specialties was the transportation industry, a perfect match for Maeve since she served on the relevant policy committee in the House. It had been Clarissa's idea to put together one last high dollar Washington fundraiser before Maeve returned to North Carolina for the remainder of the campaign. She kept track of the details, recruited generous donors, and put together the VIP guest list. It was my job to make sure Maeve showed up, prepared to schmooze.

Maeve emerged from her office with her game face on, both literally and figuratively. She'd freshened her makeup and added a finishing shine spray to her hair. A military veteran who'd seen her share of action in the Middle East, Maeve Dixon normally eschewed the heavily made-up look. In her late thirties, she was young enough to get away with a freshly scrubbed appearance. However, I'd noticed she carefully applied eyeliner, eyeshadow, mascara, and even lipstick before each fundraiser. Maeve Dixon wasn't letting anything fall to chance. Mack Hackensack might have a championship trophy under his belt, but our boss, who could double for Angie Harmon when she fixed herself up, knew what mattered to the K Street crowd. Soft on the eyes never hurt inside the Beltway.

"Time for a short run down on the attendees?" I asked.

"Sure. Let's catch a cab, and you can brief me on the way," she said.

"Meg, let's go. We're headed to the event," I called out.

Instead of Meg's voice, Brock answered. "Wait! I'm coming, too."

I raised my eyebrows, and Meg must have noticed. She tapped her phone and whispered, "He can take photos for the campaign website."

"Okay," I said under my breath. "Not sure why we need photos of lobbyists."

"Not them, silly," said Meg. "The rooftop has one of the best views of Washington, remember?"

Actually, I had no recollection because I'd never dined at Charlie Palmer's before. Unless a campaign fundraiser provided the reason, it was rare to see Capitol Hill staff there. The pricey meals and drinks didn't exactly mesh with the modest salaries of most government employees.

We exited the Cannon Building to the northeast and walked toward Independence Avenue to hail a taxi. "Can't say I'm familiar with Charlie Palmer's. Are you?" I asked.

"I've been there a few times," said Meg, smiling.

"Let me guess. With Dash?"

Meg blushed. "Perhaps."

Our boss's head was buried in her iPhone, impervious to our gentle banter. Like me, she'd switched to her campaign-issued device, which meant she was likely reading a last-minute e-mail from Clarissa about our likely guest list. I flagged down a taxi, who cut across two lanes of busy traffic to pick us up. Meg opened the door for Maeve, who got inside the car without moving her eyes from the iPhone screen. Walking without a stumble while simultaneously reading e-mails should be a prerequisite for Washington politicians.

Once we were inside the taxi, our boss seemed to take notice of our presence. "Who's going to brief me on this fundraiser? I got an e-mail with the names, but I'm not familiar with most of them."

This was my cue. I grabbed a cheat sheet out of my purse. "As you know, this is your last D.C. fundraiser before returning to North Carolina. There's not many attendees, but it's a high dollar affair. To kick the evening off, there will be drinks on the rooftop. Once everyone arrives, the Majority Leader will speak. Then Chairman Edwards will introduce you. After your remarks, we'll go inside for dinner."

Maeve wrinkled her nose. "Beef, I assume?"

"Most likely. It is a steakhouse, ma'am," I said. "I'm sure we can arrange for fish or a vegetarian meal."

"If I win this race, I'll be as big as Hackensack by the end," grumbled Maeve.

"Oh, that's not humanly possible, Congresswoman!" chimed in Brock.

Without acknowledging his comment, I plowed ahead. The restaurant was nearby so we didn't have much time. "The biggest name in the room tonight is Van Parker. Have you heard of him?"

Our boss nodded. "Who hasn't?"

"Right. The principal transportation lobbyist in Washington these days. He runs A-T-F."

"Sounds like Alcohol, Tobacco, and Firearms," said Meg, giggling.

"You wish," I said. "That's American Trucks First. Don't get between him and his eighteen wheelers."

Meg leaned in. "He'll want to talk to you about expanding highways in the district to allow more trucks to travel through to Florida."

"Should I mention truck driver fatigue and its relationship to fatal crashes?" asked Maeve, with a mischievous twinkle in her eye.

"Go ahead, especially if you want him to rip up his fat check for your campaign," I said.

"I'm joking, Kit. Don't lose your sense of humor," said Representative Dixon.

"That's what I said earlier today. She's not as much fun since she got married," said Meg in a pouty voice.

I clenched my jaw. "That's completely false. Why do I feel like I'm the one running for reelection here?"

Our boss smiled. "Kit has a point. Please continue with the briefing."

"Lauren Parker, Van's wife, will also attend. She rarely attends the same fundraisers as her husband, but she requested to attend this one because it was the last opportunity to rub elbows with you. She works at Johnson and Peale, a prominent lobbying firm in town. Other than that, I don't know too much about her. Meg?"

"Lauren's been on K Street for a while," said Meg. "She represents a wide range of clients, so you never know why she might show up at your door."

We were getting close to our destination. "Anyone else I should know about?" asked Maeve.

"Meg, would you like to do the honors concerning Dash Dugal?" I hoped she'd leave out the details about Dash's physical appearance.

My best pal straightened up, eager to talk about her latest flavor of the month. "Van Parker might be the most prominent trans-portation lobbyist in the city, but Dash Dugal is right on his heels. He's a top guy at ARF."

The corners of Maeve's mouth twitched upward. I'd seen this reaction before. She was trying to suppress a chuckle. "ARF? Does he lobby for dogs?"

"No," I interjected. "Although getting the Humane Society's endorsement would be terrific. Sixty-five percent of American families own pets. That's a lot of votes."

Meg cleared her throat. "A-R-F stands for American Railway Federation. It's the top association representing railroads." Washington was a city of acronyms. The mayor's of-fice should hand out a guide to abbreviations when transplants relocated to our fair city.

"That explains why he wants to attend the fundraiser. He wants to shake my hand as a member of the Transportation Committee," said our boss.

"Is it unusual for Dash and Van to attend the same event?" I asked. "After all, they're fierce competitors."

"You're right," said Meg. "The trucking industry and the railroads compete for scarce funding. So, they're not best buddies. But I convinced Dash he shouldn't miss this opportunity to meet you and contribute to the campaign."

The taxi arrived at our destination, and Maeve paid the driver as we got out. We started to walk toward the entrance of Charlie Palmer's when our boss called us back.

"Let's finish this conversation before it's feeding time at the zoo." She motioned toward the front door of the restaurant and faced Meg. "How were you able to convince Dash to pony up thousands of dollars for tonight's event? I'm curious."

Meg straightened the skirt of her dress. "He's a personal acquaintance, ma'am."

Maeve raised her eyebrows. "How personal?"

Meg squirmed. "We're dating."

33

Our boss exhaled a big sigh. "I hope this isn't a problem. The last thing I need is some sort of ethics investigation."

"I don't think so," I offered. "Meg might have told Dash about the fundraiser, but she only did so in her personal capacity, not as an employee of the United States Congress. Isn't that right?"

Meg nodded her head vigorously. "Absolutely."

My words seemed to reassure our boss. "Okay. I'm glad you told me. He should be easy to recognize, I suppose. He must be attractive." Her eyes twinkled. A serious legislator, Maeve Dixon didn't kid around too much. Even she knew about Meg's penchant for eye-catching men. Meg smiled and kept her mouth shut.

"Shall we?" I asked, pointing the way. "Or we could hang outside for a while longer. But you're not raising any money on the corner of First Street and Louisiana."

Maeve pursed her lips together. "Point taken."

As soon as we walked inside the fancy foyer near the bar area, Brock started snapping photos with his iPhone. He'd been with us to other off-hours fundraisers, but nothing had been as extravagant as Charlie Palmer's. His eyes widened. "Are we actually having dinner here?"

Meg had limited patience for our pup. "Don't eat anything until everyone else has been served. Understand?"

With a solemn expression, Brock nodded. "Yes, ma'am."

Meg shot him a dirty look. "Ma'am? I'm not your mother. How old do you think I am?"

Brock hailed from our home district, which made him a true southerner. I suspected his use of "ma'am" was nothing more than an attempt to affix Meg with a moniker of respect. In her mid-thirties, Meg had recently become more sensitive about her age. Our intern had inadvertently waded into a hornet's nest.

Brock stammered. "I don't know." A bead of sweat appeared on his forehead as Meg glowered at him.

Meg wasn't going to let him off the hook. "Take a guess," she pressed.

I slipped behind Meg, so Brock could see me. I held up two fingers with one hand and then five with the other.

Poor Brock wasn't the quickest on his feet. "Gosh, maybe two and five. I mean, twenty-five!"

Meg paused. She gave him a suspicious look and said, "Good answer."

Brock exhaled an audible sigh. Another crisis adverted, just in time for the arrival of Clarissa Smythe, Maeve's campaign fund-raiser.

She crossed the length of the restaurant to meet us inside the reception area. "Congresswoman, so good to see you." She gave Maeve a polite hug.

Out of the corner of my eye, Meg bristled. Clarissa wasn't her favorite person in the world. Used to being the best-looking woman in the room, Meg enjoyed a bounty of male attraction. Clarissa gave Meg a run for her money in that category. Tall and voluptuous, she had long wavy auburn hair and creamy skin that made her look like she'd just came from having a moisturizing facial. Her makeup was perennially flawless, accenting her striking blue eyes. Clarissa was in the right business. Lobbyists tripped over the opportunity to attend her fundraising events due to her knack of putting together a "who's who" for each gathering. I was thrilled when the Dixon campaign was able to land her. Although Meg couldn't dispute Clarissa's success, playing second fiddle wasn't Meg's preferred status.

Clarissa turned to me next. "Kit, I'm glad to see you survived the marathon legislative session before the campaign recess."

"It's not over yet," I said. "Final votes at eight tonight. Will we be able to get this event in before we have to head back to the Capitol?" Yes, the campaign was critically important. Nonetheless, I never lost sight that I was Maeve Dixon's chief of staff first and foremost, and I was responsible for her work as a sitting member of Congress. Besides, missing a vote for a fundraiser was bad political business, and Coach Hackensack would clean our clock if she shirked her duties while swilling French wine at a pricey steakhouse.

Clarissa hit the face of her black Fitbit around her wrist. "Not a problem. It's just after six now, and our guests will be arriving by six-thirty. We'll do a brief cocktail reception on the roof, hear some speeches of support for the Congresswoman, and then head inside for dinner."

Maeve listened to Clarissa's run down of the schedule. "Kit, I'll depart no later than quarter to eight. I don't want to be rushed. You stay here until everyone has finished their meals and enjoyed dessert or an after-dinner drink."

"Don't you want us to come back with you to the Capitol?" I asked. "In case you have any questions about the votes?"

"No, it's better if you stay here and play

host to any stragglers who want to enjoy the party. I can handle it." Her face brightened. "You and Meg should enjoy yourselves."

I groaned inwardly. After a summer of fundraising soirees, there were a thousand things more enjoyable than hanging out on a rooftop with high-priced K Street lobbyists. I took a deep breath. After all, I'd signed up as a chief of staff for a member of Congress who represented a politically divided district. This was part of the job description.

"Understood," I said.

On the other hand, Meg was delighted, since our boss had given her permission to hang out with Dash for the remainder of the evening. "Don't worry. We'll make sure everyone has a memorable evening!"

Meg's promise was easy to keep.

CHAPTER FOUR

Clarissa led us into an elevator and pressed the button for the ninth floor. "The rooftop is delightful this time of year," she cooed. Over the past several months, we'd eaten southern barbecue, Tex-Mex, seafood, and too many steaks to count. The name of the game was bringing in cash for the Dixon campaign and providing the attendees with access to the candidate. Everything else was window dressing.

However, when the elevator door opened, and we exited, I had to admit Clarissa wasn't exaggerating. A beautiful long table had been set for elegant dinner service adjacent to glass windows overlooking the rooftop balcony. "Follow me." Clarissa opened the door onto the terrace.

A middle-aged man dressed in an expensive looking suit and tie met us outside. "Welcome to Charlie Palmer's. I'm Stuart Gladstone, the manager of our private events. We are honored to host your function tonight, Congresswoman Dixon." Stuart extended his hand and shook my boss's hand lightly. He had impeccable manners, a prerequisite for his line of work.

"Thank you," said Maeve. "You certainly have a gorgeous venue."

Stuart guided us onto the large rooftop. "We're most fortunate to have the best view of two of the most famous landmarks in Washington." Walking backward, he used his right hand to gesture toward the eastern side of the terrace. "The United States Capitol Building needs no introduction to you." He smiled at our boss. "Of course, not everyone is thrilled with Congress these days, present company excluded. For those patrons, we have the Washington Monument." He extended his left arm.

"Something for everyone," I muttered.

"Yes, we like to think so," said Stuart. "And you are?"

Just like a typical Washington, D.C. veteran to ask my affiliation. Only after my answer would he assess whether I was worthy of his precious breath.

"Kit Marshall. I'm Representative Dixon's chief of staff." I extended my hand and he accepted it. But I wasn't finished. "This is Meg Peters, our legislative director. And

Brock Metcalf, our intern and campaign photographer."

Brock straightened up as he accepted Stuart's hand, clearly impressed he'd been elevated to an official title. Hey, interns worked for no money, but impressive position descriptions were free. Why not make him feel important?

Stuart nodded in their direction. "Great to see that the team's all here. We'll handle this as a standard fundraiser. We do them every night of the week," he said in a blasé tone. "I'm sure Clarissa has given you the run down. If there's any problems, don't hesitate to find me." He gave Maeve a quick kiss on the cheek. "Ciao, darlings. I hope you raise a lot of money and beat that sonofabitch Coach Crackerjack or whatever his name is."

Meg and I giggled. Stuart was a card. Sometimes it was comforting to revel in the predictability of D.C. stereotypes. However, if Hackensack defeated Dixon, this time next year, Stuart wouldn't hesitate to host a fundraiser for him instead.

We drifted over to the eastern edge of the rooftop with the Capitol in the background. There was still a glimpse of sun. A few days after the fall equinox, nightfall was coming earlier. Early autumn was a superb time in

Washington, D.C. The humidity had dissipated and with enough warmth still in the air, it would be a pleasant evening outside.

"Why don't I take your photo in front of the Capitol?" asked Brock.

"That's not a bad idea." Meg whipped out a compact from her purse and checked her makeup. Meg didn't pose for photos unless she looked flawless. It was her version of the Girl Scout motto.

I glanced at the dome before turning to face Brock. "It does look impressive after the restoration."

Over one hundred and fifty years old, the entire Capitol dome had recently undergone a complete overhaul. For the past two years, workers repaired cracks in the cast iron and repainted the entire structure. The result was spectacular, giving one of the most iconic landmarks in the world a much-needed facelift.

Maeve stood in between Meg and me. "Sixty million dollars and not one penny over budget," said our boss.

"That's a Washington first," I said.

Brock set up his iPhone for the photo. "Why don't you all say A-O-C instead of cheese?"

That stood for Architect of the Capitol, who was responsible for the maintenance

42

and preservation of the grounds. The Architect had led the dome project and received plaudits for keeping it on schedule.

We smiled for the photo and adopted Brock's corny suggestion. As soon as he snapped the picture, Clarissa approached us.

"Time to get to work," she announced. "Guests are starting to arrive."

Sure enough, a well-dressed, chiseled man in his mid-forties strode directly toward us. Over six feet tall, he cut an impressive figure. Shoving his hand at Maeve, he said, "Representative Dixon, I'm Van Parker, and I represent the United States trucking industry."

The congresswoman politely accepted his hand. "A pleasure to meet you. Thank you for supporting my campaign."

"I look forward to getting to know you," he said as he steered Maeve away from the edge of the balcony. "There's a lot of issues to discuss with the highway bill up for reauthorization next year."

"Perhaps you should meet my chief of staff and legislative director, who are here tonight as well," said Maeve in an apparent attempt to diffuse Van's strongarm tactics.

"Let's get a drink and chat ourselves. I like to get to know the politician I'm work-

ing with. I can meet with staff anytime."
Van waved his hand dismissively in our
general direction.

"Charming fellow," I whispered to Meg.

"You haven't seen the half of it. Just wait
until Dash arrives."

"Maybe you shouldn't have encouraged
him to come tonight. I don't want any
fireworks at her last fundraiser inside the
Beltway."

"Don't be a worrywart. Dash and Van
might be political rivals, but they're professional. They'll give each other enough space.
Besides, Dash really wanted to attend."

"That's your job for tonight," I said.
"Make sure they steer clear of each other."

Meg gave the thumbs-up sign and
grinned. "Will do, boss lady."

"I'm going to check in with Clarissa and
see who else has arrived," I said.

"Have fun. I'm grabbing a glass of wine.
I'll need it to keep the peace tonight."

Maeve was deep in conversation with Van
Parker underneath a small tent in the
middle of the rooftop which sheltered the
bar. I'd let the conversation run its course
for a while longer. After all, Van did pay a
great deal of money to attend tonight's
event. He deserved some precious minutes
alone with the guest of honor.

44

As soon as I reached Clarissa, another man opened the door and walked onto the rooftop. This guy looked familiar, but I couldn't remember his name. The more years I spent in Washington, the more often this scenario became a reality. The face rang a bell, yet it was impossible for the ever-expanding Rolodex inside my brain to retrieve the correct moniker. He was shorter and younger than Van, maybe our age, with the early trappings of a receding hair line. He wasn't handsome or unattractive. In other words, he looked like the majority of the male population in the District of Columbia. Yet something about his face told me I knew him. He couldn't work on the Hill; no staffer had extra cash to throw at a freshman member of Congress who might go down in flames during her first reelection cycle.

After exchanging pleasantries with Clarissa, the mystery man set his sights on me. He obviously wasn't memory challenged.

"Great to see you again," he said in a friendly voice.

It's no different than playing twenty questions. I could figure this out. "Thanks for coming to Representative Dixon's fundraiser. We appreciate the support."

"I almost didn't recognize you in a suit

45

with your hair down."

Uh-oh. I knew him somehow outside work. This was a real puzzle. I didn't have too much time outside my job. It wasn't like I joined extracurricular activities in my spare time. Perhaps he'd seen me at the gym? I'd recently joined the cardio kickboxing craze. Punching a heavy bag was an effective way to burn a ton of calories and get rid of stress without hurting anyone. Although I had to admit, sometimes I imagined I was punching a live human being, usually whomever was responsible for my most recent headaches. Coach Hackensack had made several fantasy appearances lately.

"I look a lot different when I'm not so . . ." I paused for a moment before finishing the sentence. "Sweaty?"

"Heh, heh. I know what you mean. It's hard for me to keep up with Bruiser," he said.

Bruiser! There was a hint. My brain shifted into overdrive. Of course! He owned a dog in agility training with Clarence, our beagle mutt.

"Ditto with our dog. How's Bruiser doing with the lessons?" I asked.

"I'm ready to put him forward in his first practice time trial. Hopefully later this week."

I still couldn't remember his name, but at least he wasn't a total stranger.

"I'm Kit, by the way. Dixon's chief of staff. Can you remind me of your name?"

My fellow dog owner laughed. "I should have mentioned it when I walked in. I'm Max Robinson. In addition to owning Bruiser, I'm also the chief lobbyist for BAM." He pronounced it as a word, rhyming with "lamb."

I shook my head. "I'm sorry. BAM doesn't ring a bell with me, except for Barbara Ann Mikulski." The longest serving female member of Congress in American history, who hailed from the nearby state of Maryland, had retired recently. Her legendary initials were well known amongst Hill insiders.

"Don't worry. We get that a lot and it doesn't bother us because Senator Mikulski supported our cause," he explained. "These days, BAM stands for the Bicycle Advocacy Movement."

I tilted my head to the side. Never heard of it. Bluffing with Max was exhausting. I gave up. "Sorry. I don't know your organization."

A frown telegraphed Max's disappointment. Remembering he'd paid a hefty sum to attend tonight's event, I recovered quickly. "But I'd love to learn more about it," I offered in a gracious voice.

His eyes brightened. "We're the umbrella organization for bike advocates across the country. Are you familiar with our policy issues?"

Meg covered the transportation portfolio in our office. She kept me informed about the big decisions, like proposed changes to federal aviation policy and funding for highways in our congressional district. Somehow bicycles had gotten lost in the shuffle.

"Um . . . I can't say I do," I said lamely.

"Let's grab a drink, and I can tell you about them," he said. We headed toward the tent. Under his breath, Max muttered something.

"Excuse me," I said. "I'm not sure I heard what you said."

"Nothing. I see that Van Parker already arrived." Max's face had grown dark, a dramatic change from the upbeat guy I'd just met.

Van had apparently ended his discussion with the Congresswoman and was now walking in our direction toward the bar. He spotted Max and acknowledged him with a dismissive wink. "Did you cycle over here, Robinson? I'm not sure Charlie Palmer's has a bike rack."

Creases on Max's forehead appeared as he grimaced. "You're a real jerk, Van."

Parker didn't seem fazed by Max's harsh pronouncement. The placid look on his face indicated that Van viewed Max as an annoying gnat who could be swatted away without a second thought. He stared at Max for a long moment, considering a retort. Then he must have decided Max didn't warrant wasted breath. He ordered a Cabernet Sauvignon at the bar and walked away.

I couldn't hold my tongue. "Charming personality," I commented.

"Believe me, you don't know the half of it," said Max.

"Would you like a drink? You could use one," I said in a light tone.

"I don't drink alcohol, but a club soda with lime would be great."

"You got it." I grabbed Max's drink from the bar, along with a Riesling for myself. I allowed myself one glass of vino at evening fundraisers. Anything more was irresponsible, but it was downright impossible to get through the endless chitchat without some liquid courage.

When I returned to Max, Meg had joined the conversation. "Kit, Max tells me you've already met."

"He was about to tell me more about the bike lobby's legislative agenda," I said.

Max started to say something, but Meg cut him off. "No need to go through it. We're big supporters of cyclists in the Maeve Dixon office."

I'd known Meg long enough to surmise she wasn't lying, but also wasn't exactly telling the truth, either. We were in a difficult spot. Our boss needed to raise money for her campaign, yet she wanted to avoid selling the farm, if possible.

"I'm glad to hear you say that, Ms. Peters. When Maeve Dixon is reelected, we'll count on her support as a member of the key committee to make sure that cycling is included at the table as one of the key players for the next major transportation bill," said Max.

Meg gulped. Max had gone one step too far. She sipped her wine. "Of course. We're supportive of the rails to trails initiative. And you know we advocate for bike sharing programs in cities across North Carolina." Meg flashed a thousand-watt smile. At the same time, she snuck a sideways glance that screamed "Get me out of here right now."

Max shook his head. "That's helpful, but it's not the direction BAM is headed. We want to be treated as an equal player. Bike commuting has increased over one hundred percent in the past decade. Can you say that about any other method of transportation?" Max didn't wait for Meg to feign a response. "You can't. Face it. Bicycling is a growth industry, and cyclists demand their share of the pie." He straightened his tortoiseshell glasses, which had fallen askew during his brief tirade. I had newfound respect for Max Robinson.

Meg was no novice and didn't like bullies. Given the venue, I hoped she'd mind her tongue. Her eyebrows furrowed for a moment, but she quickly recovered. She patted Max on the hand appreciatively. "That's very exciting, Max, about the new strategy. We'll have a lot to discuss next year, won't we?"

Max might have been a crusader for cyclists worldwide but even he couldn't resist Meg when she turned on the charm. The edge disappeared from his voice. "I look forward to it." He raised his club soda. "Let's toast to the reelection of Maeve Dixon."

"We can all drink to that," I agreed. "Thank you for attending, Max. Other guests have arrived, and I need to check in with Clarissa. Please excuse me."

There was certainly a backstory to Max Robinson. I'd have to ask Meg later to fill me in. She'd been dead on about Van Parker. He was certainly the dean of transportation lobbyists and knew it. I didn't mind powerful people in Washington; they were everywhere. What yanked my chain were the idiots who acted like they were better than everyone else. On the other hand, the Dixon campaign wasn't in the business of turning down donors because they were narcissists. If we did that, there wouldn't be enough money to run a television ad on cable access.

Clarissa snagged me as soon as she saw I'd broken free. She knew exactly what had happened. "Max can be tenacious as hell," she said.

"That's an understatement. Boa constrictors are easier to escape."

She laughed and gestured to an attractive woman who was walking toward the small group of people gathering around the bar area. "Have you ever met Lauren Parker?"

"No, but I saw her name on the guest list you sent over. Van's wife, right?"

Clarissa nodded. "She's a tough cookie."

"You'd have to be if you were married to Van."

"She's small in stature, but believe me, she can hold her own," said Clarissa.

"Why was she so keen on attending this

fundraiser?" I asked.

"She was a late addition. Your boss is in one of the hottest races this fall, and Lauren wanted in on the action," said Clarissa. "You know me, Kit. I do my job. Everyone who is anyone knew about tonight's event."

"I get it, but there were other fundraisers this evening. She chose this one over the other ones being hosted around town," I said. There had to be a reason why Lauren was here, and I wanted Clarissa to tell me before I got caught in a conversation with her.

Clarissa looked left and right and then leaned closer to me. She beckoned me with her hand, so I'd do the same. "Chairman Edwards," she whispered.

"She's wants to get in good with Rory Edwards?" I asked. Why was this such a secret? Although it might have been easier for Lauren to attend a fundraiser for Edwards' political action committee.

"That's already happened," said Clarissa.

I could read between the lines and knew how to veil my language. "Lauren and Chairman Edwards have a special relationship?"

Clarissa nodded. "I think he persuaded her to attend this event. Maybe she didn't know Van was attending."

"She'd already paid up so there was no way for her to get out it," I said.

"Basically. I'm sure Edwards thought this would be a cozy rooftop evening with his secret paramour."

"Damn husbands. They always get in the way," I said sarcastically.

"Exactly. But don't spread it around. I don't want to be the source of gossip."

That was like the Pillsbury doughboy saying he didn't want to be responsible for those pesky five pounds you'd just packed on. I told Clarissa what she wanted to hear. "Don't worry. I won't say anything about the affair."

She swept a strand of auburn hair that blew across her face due to the gentle breeze on the rooftop. "Thanks. My reputation is the only way I survive in this town."

Clarissa was right, especially in her job as a campaign consultant. First and foremost, her clients needed to trust her.

"Can you introduce me to Lauren?" I asked. "Meg told me she's been a lobbyist for a while. I'd better make her acquaintance."

"Absolutely. Let's do it now," said Clarissa. Under her breath, she said, "By the way, Lauren is a doppelgänger for Meg."

She took a few steps forward. "Lauren,

darling! Come here. You have to meet someone after you secured a beverage!"

I followed Clarissa and a minute later, proper introductions had been made. When I got a good glimpse of Lauren Parker up close, I was intrigued. She did strongly resemble Meg, only about ten years older — but fully equipped with a sleek blonde bob and a killer shape. Gorgeous blue eyes adorned with black eyeliner and skillfully applied eyeshadow enhanced her natural beauty. Her brows had been sculpted into a perfect arch, no doubt the product of a skilled aesthetician at a highly priced salon. She wore a black and white skirt suit ensemble that leapt off the pages of *Vogue*. Ebony stiletto sandal heels perfectly accented the outfit and boosted her small frame. Van might be the king of transportation lobbyists, but his wife was a well-coiffed masterpiece of K Street.

Lauren was juggling two phones in her left hand, including one with a hot pink Michael Kors leather case. Her right hand held a glass of wine filled to the brim. With the impressive dexterity of a woman who'd lived in Washington for years, she placed her phones inside her purse, transferred her drink, and extended a manicured hand as Clarissa did the official honors. "Pleased to meet you, Kit."

I accepted her hand and expressed my gratitude for her contribution. "If you'd like to speak with my boss, let me know," I offered.

"I'm sure we'll say hello this evening" said Lauren. Clarissa must have been right. Lauren was more interested in other guests at the fundraiser, namely Chairman Edwards.

Well accustomed to lobbyists launching into a pitch almost immediately after pleasantries were exchanged, I was momentarily at a loss for words. Small talk wasn't my strongest suit.

"Beautiful view, isn't it?" I asked.

"Yes, and I always forget to snap a photo," she said. "I'll make sure to do it this time."

"Do you dine here frequently?"

"It's a popular place for fundraisers. Not a bad restaurant, as far as these venues go. I patronize my fair share these days." She sipped her wine.

I couldn't resist asking about Van. "Do you attend many with your husband? I met him earlier for the first time."

Lauren gazed across the rooftop when I mentioned Van. He was leaning against a high table, engrossed in what appeared a deep conversation with Meg.

Lauren turned back to me quickly. "Not

often. These are work events. As you can see, his attention is elsewhere."

"That's our legislative director for Congresswoman Dixon," I said. "I'm sure he's talking to her about the legislative agenda for the trucking industry."

"He's got an agenda, for sure." Lauren didn't bother to mask the annoyed tone.

"Hello, Lauren." A deep masculine voice greeted us from behind.

It was Rory Edwards, chairman of the Transportation Committee and one of our two VIP guests for the evening. His salt and pepper hair glistened underneath the retreating sunlight. Not a bad looking guy, although if truth be told, he couldn't hold a flame to Van Parker's ruggedly handsome good looks. Nonetheless, Lauren's gloomy expression disappeared instantly.

"Rory!" she exclaimed. They hugged politely, although I noticed his hand lingered on the small of her back. Or it might have been her rounded butt. If it wasn't already, their affair was well on its way to becoming one of the worst kept secrets in Washington. In general, I adopted the old adage, "don't ask, don't tell." But bearing witness to extramarital shenanigans seemed beyond the call of duty. After all, I was practically a newlywed myself. I didn't need bad relationship karma, and negative juju oozed from Lauren's pores.

"Excuse me, I'd better find Representative Dixon to let her know Chairman Edwards has arrived," I said.

The two seemingly clandestine lovebirds paid me no attention. I slipped away as they stared hauntingly into each other's eyes. Only in our nation's capital could one spouse ogle a younger woman while the other publicly flirted with a senior member of Congress. Sometimes this city could be too much.

On my way to give Maeve an update, I ran into Meg. "Enjoy your chat with Van Parker?" I asked.

"He's a piece of work. I don't mind the hard sell on the trucking industry," she said. "But I don't need it on anything else, if you know what I mean."

"Well, you do look a lot like his wife. Just a bit younger."

"A bit? Now you're insulting my age, too." Meg pouted.

"Five years?" I asked in teasing voice. At this point, I was messing with my best friend.

"Double that." Meg's eyes wandered across the room and lit up. "Thank goodness. Dash has arrived. Kit, come over and say hello." Giving me no choice in the matter, Meg grabbed my arm and pulled me toward her new beau.

Meg may have embellished Dash's good looks, but not by much. His dark brown skin, a product of his Indian heritage, contrasted handsomely with his light grey tailored suit and blue pastel dress shirt. As we approached, he removed his aviator sunglasses to reveal his sparkling green eyes. Even at a soiree filled with impressive people, Dash Dugal stood out.

Meg ran up to him and linked her right arm under his, and he returned the gesture with a friendly grin. "Dash, I'd like you to meet my best friend Kit Marshall, Maeve Dixon's chief of staff."

"A pleasure to finally meet you," he said. "I've heard so much about you, I feel as though we know each other already."

"Thank you for attending. I know you don't always choose fundraisers in which competing interests are also making an appearance." I gestured in the direction of Van Parker, who was sipping his drink at the bar. At least he was enjoying himself.

Dash rolled his eyes. "He's a real pain in the you-know-what," he said.

"That's because high speed rail is the future, and Van knows it," said Meg.

Dash puffed up at Meg's praise. "Thanks, babe. The proof will be in the pudding. And by pudding, I mean next year's transportation bill."

If Maeve survived the election, we'd have to prioritize requests for funding in the legislation. As a member of the relevant committee, she could play an important role. But there were only so many chits to distribute, especially as a junior member of Congress with low seniority. I'd might as well hear what Dash wanted.

"What are you looking to accomplish?" I asked in a clipped voice. The small talk was grating. I preferred to cut through the fluff and get to the heart of the matter. An attraction to Meg notwithstanding, I knew why the American Railways Federation paid thousands of dollars for Dash to eat dinner at Charlie Palmer's tonight. And it wasn't to enjoy the nice view.

"It's a pretty ambitious agenda," Dash said slowly.

Before I could keep expectations reasonable, Meg piped up. "That's not a problem. We work for an ambitious member of Congress. Don't we, Kit?" Meg twirled a lock of her blonde tresses around her finger. Oh, brother. Best to play along — for now. I'd berate Meg later for mixing business with pleasure.

"We sure do. Lay it on us, Dash," I mustered as much enthusiasm as possible without sounding like a used car salesman.

"Right now, there's no passenger rail service to Wilmington. Charlotte, Rocky Mount, Durham, Raleigh, and Greensboro are covered." Dash waved his aviators at us. "But what about the coastline?"

"You want to expand Amtrak service to Wilmington? Is that what you're proposing?" I asked.

"You got it. Right now, if you want to head to Cape Fear, you must catch a bus after riding the train," Dash explained. "That's ridiculous. Who wants to take a train and then a bus to the beach? Let's get passenger rails headed to your district. Wouldn't that be a major victory for Maeve Dixon in her second term?"

I had to admit a train to the coastline had a certain cache to it. But with a quarter of the district's families living in poverty, somehow focusing my boss's efforts on a train that would likely service tourists outside her jurisdiction sounded foolhardy. Fixing and building roads employed a lot of people, and as offensive as he might be, Van Parker from American Trucks First would be pushing that agenda.

"What an interesting idea, Dash," I said. "I look forward to hearing a full cost-benefit analysis in the months to come."

Meg narrowed her gaze. She could smell a brush-off from miles away. "We'll be sure to give it our fullest attention," she promised. Privately, I wondered whether Dash would be around this time next year. Meg switched paramours more frequently than most women cleaned out their closets.

The Majority Leader of the House had just arrived. Time to get this show started. I nodded curtly and extended my hand to Dash. "A pleasure to meet you. I hope you enjoy the evening."

Clarissa had already corralled Maeve and our two guest speakers. "Are you ready to start?" I asked my boss.

"As ready as I'll ever be." She glanced at her watch. "Let's roll."

The Majority Leader was an outwardly friendly pol who had been around the political block more than once. A septuagenarian Irishman with a head full of snow white hair, he was loved by most and feared by many. I remembered the quote from my undergraduate lecture in political philosophy on Machiavelli's *Prince* that had stayed with me for well over a decade: "He who wishes to be obeyed must know how to command." The Majority Leader certainly knew how to command the attention of a crowd. From my experience in Congress, very few disobeyed him and survived to tell about it.

But there was no semblance of shock and awe in tonight's performance. He was there to delight the crowd, entertain them, and boost my boss's reelection efforts. All three goals crossed off his list, he kissed Maeve on the cheek, wished her good luck campaigning, and headed for the hills. Or more accurately, he caught an Uber for the next fundraiser.

Next up was Chairman Rory Edwards. As he sang Maeve's praises in a litany of platitudes everyone in the room had heard twenty times before, I scanned the group to find Lauren. She wasn't hard to find in such a small group. It appeared she was working hard to keep her face neutral. Her line of sight never once left Rory Edwards. Where was her husband? He certainly wasn't standing next to Lauren. After surveying the rooftop, I finally located him. Van Parker was sitting at a table situated in the furthest corner of the tent, far apart from the other attendees. His head swayed slightly from side to side, and he didn't seem focused on the speeches.

I pulled out my phone and texted Meg.

Van seems out of it.

Ten feet away, I heard Meg's iPhone buzz. After taking her own peek at Van, she replied.

Too much wine.

Great. We had this before at fundraisers, and it was always a pain the neck. After paying thousands of dollars to attend, it was difficult to ask a donor to leave, even if he or she had indulged in one too many.

I replied to Meg.

I'll check it out.

The corners of her mouth twitched upward.

Have fun :)

Wrangling an egotistical, detested lobbyist who imbibed too much was not exactly my definition of fun. But it was part of the gig.

Chairman Edwards had just finished his shtick and turned the floor over to our boss. Maeve smoothed her hair and smiled widely. After thanking everyone profusely for their donation, she launched into her ten-minute spiel about why she needed to remain the elected representative from the seventh district of North Carolina. She'd given this talk so many times, I'm sure she recited it in her sleep.

She paid homage to several different

interests in her short speech, including the importance of discovering alternative fuels for transportation and investing more strategically in our nation's infrastructure. Then she added, "None of this means that we shouldn't build roads to support traditional modes of transportation. For example, our national trucking industry is a vital part of interstate commerce and an essential component to a healthy economy."

I hadn't told her to include those statements in her speech. By the look on Meg's face, she hadn't, either. Maeve wrapped up her talk and greeted a few attendees she hadn't spoken with earlier in the evening.

Out of the corner of my eye, I spotted Dash Dugal. His face had turned a shade a crimson only donned previously by Harvard grads. He was fuming. If steam came out of his ears, I wouldn't be surprised. Meg was headed in his direction, thank goodness. She could mollify his anger about Maeve's apparent effusion with Van Parker and the trucking industry.

Speaking of Van, I was supposed to check in on him. He'd gotten up and was headed in the direction of the bar. Maybe I could cut him off at the pass.

While making a beeline for him, I waved to get his attention. "Hey, Van!"

He raised his head when he heard his name. His eyes were unfocused, giving him a glazed look of general confusion.

"Are you a staffer for Dixon?" His speech was slow and staccato, like he had to concentrate before pronouncing each word.

"Yes. We only met briefly when you arrived tonight. I wanted to introduce myself and give you my contact information personally." I fumbled in my purse and produced my business card. Much of the world had moved to virtual cards or digital methods of swapping contact information. Washington, D.C. still ran on old standards. We swapped paper cards and dutifully inputted them the next day in our e-mail address books. I even kept mine in an alphabetical Rolodex, just in case Outlook decided to crash and burn on a whim.

He took my card. Squinting, he shook his head and pulled out a pair of reading glasses from his breast pocket. "Damn pain in the ass that I have to use these to read these days," he said.

"I got Lasik a while ago," I said. "Perfect vision without glasses."

"Believe me, your day will come," he murmured.

After he put on his cheaters, he read my card out loud. "Kit Marshall, Chief of Staff,

The Honorable Maeve Dixon, North Carolina Seven."

"That's me," I said. This was going from bad to worse. Time to wrap it up. "Like I said, we look forward to working with you in the future." That was my emptiest line ever. Translation: I need to get out of this conversation now. See you later, alligator.

"Looks like we'll be seeing a lot of each other, according to your boss's remarks." He shrugged in the direction of Maeve, who was easing toward the door.

"Who's not a fan of roads?" I asked lightly. Van's smugness irked me.

"Lots of people. We can move freight on highways via trucks or on the railroads. Maeve Dixon seems to be on the side of the truckers."

"She's also a fan of clean energy. I'm not sure she'll be thrilled when we give her the environmental statistics associated with trucks."

Van seemed unfazed. "Everyone's an environmentalist until they have to make a choice between trees and jobs." His grin was lopsided, giving it an almost goofy appearance. How many drinks had he managed to imbibe? He added ominously, "I'll give you a hint. Jobs always win."

"I'm guessing your membership card for

the Sierra Club got lost in the mail," I said sarcastically.

Van stared stonily after my last comment. I thought he might come back at me with a clever retort. Instead, he stood up. "Enough chitchatting." He glanced at his empty glass. "Will there be wine service with dinner?"

"It seems like you've had your share already," I blurted out. To soften my rude comment, I quickly added, "We wouldn't want you to become ill during dinner."

Van Parker put his hand to his forehead, appearing deep in thought. "I've only had two drinks tonight. A glass of Cabernet and something else. But now that you mention it, I do feel a little tired."

It seemed he'd drank an entire bottle of wine rather than what he claimed. But I wasn't about to argue with the man. I'd already acted way too cheeky for my own good. Thankfully, Van would likely forget this conversation ever occurred, especially if he continued to imbibe more during the meal.

"We're heading inside for dinner," I said. "Follow me, it's this way."

We walked across the rooftop terrace and inside the building. A long table with a pristine white tablecloth had been set beautifully within the alcove. A ceiling to floor window provided an indoor dining experience while preserving the benefits of the breathtaking views from east to west.

Congresswoman Dixon was seated in the center of the table, so she could talk to as many guests as possible. The Majority Leader had already left for the next fundraiser on his list, but I noticed Chairman Edwards had decided to stick around for dinner. Sure enough, Lauren Parker had finagled a seat next to him. Predictably, Max Robinson was situated on the outer edges. Although I never asked Clarissa about amounts donated, I guessed that the bicycle lobby had less resources than trains or trucks. BAM had probably given the minimum to attend, hence Max's seat in the outer edges of the universe. Dash Dugal, on the other hand, had secured a position between Maeve and Rory Edwards. Maybe Meg was onto something about Dash's political skills. He certainly didn't lack ambition.

Maeve motioned privately that she wanted to speak with me away from the table. We met by the exit, several steps removed so no one could hear our conversation. "I'll stay for the first course and eat a few bites of dinner. But I'm headed out after that."

I consulted my iPhone, which served as

my watch. "You can stay longer than that. Last votes aren't until eight. It's only a five-minute ride back to the Capitol, especially after rush hour."

Her body tensed. "I know where we are. I'm at my limit for these fundraisers. We've been doing them for months."

I'd only been working for my boss for about a year, but I knew when I shouldn't push matters with her. This was one of those times. Her mind was made up. "Take Rory Edwards with you," I said. "Otherwise it will look strange if he stays and you go."

Maeve glanced at the table. Edwards was laughing at something Lauren had said. "If I can pry him away from Parker's wife."

"No kidding," I said. "We've got a love triangle at our fundraiser this evening."

"Remember, you stay for the whole event," said Maeve. "I want to make sure our donors feel as though they got the royal treatment. Be sure you're the last one out the door."

I scowled. "Really? God only knows when this will wrap up."

"You or Meg. Flip a coin," she said. "We need to make sure the Dixon team shuts this down with Clarissa."

"No problem," I agreed quickly. Meg would likely want to babysit Dash all night.

That meant I was off the hook, hopefully after dinner was finished.

Maeve put her hands on my shoulders. "Next time I see you, it will be in North Carolina. Wish me luck."

"You'll knock 'em dead on the campaign trail, boss. Don't worry."

I should really consider removing all idioms referencing "dead" from my spoken vernacular.

CHAPTER FIVE

Once we took our seats, the dinner seemed to fly by faster than summer vacation. Charlie Palmer's had a reputation for classy dining, catering to those with fat expense accounts. Close to the Hill with lavish surroundings, it was hard to beat for a fundraiser. I'd eaten at my share of soirees over the summer, and the heirloom tomato salad with watermelon, cucumbers, basil, feta cheese, and light balsamic hit the spot. Of course, it couldn't outshine Palmer's signature dish, the filet mignon, served with pancetta corn succotash and black truffle mac and cheese. Blueberry cobbler rounded out the menu for the evening.

Sound extravagant? It was. As much as I loved the food at these events, if I ate everything on my plate, I would soon find myself unable to fit into the ten standard black suits that hung in my closet. Instead, under the premise that French women don't get fat, I typically ate half of everything. That approach worked reasonably well, although it took considerable discipline (such as tonight) to push away the plate after fifty percent of the portion had been consumed. Particularly when my partner-in-crime and colleague Meg, whose metabolism somehow defied the norms of human caloric consumption, practically licked her plate clean. For the life of me, I couldn't tell the difference between her and Clarence's dishes after they finished a meal.

I'd been seated next to a wealthy donor Clarissa had brought into the fold through her litany of contacts. My dinner companion, a retired lawyer from a big D.C. firm, would be lucky to see eighty again, yet he dazzled me with his encyclopedic knowledge of close congressional races and the Democrats' challenge of maintaining majority control. He understood my boss's race was a pivotal one and decided to donate generously to her campaign. As the evening ended, I graciously accepted his business card and joked that Chris Matthews should consider him as a future guest on his famous political talk show "Hardball."

It was close to eight in the evening, and we'd motored through the entire event. With a little luck, our attendees would be thrilled by the efficiency of the Dixon campaign operation and call it an early night. Maeve had headed out with Chairman Edwards in tow. He'd looked remorseful about leaving, perhaps one of the few members of Congress who'd rather raise money rather than legislate. Of course, it didn't hurt Lauren Parker was still around.

As I'd hoped, our dinner party was breaking up. As soon as the members of Congress left, the incentive for lobbyists to stick around diminished. Unfortunately, not everyone had bolted for the exit.

Clarissa smiled brightly. "On behalf of the Maeve Dixon reelection campaign, thank you again for your generous donation. Since it's such a beautiful night, feel free to have one last drink on the balcony while enjoying the view."

Dash was now sitting between Meg and Lauren. His head swiveled back and forth between the two of them. If he wasn't careful, he'd develop whiplash. Finally, Meg took her eyes off him, and I was able to give her the high sign. She followed me to the corner of the table.

"Do you mind staying for the final drink?" I asked.

"Of course not," said Meg cheerily. "Don't tell me you're going home!"

74

"I'm tired, Meg. It's been a long day." My shoulders slumped.

"Kit, after this election is over, I hope you perk up. You've got to relax more." She gave me a pouty look and sipped her red wine.

"Doug called me at the office, but I didn't have time to speak with him. He wants to talk to me about something." I rubbed my temples. "Although the idea of having a long conversation tonight makes my head hurt."

I felt the weight of Meg's stare as she gave me the once-over. "You'd better go home and get some sleep. We'll both be heading to North Carolina soon, and you know that campaign schedules are worse than long days on Capitol Hill."

"Maybe we'll get sent somewhere on the beach," I said wistfully.

Meg snorted. "Fat chance. Do you think the Dixon campaign staff are going to send snobby Washington, D.C. types to the coast? We'll be lucky if we ever get out of the Raleigh suburbs. I wouldn't pack your swimsuit."

Meg was being snarky, but as usual, she was right. I sighed. "All the more reason I should make a break for home. You'll stay here and babysit the stragglers? Maeve asked that either me or you remain until the bitter end."

Meg gave me a two-fingered salute. "No worries, boss."

"Thanks. I'll see you in the office tomorrow," I said. "Hopefully we can wrap up any loose odds and ends this week before we hit the campaign trail."

"Got it." Accompanied by a look of genuine concern, she added, "Kit, try to get some rest, okay?"

I nodded. Meg turned around and ran right into Dash, who had approached her from behind. She'd whipped around with her almost full wineglass, which teetered and then spilled on the floor.

"I'm so sorry," sputtered Dash. He grabbed a napkin and started dabbing at Meg's blazer, now collateral damage. I waited for the inevitable explosion. It was hard to say what designer Meg was wearing. Her couture trended toward the sophisticated, particularly for Capitol Hill standards. Today she was wearing a dark blue Navy-inspired jacket with a tan pencil skirt. Whatever the label, I knew it wasn't bargain basement leftovers. Meg prided herself on her clothes, almost treating her outfits as children. Dash had no idea what he'd just done.

My best friend's eyes protruded, and she clenched her fists. I braced myself for

Mount Saint Meg to erupt. But instead, a minor miracle transpired before my eyes. After taking a deep breath, Meg said, "Don't worry, Dash. I'm sure the dry cleaners can fix it."

My jaw dropped faster than Donald Trump's approval ratings. Had I witnessed Meg letting Dash off the hook?

Dash flashed a thousand-watt smile and put his arm around Meg. "Thanks for being so understanding, babe."

That was my cue to depart. "See you tomorrow, Meg."

"I'll follow you out," she said. "I'd better go to the ladies' room. I can't let this red wine stain set on my jacket."

"Good idea." Dash picked up her now empty wineglass. "I'll make sure you get a refill for our romantic stroll on the patio."

Barf. Were Doug and I this annoying when we first started dating? I hoped not.

We walked off together, and I stopped at the elevator. I couldn't resist adding a few cautionary words. "Remember, you're still on duty. We have other donors here besides Dash."

Meg crossed her arms. "You don't have to remind me, Kit. I'm a professional."

"I know," I said. "Have fun and see you tomorrow."

Inside the elevator, I checked the time. It was eight o'clock. Final votes were starting. I doubted Maeve needed any help, but I flipped my phone off silent mode, so I could hear it ping in case she texted me.

I could either walk two blocks to Union Station or catch an Uber home. My mind shuffled through the cost benefit analysis. I'd shelled out more cash this summer for late night rides home than I cared to remember. On the other hand, the subway was slow and unpredictable. Years of mismanagement, safety violations, and inadequate funding had made the Metro the bane of every Washingtonian's existence. Remembering that Doug wanted to talk to me about something, I opened the Uber app. My ride was scheduled to arrive in three minutes at the corner of First and Louisiana.

I caught up with today's news as I waited. Finally, a Camry arrived with the license plate matching my driver's car. He slowed as I waved him down. As I opened the rear passenger door, I heard spine-tingling screams behind me. My hand froze on the door handle. Without thinking, I spun around. Two older women were standing at the entrance of a narrow passageway that separated Charlie Palmer's from the building directly behind it. I didn't have to move to figure out the source of their bloodcurdling cries. Near the far end of the alley, a body was sprawled on the pavement.

CHAPTER SIX

Abandoning my ride home, I ran to the edge of the alley. Several other bystanders stopped, and we peered down the narrow passageway. The eyewitnesses had now traded in their screams for waterworks. I grabbed hold of the one who seemed like she was in better shape and forced her to look at me.

"Did you see what happened?" I asked.

"He fell . . ." she gasped in between sobs. "From up there." She managed to point a shaky finger to the top of the building.

A beefy guy in a Redskins jersey stared into the sky. "He committed suicide?"

The other woman wailed. "How do we know? We just saw him fly through the air and then . . ." Instead of finishing the sentence, she burst into another round of tears.

There was no way of identifying the man from where we were standing. And I certainly didn't want a closer look. No one could have survived that fall. I knew every person on the rooftop, which meant the victim was no stranger.

"Someone call the police," I yelled. "I'm headed inside."

My Uber driver had gotten out of his vehicle. "Lady, do you want this ride? I'm gonna have to charge you if you're canceling."

"Bill me!" I called over my shoulder as I bolted inside the restaurant.

An attractive hostess, clad in a fancy black cocktail dress and sexy high heels, looked up from the computer in front of her and smiled invitingly. "Welcome to Charlie Palmer's. Would you care to join us for dinner this evening?"

"I was just here for Representative Maeve Dixon's fundraiser on your rooftop. Can I speak to your manager?" I paused for a moment while I collected my thoughts. "I think his name is Stuart. Please hurry. There's been an accident outside." I pointed to the sidewalk, where a group of people had now gathered. Police sirens were growing louder.

"Oh, we don't own the sidewalk. If there's a problem, it's best to call the D.C. Police." Her gaze returned to the computer as she clicked the mouse in earnest.

"What about if someone fell from your rooftop on the sidewalk?" I asked. "Would that be your problem?"

The hostess jerked her head upward. "Did you say a patron fell from the ninth floor?"

"I'm not sure who it was, but you've got two very upset eyewitnesses, and the cops are on their way. Now can I speak to your manager?" I demanded.

"Certainly," she said in a shaky voice. She darted off as fast as her five-inch spiked heels could take her.

I hadn't witnessed the incident first-hand, but the two women had seemed certain it was a man. About a hundred feet away, it had been impossible to identify the victim. Meg was still upstairs. Did she know what had transpired? A wave of panic overcame me. I had a sudden urge to make sure she was safe. I pulled out my iPhone and texted her.

What happened? Someone jumped off roof?

I held my breath as I waited for her reply. Thirty agonizing seconds later, three dots appeared to indicate she was typing a response.

Van.

Exhaling in relief that my best friend was indeed safe, I gaped at her single word response. Van Parker was the victim? No point in asking more questions via text messaging.

I'm coming up.

I hustled around the corner to the back of the restaurant where the elevator was located. I almost ran into a man dressed in a fashionable suit carrying a stack of menus. "Are you the manager? Can you take me up to the ninth floor?"

His forehead glistened with sweat as he answered my question with a question. "Did you report a suicide from our rooftop?" He pulled out a handkerchief from his pocket and wiped the moisture from his face. The poor man was used to customers sending back their fifty dollar steaks if they weren't cooked properly. Patrons tumbling off buildings was clearly above his pay grade.

I shook my head. "I was outside when it happened. But I attended the Dixon fundraiser upstairs this evening and my colleagues are still there. Let's go find out what happened."

Mr. Nerves-of-Steel rubbed the back of his neck. "Shouldn't we let the police handle it? They'll be here any minute," he whined.

I'd tried the police route, but now it was time to take charge of the situation. My months as a chief of staff for a member of

Congress kicked into high gear.

"Sir, I demand that you take me to the rooftop." I pointed diagonally in the direction of the elevator bank.

The man wrung his hands. "I don't know if I should."

"I'm a paying customer, and I need to check on the rest of my party. We just dumped thousands of dollars at your restaurant this evening!" Personally, I hadn't paid a dime for dinner. But the Dixon campaign had certainly shelled out a small fortune. It was close enough in my book.

I'd said the magic words. When I looked into his eyes, green dollar signs flashed back. "Of course," he stammered. "We'll go right up to check on your friends."

I corrected him. "Not friends. Donors."

We entered the elevator and began our ascent. "In Washington, that's even more important," he said wryly.

The elevator dinged, and we exited. No one was inside the room where we ate dinner. We pushed through the glass doors and walked onto the rooftop. Clarissa, Meg, Dash, Lauren, and Max were standing underneath the rooftop tent. Only a few hours earlier, we'd enjoyed drinks at the bar at this exact location, making small talk and discussing future legislative agendas. A completely different scene presented itself now. Five worried faces, contorted in varying displays of disbelief, greeted us as we approached.

Meg broke away and gave me a big hug. After our quick but firm embrace, she leaned back and lowered her voice so only I could hear. "It's so awful. Did you see him?" Meg paused for a moment before finally finishing the sentence. "Fall from the roof?"

I shook my head. "Thank God, no. My ride had just arrived when I heard screaming behind me. A couple bystanders saw him fall. Or at least they claimed they witnessed it. Then I ran inside and convinced someone from the restaurant to bring me up here."

Meg wiped away a tear streaming down her cheek. "Why would Van Parker do this?"

"Good question. You didn't see what happened?"

"I was in the bathroom, remember?" She pointed to the wet spot on her blazer.

"How long?" I asked.

"I don't know. About five minutes? I took care of the stain, used the restroom, and fixed my makeup."

"When you came out of the bathroom, what happened?"

"I went outside on the rooftop. Dash said he'd get me another glass of wine, so I wanted to find him. I did, and he handed me a glass of red wine. A second later, Lauren started screaming about Van jumping off the roof. Dash ran to her to ask her what happened." Meg rubbed her temples. "Then the elevator dinged, and Max got off. He joined us outside."

"What about Clarissa?" I asked.

Meg bit her lip. "She was on the rooftop, too. She may have followed me outside."

"Someone called the police, I assume?"

"I think Clarissa called them. Lauren was too upset to do it. Dash suggested we head downstairs to meet them, but Lauren said she couldn't bear it," said Meg.

"What happened next?" I hated to prod Meg, who looked like she might burst into tears at any moment, but it was important to get the details about what happened before she forgot anything.

"You arrived," said Meg. "That's it. I don't have much more to share, unfortunately."

"Do you think anyone saw him jump?" I asked.

Meg shook her head. "Lauren and Dash both said they didn't see anything. I'm not sure where they were on the rooftop, but they both said they didn't see him do it."

I fiddled with my earring, a nervous habit I'd developed recently. "Do we really know he jumped?"

Meg sucked her cheeks in. "What do you mean, Kit?"

"There's another plausible explanation," I said evenly. "Maybe Van Parker was pushed."

CHAPTER SEVEN

"You have murder on the brain," said Meg.

I looked Meg directly in the eye. "That's because in the past year, murder has been everywhere we've been."

Meg muttered under her breath, "I need to find new friends. If I keep hanging out with you, I might as well sign my own death certificate."

"All I'm saying is that we don't know this is a suicide yet," I said. "Let's see what the police can sort out."

The cops had to be occupied on the street below. Surely, they'd make their way up to the rooftop soon. In the meantime, I scanned the rooftop and rested my gaze on Lauren Parker. Her perfect makeup was streaked with tears. Dash Dugal had a protective arm around her as she rested on a white vinyl foldout chair from the fund-raiser.

I dragged a chair next to Lauren and sat

down. "I'm very sorry about your husband."

She dabbed her eyes with a rolled-up Kleenex. "He was having a tough time, but I never thought he'd kill himself."

I fidgeted in my chair. These things were damn uncomfortable, even though they'd likely cost the campaign a fortune to rent. "I didn't know that. He seemed pretty upbeat when I met him earlier this evening."

Dash shot me a questioning look. "He put on a good face for these events."

Lauren nodded. "Dash is right. He was having trouble sleeping. He had a prescription for anxiety. I think it was linked to depression. But Van was the kind of guy who didn't like to talk about these things. And I kept his struggles private, too."

"What things?" I asked.

Lauren smoothed her hair. "Mental problems. Stuff like that. He was under a lot of pressure at work and it was only going to get more intense next year with a highway bill on the agenda."

I started to answer her, but then thought better of it and shut my mouth. It didn't seem like Van was worried about the prospect of legislation moving next year. In fact, he'd been smug about his chances in getting preferential treatment for the trucking industry. If he was only minutes away from ending it all, would he have been pressing Maeve Dixon on his issues and gloating about his apparent victory to me? Something was rotten in the state of Denmark, and it smelled like K Street.

Max Robinson, bike lobbyist extraordinaire, was standing several feet away. He'd unbuttoned the top button of his dress shirt and loosened his tie. I got up and sauntered over to him. "Did you know what happened here?"

He looked at me quizzically. "Van Parker killed himself," he said matter-of-factly.

"Were you on the rooftop when he jumped?" I asked.

"No, but others were. I'm sure someone saw something," he said.

"I don't know about that," I said. "Why weren't you on the ninth floor? Weren't you staying for another drink?"

"I went downstairs to retrieve my briefcase from the coat check," he said. "I wanted to share a new fact sheet about building bike lanes with your colleague Meg. She was quite interested in securing funding for a project in Dixon's district."

I doubted Meg was intensely interested in bike lanes, but that didn't matter. Max's story made sense. If Meg had shown any semblance of enthusiasm, he would have wanted to capitalize on the opportunity and provide her with the relevant information.

Clarissa joined us. She chewed at a fingernail and glanced at the entrance to the rooftop deck. "Where are the police?"

"They should make their way up here any minute," I said.

"What a disaster," she mumbled. "A suicide at one of my fundraisers. This will be the death of my career, no pun intended."

I patted Clarissa on the shoulder. "Don't worry. I'm sure this will be cleared up. It's not your fault this happened."

She shook her head slowly but didn't reply. She didn't need to verbalize dismay. Her normally flawless skin had grown blotchy, likely the result of the evening's added stress. Even though the early fall air was crisp and cool, beads of sweat glistened on her forehead.

Max must have noticed her distress. In a flat voice, he said, "I'm sure people will still come to your fundraisers."

"You don't understand. There won't be any more events to organize. Without clients like Maeve Dixon, I'm sunk." She paced back and forth between me and Max.

"Members of Congress won't remember what happened here," I said. "What they care about is that you can pull in the money

91

to fund their expensive campaigns."

Clarissa seemed to consider my reasoning. "That's the bottom line. But politicians want to throw a good party. Someone tumbling off a rooftop at Charlie Palmer's hardly qualifies."

"I'm sure the police will determine what happened. After that, no one will blame you for Van's death," I reasoned.

"You have a lot of confidence in D.C. Metro police," she said. "Excuse me. I've been trying to quit smoking, but I really need a cigarette." She pulled a pack out of her purse and walked away to light up.

As if on cue, the glass door connecting the interior of the building to the rooftop opened. A petite woman with her hair in a ponytail led a small team of uniformed police officers. When she spotted me in the distance, her mouth slackened in apparent disbelief.

"Well, we meet again, Ms. Marshall." She extended her hand.

I politely accepted it. "Detective Maggie Glass. Good to see you're on the case."

"Case? I hope not. The rumor is suicide. Lobbyist decided the K Street backstabbing wasn't worth it anymore and decided to end it all after a nice meal at Charlie Palmer's."

She whipped out a small notebook from

92

the pocket of her black blazer. Detective Glass wouldn't make an appearance anytime soon on Fifth Avenue, but she did have a business-like style I appreciated. Her suits were functional, like she could take off at any moment and chase a thief down Pennsylvania Avenue with no problem whatsoever. On the other hand, I often had trouble keeping my blouse tucked in.

"We'd just finished up a fundraising dinner for my boss. I work for Maeve Dixon in the House of Representatives," I reminded the detective. We'd met months ago at a crime scene away from Capitol Hill. I wasn't sure she remembered my background.

"I figured it was something like that. This place isn't exactly a casual dining experience." She surveyed the rooftop area. "Most people probably live their whole lives in Washington and never see a view like this."

Glass had a point. But when wealthy contributors write checks for thousands of dollars, they don't expect Sizzler. Wining and dining was part of the expectation. Clarissa often talked about "making the experience memorable." She'd hit the mark with tonight's event, although not in a good way.

Glass opened her notebook and plucked a pen from behind her ear. "So, tell me your story. What did you see tonight?"

"Not much concerning Van Parker's death. I was already headed out when it happened." I explained to the detective about the discovery of the body and my movements after the fact.

"We'll verify all this information. Did you interact with the victim earlier in the evening?" she asked.

"Absolutely. He's one of the top lobbyists in the city. We wanted to make sure he had an enjoyable time at the event, especially since he could have chosen to spend his association's dollars elsewhere."

After scribbling in her notebook, she asked, "Anything out of the ordinary? How did he behave?"

I shifted my weight from one side to the other.

My fidgeting caught her attention. "You noticed something?" she pressed.

Everyone else on the rooftop was watching me converse with Detective Glass. I didn't think they could hear our conversation, but just to make sure, I lowered my voice. "He didn't seem like someone who was contemplating suicide."

"People react to stressful situations in unusual ways, Ms. Marshall. What did you observe? I'm not terribly interested in your impressions."

Ouch. Maggie Glass was a tough customer. I cleared my throat. "He was smug and overconfident. Just as you might expect from someone at the top of his game. We chatted briefly about the transportation bill scheduled for next year. There was nothing to indicate he planned to take himself out of the game, so to speak."

Glass's pen flew across the page of notepad. After flipping the page over, she peered up at me. "Anything else? You seem like there's something more to the story."

Damn impressive intuition. This wasn't Maggie Glass's first rodeo. "He seemed intoxicated," I said.

She looked at the empty wineglasses arranged haphazardly on the skirted hightop bar tables. "Is that really a surprise? There's a lot of booze at these fundraisers, I suspect."

"There was an open bar. But Van caught my eye. He was woozy. When I chatted with him, I asked how much he'd had to drink."

Detective Glass raised her eyebrows. "Isn't that a gutsy comment? From a lowly congressional staffer to a big donor?"

I straightened up. "Well, I am the chief of staff for Representative Dixon. Besides, he seemed like he'd had one too many before dinner. I didn't want anyone passing out on top of their filet mignon."

Glass snickered. "We couldn't have that, now could we? What did he say?"

"About the filet mignon?" I asked.

"Ms. Marshall, try to keep up, please. About how much he had to drink?"

"Oh, I'm sorry. It's been a long day," I said. "He said he'd only had two glasses of wine, but he didn't feel good. I remember because I thought he might have lied."

Detective Glass tilted her head. "But why would he fib?" she asked, almost to herself.

"Maybe he was embarrassed because he'd drank too much."

"Still, why would he care what you thought? A bigwig lobbyist is entitled to a few too many drinks at a fundraiser. It doesn't make sense." She jotted more down in her trusty notebook before looking me in the eye. "Thank you for your help. I need to talk to some of the other witnesses now."

"You should talk to my colleague Meg Peters." I stopped myself before mentioning that Meg had been on the rooftop during the incident. No need to buy Meg any trouble. Instead, I added, "She's very savvy. You met her last spring. Remember?"

"How could I forget?" asked Detective Glass.

Detective Glass was referring to the role

Meg played in catching a killer at the famous Continental Club in Washington, D.C. I motioned for Meg to join us. After introductions were done, I left the two of them alone to talk.

Dash had walked over to the southeastern corner of the rooftop. While sipping from a tumbler, he stared directly at the Capitol dome, brightly lit from underneath the dark evening sky. Had that been Van's last view of the world before he flung himself over the railing into the alley below? Had it been some sort of ironic act of desperation on Van's part, killing himself at the footsteps of power and influence he'd traversed so often in his career? I couldn't shake the feeling that something seemed out of place. If he'd been bested by a competitor, then a deep depression was plausible, or even expected. To my knowledge, Van hadn't lost any major political battles lately.

"Penny for your thoughts?" I asked Dash.

He jerked backward, caught by surprise at my question. "Oh, it's you." He rubbed his eyes. "I don't think you can buy anything for a penny these days in Washington."

"How about two thousand seven hundred dollars?" I quoted the maximum amount an individual could donate to a federal election candidate.

Dash smiled. "Now you're talking."

I joined him at the railing, which only reached my hips. "What do you think happened here tonight?"

He motioned toward the dome. "Washington, D.C. killed one of its own."

I blinked. "What do you mean?"

Dash's eyes glazed over. He didn't look at me directly but focused on the skyline. "This city has a way of eating its young."

"I'm still not following you, Dash."

"Van Parker was a major player. But he didn't have much success this year. You don't get too many swings and misses in the high price world of lobbying."

"He seemed pretty confident about his chances with the big transportation bill next year," I said.

"That was his last shot. I guess the pressure got to him," said Dash. "It could have been a moment of insanity."

What was insane was that somehow, I'd found myself in the middle of another suspicious death. Whatever happened, the investigation would surely throw a wrench in my plans for making a fast exit to help my boss in North Carolina.

"I suppose the police will have to sort everything out. Did you see what happened?" I asked.

Dash shook his head. "I was inside the room where we had dinner. You see where he went over, right?"

He pointed to the northern edge, which wasn't the scenic portion of the rooftop. It faced another tall building. Between the two structures was a narrow alleyway where Van's body had landed. From where we were standing, I could see the spot. But a person situated on the western side of the rooftop wouldn't see it. The sizable white tent, which housed the bar for the evening's festivities, obscured it.

I was keenly aware that Dash was being as parsimonious as possible with his words. I'd have to press him to get some answers. "So where did you go after I got on the elevator to leave?"

He raised his glass, filled with amber-colored fluid, in the air. "Had to find a drink for Meg, remember?"

"Sorry, I don't. Maybe it was the dead body on the sidewalk that's caused my memory to fail."

He shook the glass at me before taking a sip. "You're funny, Kit. I can see why Meg likes to hang out with you."

I stiffened up. "We don't just hang out together. We're best friends." It sounded a little defensive, like something a fifth grader

99

might say. It came out of my mouth none-theless. For whatever reason, I sensed Dash would become a rival. Had Meg felt this way about Doug? Maybe now I better understood the loggerheads I frequently navigated when the three of us got together.

"Of course, of course," said Dash in a know-it-all voice. "She's told me about your friendship. I wouldn't have expected any-thing else. After all, Meg is quite a lady. The total package." He grinned from ear to ear.

"She certainly is. But we're getting off topic. I asked you where you went after I left the party."

"And I told you the answer. I went to find another glass of wine. For Meg."

Now it was coming back. "Because she spilled her drink right before I left."

"Bingo." Dash raised his glass in mock congratulations.

"You couldn't see the part of the rooftop where the incident occurred?" I asked.

He pointed to the tent. "The bar was already shut down outside. I couldn't find a waiter to help me. After searching around the table where we had dinner, I found an already open bottle and poured her a glass."

"You didn't see anyone else?" I asked.

"When I was looking for a drink, I did see someone."

This was worse than pulling teeth. "Who?" I tried to keep the exasperation out of my voice.

"A waiter. He was outside on the rooftop. I remember him because I opened the door to the rooftop and asked him for a glass of wine."

"What did he say?"

"Nothing. He heard me, but he didn't stop. He pushed open the door to the stairwell, and I never saw him again."

"Was he one of the waiters who served dinner?"

"I don't really remember," he admitted. "I don't scrutinize the wait staff at these events."

How progressive. "Well, what did he look like? Do you remember? He might have seen something that could help us put this to rest."

"He had dark, wavy hair. A big guy. Tall and not a slight build. Possibly Hispanic, but it's hard to say."

"Have you told the police about him?" I asked.

"Haven't had the chance. You beat them to the interrogation."

I glanced over my shoulder. Detective Glass was still talking to Meg. Maybe she'd seen the waiter, although she hadn't mentioned it when we talked briefly.

Something was bugging me about Dash's story. Then it hit me. "Did you say the waiter opened the door to the stairwell?"

He nodded. "It's right next to the elevators."

"But we're on the ninth floor of this building. That's a lot of stairs."

Dash shrugged. "Who knows? Maybe the guy has a Fitbit, and he has to get his steps in for the day."

Or maybe our mystery waiter wanted to avoid the surveillance camera inside the elevator.

CHAPTER EIGHT

I left Dash to his tumbler of booze and stellar view of the Capitol. Detective Glass had moved onto Lauren. Meg was making a beeline to join Dash, but I intercepted her.

"How did it go?" I asked.

"Routine questions. Where was I when it happened. She also wanted to know about Van's demeanor during the fundraiser."

"What did you say?"

"I told the truth," she said. "He didn't seem like a guy who was ready to commit suicide, but he was acting weird."

"Something was definitely off about him. By the way, did you see a dark-haired waiter on the rooftop after I left?"

Meg took a sip of her wine, which she was clutching like a security blanket. She made a face. "This isn't very good. It figures. Just when I desperately need some alcohol." She put down the glass on an empty high top table.

"Dash said he got you that drink when you were in the bathroom. From an opened bottle somewhere," I explained.

"It was probably still full because no one wanted to drink it." She wrinkled her nose. "What did you say about a waiter?"

"Dash saw a server leaving the rooftop and entering the stairwell next to the elevator. You didn't happen to see him when you came out of the bathroom?" I asked.

Meg shook her head. "Nope. I walked by the elevators and right outside. I didn't see anyone except Dash and Lauren."

"Where was Clarissa? You didn't see her?"

Meg's forehead wrinkled, and she spoke slowly. "I don't think so. She wasn't outdoors."

"Okay, got it. I'm going to try to talk to her next," I said.

"Do you mind if I sit out that conversation? She's never been my favorite person, and I'd like to check in with Dash." She looked longingly in his direction.

"You have a reprieve on sleuthing," I said. "At least for tonight."

She grinned. "Thanks, boss."

I scanned the rooftop until my gaze rested on Clarissa Smythe, who had just thrown the butt of her cigarette on the ground and put it out with the toe of her high heel. She headed toward the door that led inside, so I jogged across the rooftop to catch her.

"Clarissa!" I called out.

She turned around, and I was surprised to see her eyes were red and her creamy complexion was still dotted with blotches.

"Are you alright? Would you like a tissue?" I fished in my purse for one.

She waved me off. "No, I'm fine. I had a moment, but now it's over."

"Are you upset about Van's death? I didn't know you were close."

"We weren't. I'm not sure anyone really knew Van Parker, including Lauren. I'm worried about my business. I've worked hard to build up a profitable clientele base, and I'm sick to my stomach that it could disappear in an instant." Her voice cracked.

Clarissa certainly had a one-track mind. The political fundraising business was a cut-throat, competitive industry inside the Beltway. It wasn't for the faint-hearted, and it certainly took years to make a substantial mark. I still thought she was exaggerating the effect of Van's death on her reputation. If I tried to reassure her again, who knows how long she'd get stuck on the topic. Time to pivot.

"Did you see what happened? Is that upsetting you?" It was a shot in the dark.

"No. I suppose I need to wait and talk to the police before I leave, but I'm not going to be very useful as a witness."

"Were you outside on the rooftop?" I asked.

She shook her head. "I was inside. I spoke briefly with Stuart. You met him earlier. He handles private events for the restaurant. We went over final numbers and the bill. I told him that a few people wanted to have one last drink on the rooftop. I found a seat in the food prep area behind the dining room and read my e-mail and text messages. Even though Members of Congress will be headed to their home districts starting tomorrow, I still have other events scheduled around town in October. I needed to catch up on those commitments."

"Did you see anyone come inside while you were checking your phone?" I asked.

"No, but that would have been impossible. I didn't have a view of the door that connects the dining room with the rooftop."

"So, you didn't see Dash Dugal pour Meg a new glass of wine?"

"I heard ruckus, which must have been Lauren screaming. I followed the noise, and I saw Dash by the table," she said. "Now that you mention it, he did have a glass of wine in his hand."

"What about a dark-haired, tall waiter? Male, with darker skin. Could be Hispanic. Did you see someone matching that description?"

"Nope. Why do you ask?"

"Dash said he saw a guy from the wait staff leave the rooftop and rush downstairs. It could be important," I said.

"No, but like I said, I didn't have a view of the door leading to the outside. Why do you think that's important?" Clarissa asked.

"He could have seen what happened. Who knows what else?"

Clarissa fished in her purse for another cigarette. I noticed her hand was shaking. "Do you mind?"

I did, but Clarissa seemed like she needed it. I shook my head. "Go ahead."

She lit her cigarette and inhaled. "Thanks. Like I said, I'm trying to quit. Today's not the day to push it."

"Probably not. I hope you're able to kick the habit, though," I said.

The corners of her mouth curled upward. "I'm getting there. But what do you mean about the waiter besides being a witness?"

"Nothing, don't worry about it. Let me ask you something else. Do you think Van Parker was depressed enough to commit suicide?"

Clarissa exhaled a cloud of smoke and considered my question. "Like I said, I'm not sure anyone really knew Van Parker. He was a powerful player in the lobbying world, a who's who in Washington. When you're that successful, you don't have many friends. Take my word for it."

"He was a loner?" I asked.

"Van was plenty social, given the requirements of his job. Even so, I doubt he had many true confidantes."

That was a sad commentary on Washington, D.C. but sounded plausible to me. The more time spent at work, the less time available to spend with friends or family. Professional acquaintances often substituted for genuine friendships or relationships. That's why I was so lucky to have Meg and Doug, my yin and yang.

"That could be a challenge," I muttered, mostly to myself. But my voice was loud enough for Clarissa to understand what I said.

"A challenge for what?" asked Clarissa.

I waved my hand. "Oh, you know. Determining whether he actually committed suicide."

Clarissa raised her eyebrows and took an especially long drag. "Is that in question? Didn't he jump off the roof?"

"That's the working assumption but I'm not sure there's substantial evidence to make a definite conclusion." Now I was starting to sound like a cop.

"What you're saying is that Van might have been murdered," said Clarissa.

"Yes. Maybe his fall was assisted."

Clarissa snorted. "That's a euphemism if I ever heard one."

"Touché. But now you understand why I wanted to know if you saw the dark-haired waiter. He could be a witness or even a suspect."

"Sorry. I wish I could help." She took one last pull off her cigarette and extinguished it. I would have politely asked her to use the trash receptacle for her butt to keep the rooftop clean, but given what recently transpired, it seemed nitpicky.

"Do you know the waiter they're talking about? I know you do a lot of events at Charlie Palmer's."

Clarissa thought for a moment before answering. "I can't say that I do. Only a portion of the wait staff work rooftop events since these are high profile affairs. Everyone who works at a place like this is the best in the hospitality game. The rooftop is the crème de la crème, if you know what I mean."

I certainly did. I worked in catering in college to make extra money, and management was particular about which of the staff worked important events. By the time I was a senior, I was working the President's box at football games. I'd even had the pleasure of serving a hot dog to Bill Clinton. Not many people could claim that on their resume.

"You've never seen a person matching that description?" I asked.

"Not for a private dinner I've hosted here before. Maybe he's a new hire."

"Could be. Although all wait staff don't have access to this floor, do they?" I asked.

"No way. As you know, access to the ninth floor is restricted. Only guests and people who have a reason to be up here. A waiter from the main restaurant can't come up here to look around or admire the view."

"Have you told the detective your story?"

"Not yet." Clarissa glanced at her watch. "But I'm going to speak to her as soon as she's done with Lauren. I need to make some phone calls tonight about this debacle."

"Not the press, right?" I asked.

"Definitely not. Although I'm sure they'll get wind of this tomorrow. I need to call your boss."

"You're going to call Maeve?" I asked.

"Of course. She's my client, and someone died at her fundraiser," Clarissa said.

"Don't do that. Let me call her. I think it might be better if it came from me."

Clarissa considered my request for a few seconds before answering. "Okay. But I'm going to follow up with her tomorrow. I work for members of Congress and I take care of them. This is a business relationship. You understand?"

Clarissa had a good point, and she was not someone I wanted to tangle with. "It's a deal. She might head out early for North Carolina."

Clarissa waved her hand. "It doesn't matter. I have her cell numbers, official congressional e-mail, and personal e-mail. If all else fails, I can send her a private message on Facebook."

"No chance of her going off the grid," I agreed. "Thanks, Clarissa."

She nodded and headed in the direction of Detective Glass, who seemed to be wrapping up with Lauren. It was a perfect opportunity to switch conversation partners. I waited until Lauren had stepped aside, and I approached her.

In my most soothing voice, I said, "I know we just met, but once again, I'm really sorry about your husband."

"Thank you. That's very kind." Lauren had stopped crying, but she still dabbed at her eyes with a tissue.

"Were you outside when it happened?" I asked.

"Yes, but I wasn't anywhere near him. Thank God," she said.

I hated to interrogate her now, but establishing where everyone was when Van died would be important. Details about the night would soon be forgotten.

"You were on the other side of the rooftop?" I asked.

She nodded. "Over by the Washington Monument."

Right in the middle of the rooftop was the large white tent which housed the outdoor bar, it obscured the view of the rooftop's other side.

"You were enjoying the scenery?" I asked.

"When I went outside, Van walked in the other direction. I asked him to take a photo of me in front of the monument, and he declined. He muttered something, but I'm not sure what it was." She paused to dab at her seemingly dry eyes. "He seemed out of it to me. He was probably drunk. I don't know. Par for the course these days."

"So, you decided to take your own photo?" I asked.

"Yes. Van hated taking pictures of me. Always complaining on vacation when I wanted to have my photo in front of the Eiffel Tower or the Grand Canyon. He thought it was annoying."

Wasn't it in the husband's list of unwritten vows that as soon as he said, "I do," he became his wife's enthusiastic photographer for the remainder of her days on earth? That's how I viewed it, and I hoped Doug agreed with me.

She rifled through her purse and found her phone. "I didn't use that one," she said. She finally found the right device and swiped it open. "There I am."

Sure enough, there was a photo of Lauren with the Washington Monument in the background. "I posted the best one on Instagram," she said.

I checked the time it was posted, and it fit the timeline of events. She'd shared the picture on the social media site a few minutes after I left the fundraiser.

"Then what happened?"

"After I posted it, I decided to show Van, so I walked in the direction where I saw him go. Then I heard the screaming."

"From below?" I asked.

113

"It was really loud. I followed it and looked over the edge. That's when I saw a man lying on the ground below. I knew it had to be Van." Her chin trembled as she recounted the story.

I put my arm around her. "That must have been horrible."

Lauren breathed deeply. "I don't know if I'll ever get that image out of my mind."

I gave her a squeeze. "Did you see anyone else on the rooftop?"

She pulled away from me. "What do you mean?"

"Dash says he was inside the room where we had dinner, looking to refill Meg's wine. Clarissa talked to the manager and checked e-mails on her phone. Max was coming back upstairs after retrieving a document from his briefcase. Meg was inside the bathroom."

"I guess so," she said. "It wasn't like I kept track of everyone's movements."

I leaned back from her. "I'd already left. I'm recounting what everyone told me after the fact."

The grieving widow disappeared faster than free beer at an intern reception. Lauren's face tightened. "You must have a very good memory to recall those details."

"Not especially," I said. "There were only

114

five people left at the party, besides Van. It's not terribly difficult to keep track."

Lauren looked me directly in the eye. "I don't think it matters if there were five people or fifty people on the rooftop. My husband was distraught and jumped to his death. I don't know if it was planned or a moment of insanity. Either way, he's no longer with us."

Whether or not Lauren was intentionally trying to mislead me, she hadn't answered my question. "Are you sure there wasn't anyone else on the rooftop with you and Van? It could be important."

"I'm not sure why you want to know everything, but actually, there was someone else." She crossed her arms.

"And who was this mystery person?" Newly widowed or not, Lauren was stretching the limits of my patience.

"Someone on the wait staff. I don't know his name. I saw him as I walked over to take my photo in front of the Washington Monument."

"Was he familiar to you? Someone who served us drinks or dinner earlier in the evening?" I asked.

"I don't remember him. He had dark hair and was a big guy. Probably the same size as Van."

That description matched the one Dash had given. There was another person on the rooftop during the time of the incident who no one could identify.

"Did you tell Detective Glass about this person?" I asked.

"Of course. Her questions were almost the same as the ones you just threw at me. Perhaps you should share notes," she said.

I tilted my head. "Not a bad idea."

"It would be more efficient. I don't need to go through the third degree more than once." Lauren sniffed. "After all, I just lost my husband." The grieving widow had suddenly reappeared.

"Of course. I won't take up any more of your time. I am interested in figuring out what happened here tonight. This was my boss's fundraiser, and she will feel responsible, even if she wasn't actually here when Van died."

Lauren glared. "Isn't that the job of the police?"

"Mostly, but I've had some luck solving crimes, too." Just inside the glass doors, I spotted Stuart, the events manager we'd spoken to earlier in the evening. I nodded to Lauren politely and hurried over to catch him.

"Excuse me, it's Stuart, correct?" I asked.

Studying a clipboard loaded with papers, he lowered his reading glasses and glanced at me. "Yes. Who's asking?"

"Remember me? I'm Kit Marshall, Representative Dixon's chief of staff. We hosted the event on the rooftop tonight."

"Oh yes. It seems like a lifetime ago when we met."

"Unfortunately, a life has been lost since we talked earlier."

Stuart blinked several times. "It's a tragedy. Of course, the restaurant isn't liable. The rooftop terrace is up to code. We did nothing wrong."

I waved my hand. "No argument there. However, I'm sure you can understand how concerned Maeve Dixon will be about this incident."

Stuart's cheeks became flush. "That's certainly understandable. I hope she'll remain a client of Charlie Palmer's in the future." He forced a smile. "The congresswoman is a rising star in Washington. We'd like to host more memorable evenings for her political fundraising."

With an edge to my voice, I said, "It can't get much more memorable than this, Stuart."

He winced at my pointed comment. "A valid point, Ms. Marshall."

Now I had him painted into a corner. He'd answer any question I wanted to ask him. "You were on the ninth floor when Van Parker died?"

"I'm not exactly certain." Stuart cleared his throat. "Let's see. I spoke with Clarissa briefly about the final numbers for tonight's event. I told her the rooftop was open until nine. We weren't going to serve any more bottles of wine, but the remaining guests could help themselves to what was already open. Then I got on the elevator and came back downstairs. So, I'm not sure if I was there when it happened."

"Did you see anyone else on the rooftop?" I asked.

"Not that I can recall. But I was busy double-checking my accounts for the night. This wasn't the only private event. We had several other smaller events in dining rooms on the main floor."

"What did you do when you got off the elevator?" I asked.

"I let someone else on it, a guest who was heading back up to the rooftop."

That had to be Max Robinson. "A white guy in his mid-thirties or early forties? Average build and dressed in a suit?"

"Sounds right. He wasn't memorable to me, but I believe I'd seen him upstairs dur-

118

ing dinner, so I knew it was okay to send the elevator back up to the rooftop," he said.

"You didn't see a waiter with dark brown hair when you got on the elevator?" I asked. Stuart might have forgotten the waiter. After all, his presence wouldn't have seemed out of place. "He might have exited the stairwell."

Stuart rubbed his chin as he considered my question. "No one else was in the corridor by the elevator that I recall. But my nose was in my clipboard, I'm afraid."

"You didn't see anyone else on the rooftop?" I asked.

"No, but admittedly, Ms. Marshall, I wasn't paying attention. Like I said, I'd just finalized the bill with Clarissa and had had to do the same with other private soirees. I was reviewing my spreadsheets to make sure everything was in order."

"Does someone work private events on the rooftop matching that description? A big guy with wavy brown hair and a darker complexion?"

Stuart smoothed the lapels of his trim fit designer suit jacket. "You'd have to ask the manager in charge of our servers. They're constantly hiring and firing people around here. We have impeccable standards and not everyone can meet them."

"But that description doesn't ring a bell for you?"

He sniffed. "No, it does not, Ms. Marshall. As you suggest, I'm familiar with the wait staff who work our private events. I'm very particular about good service, and I hadn't heard about someone new being brought onboard for tonight's dinner."

Good enough. Stuart had been a good sport, so perhaps it was time to put his mind at ease. "I'll be sure to let my boss know you've been helpful. She'll appreciate it."

Stuart let out a sigh. "Thank you. We hope to see Representative Dixon at our restaurant again soon." Then he added, "And you, too, of course." With that, Stuart hustled off in the direction of the elevator, undoubtedly way behind in attending to his other important clients.

Meg opened the door and walked inside. She looked up and down the long table where we had dinner, which hadn't been cleared yet. "Looking for something?" I asked.

"I'd love a glass of water or something to drink. I can't find anything," she said.

"Considering the circumstances, maybe we can ask Clarissa if the restaurant can provide us with some refreshments while we wait for the police to release us."

Meg's face brightened. "Good idea, Kit. Did you find anything out when you spoke with Clarissa?"

"I've spoken to everyone who was still at the restaurant when Van went over the edge," I said.

As we were talking, Meg pulled out a compact from her purse and reapplied lipstick, no doubt wanting to look her best for Dash. "And what do you think, Ms. Sherlock?"

There had been a multitude of adaptations of the world's most famous detective, although not one with Holmes as a woman. Not a bad idea. Meg's eyes twinkled. She loved a good mystery almost as much as I did.

"It's too early to tell," I said. Then I added, "Ms. Watson."

She giggled. "I wish I had Lucy Liu's wardrobe."

"That makes two of us. But back to the Van Parker situation. Lauren claims she was on the other side of the roof when it happened, taking a selfie. You were in the bathroom. Dash was inside, looking for a glass of wine. Clarissa spoke with Stuart and then answered messages on her phone."

"Seems like Van took advantage of the situation. He had the opportunity and decided to end it all."

"That's what Lauren, Dash, and Max say. Clarissa isn't convinced," I said.

Meg put her hand on her right hip. "What does Clarissa know? She wasn't friends with Van Parker. She didn't work with him."

"You're right," I said slowly. "But given her position as a fundraiser, she saw Van a lot. Clarissa definitely was privy to his behavior and state of mind."

"I agree it doesn't make complete sense. Listen, Kit. We need to be on the road to North Carolina in the next couple of days. Maeve needs us there for the campaign."

"Absolutely. It's critical we're there for the weeks leading up to the election."

"We can't help her if we're solving a pretend murder. Just this once, maybe you should let it go. The police can handle it. Maggie Glass is a good detective," she said.

Meg was usually the daredevil. Usually, I could be convinced to take a risk, such as snooping where I shouldn't. This was an unexpected twist. She was right about the need for us in North Carolina, but delaying our arrival for a few days shouldn't affect the results of the election. It made me wonder if there wasn't another motive for Meg's sudden reticence.

"I haven't spoken to our boss yet. Let me

see what she says about it," I said.

"She'll want us on a fast train to North Carolina."

I kept my mouth shut, but I strongly doubted Meg's emphatic statement. We had gotten ourselves in a quagmire, and it was going to take a herculean effort to get out of it.

CHAPTER NINE

After saying good-bye to Meg, I scanned the rooftop for Detective Glass. Deep in conversation with a uniformed police officer, she was done with her interviews or had taken a break from them. Either way, it was my opportunity to speak with her.

I pushed open the door and waved my hand in her direction. "Detective, can I speak with you for a moment?"

Glass looked up. It was dark outside, but I'm pretty sure she shook her head when she heard my voice. Truth be told, I'm a homicide detective's worst nightmare during an investigation. But when the case was solved, my assistance was always appreciated. Mostly.

"How can I be of service, Ms. Marshall?" The detective tapped her pen against the side of her face. I'd better keep this brief.

"Did your conversations shed any light on what happened to Van Parker?"

Glass tilted her head and considered my question. On another woman, the detective's ponytail might send a subtle message of unprofessionalism. My first supervisor used to liken such a hairstyle to a "horse's tail," scoffing at it as artless. But Maggie Glass pulled it off with grace. There was an aura surrounding her that let everyone know no matter her choice in hair accoutrements, she meant business.

"We know *what* happened to him. The better and more precise question is *how* it happened," said the detective. "Any first impressions you care to share with me, Ms. Marshall?"

The turning of the tables caught me off guard. I chose my words carefully. "There were several people in the vicinity of the rooftop when Van Parker went over the edge. Yet no one saw or heard anything of consequence."

"That does seem to be the case," she conceded.

"And then there's the report of a waiter on the rooftop at the time, who may or may not work here."

"Roger that. I'm checking out that description with the wait staff supervisor as soon as I head downstairs."

"Identifying that person could be critical

to discovering the truth about Van Parker's death," I said.

"You may be right, Ms. Marshall." Detective Glass extended her hand, and I shook it lightly. "Until we meet again. I assume I can track you down at your House of Representatives office location."

"Yes, ma'am. But we do have a tight election right now in the Congresswoman's district. Meg and I were planning to head to North Carolina soon."

Detective Glass tightened her ponytail. "I'll check in with you tomorrow. You're not headed out that soon, are you?"

"No. But we're not prohibited from going, are we?" I asked.

"Like I said, you'll hear from me tomorrow." She nodded curtly. "Have a pleasant evening."

Sure thing. A body on the pavement won't ruin my evening. A mere inconvenience, like a traffic jam on the Beltway or a weak margarita at Tortilla Coast.

I remained silent and returned the head nod. No point in getting sarcastic with the woman who could determine whether Meg and I were grounded for the foreseeable future. As the days went by, I only saw more votes piling up for Coach Hackensack. We had no utility in Washington, D.C. The only

126

way to help our boss was to head for the campaign.

Before I turned around and headed inside, I took one last look at the beautiful night-time landscape before me. The glittering Capitol could only be challenged in majesty by the stately Washington Monument. Was Dash Dugal onto something? Even if he wasn't pushed by another human being, perhaps Van Parker's death was murder. Had the pressure cooker of our capital city burned out one of its most successful denizens? Although it seemed odd for Van to end it all at a fundraiser, it was possible that was precisely the message he wanted to send. The ultimate condemnation of *Citizens United*? I tried to imagine Van Parker as the martyr for campaign finance reform. I couldn't picture it. Van Parker didn't seem like the modern-day John Brown of Harper's Ferry fame. Whether he killed himself or someone murdered him, there was something eerie about the death of a powerful lobbyist occurring with this picturesque backdrop. I shuddered, and it wasn't because of the autumn chill in the air.

It was half past nine. Maeve would have been done with final votes by now. She might already be at home in her studio apartment, undoubtedly packing up for the trip to North Carolina. I needed to give her a head's up about what happened tonight after she left. Some privacy for the conversation would be nice, at least, away from the police and other interested parties. I got inside the elevator and exited on the ground floor. The restaurant was still busy, but there were only a few stragglers at the bar. I grabbed a barstool on the corner and ordered a club soda with lime. I would have liked something a little stronger, but I needed a clear head to get through this conversation.

Maeve picked up after only two rings. "Kit, are you checking up on me? You know I'm perfectly capable of voting without your assistance." Her upbeat voice gently goaded me. I hated to burst her bubble before her trip, but I had a bad feeling this wasn't going to be an open-and-shut case.

"I'm sure the votes were fine. Congresswoman, we, uh, had an incident after you left the restaurant tonight."

"An incident? Did someone have too much to drink and get into a fight?" she asked.

Not a bad guess, especially with tensions running high before the election. "Not exactly. It's more serious than that."

Maeve's voice lost its teasing tone. "Who

got arrested?"

At least she was headed in the right direction. "No one," I said. "At least, yet."

Maeve emitted what I imagined was a sigh of exasperation. "I give up. Tell me what happened, Kit. I need to leave early tomorrow morning, and I still have a lot to do tonight."

Typical Maeve Dixon. Polite, yet she possessed finite patience. "Van Parker is dead. He fell off the rooftop after dinner was over."

Silence on the line. Finally, Maeve spoke. "An accident?"

"Not likely. It's either a suicide or homicide."

"A homicide? Someone pushed him?" Maeve asked in a shaky voice.

"No one saw anything. The police aren't exactly sure what happened." I summarized everyone's whereabouts at the time of Van's death, including my own.

After I finished, Maeve said, "Let me think for a moment."

Almost a minute ticked by. Finally, I spoke up. "I think you can still go to North Carolina. You weren't involved. Detective Glass never mentioned detaining you."

"She may need to speak to me if this turns out to be a criminal investigation. Of course,

I'm available to talk to her on the phone," she said.

"Right. But you're not a suspect."

"Thank goodness I dodged the bullet this time." She was referring to a recent murder I helped the Capitol Hill Police solve involving a top aide to the Speaker of the House. In that case, Maeve had indeed been the prime suspect until I was able to identify the real killer.

A business-like tenor returned to Maeve's voice. "I agree that I should leave for North Carolina tomorrow as planned." She paused briefly before continuing. "But you need to stay put."

"What do you mean? Don't you need me in the district for your campaign?"

"Of course, I do. News of Van's death will hit the airwaves tomorrow. It will be a Washington story primarily, but the local North Carolina press may pick it up."

"Don't you want me to help you manage it?" I asked.

"Of course. I need you to stay on top of the investigation in Washington. We have press aides on the campaign to help me spin it on the ground, if need be."

I finished my club soda and rubbed my temples. This day had gone south in record time. "I'm helpless here. What matters right now is your election." I tried to keep the whiny pitch out of my voice as much as I could.

"Let's put it this way, Kit. If Van Parker's death is ruled a suicide, then come to North Carolina as planned. But if it's not, I need someone in Washington keeping track of the investigation. A man died at one of my fundraisers. Do you think that's something Coach Hackensack is going to let slide by?"

"Not on your life," I admitted. "In a close race like this, anything is fair game."

"Spoken like an experienced politico," said Maeve. "Kit, there was a reason why I hired you as chief of staff. I trust you to be my eyes and ears. Until this is resolved, you need to play that role in D.C."

"What about Meg?" I asked.

"Didn't you say she was at the restaurant when Van died?"

"Yes, that's right."

"If this is anything but a case of Van taking his own life, she's not going anywhere. Of all people, you should understand that, Kit."

I gulped. Maeve had a point. If Van Parker was murdered, Meg could be a suspect. She didn't mention anyone who saw her inside the bathroom. From the police's point of view, her alibi was as flimsy as the rest.

"Okay, Congresswoman. I understand, and I will be in touch when I have more information."

"Thank you, Kit. I hope I see you soon." The phone clicked off.

Chiefs of staff played many roles for members of Congress. They were political advisers, policy wonks, strategists, and oftentimes personal confidantes. In the best circumstances and relationships, they acted as the elected politician's alter ego. Maeve was needed on the campaign trail and that meant I had to take care of the fiasco in Washington. We'd carefully managed her votes and policy endorsements over the past several months. I hadn't foreseen another murder on the horizon.

After paying my bill, I ordered an Uber for the second time this evening. A few minutes later, my driver pulled up, and I got inside. This time, we sped away without interruption.

"Did you call for a ride earlier tonight and cancel?" asked my driver. Uber provided your customer history to their drivers so they could select clients with good track records.

"Something unfortunate happened so I

had to delay," I said.

"You don't want to do that too often. You'll hurt your rating."

"Duly noted," I said dully.

"I almost didn't pick you up. Not because of your rating, but because I heard on the radio someone died at Charlie Palmer's tonight."

Maeve had been right. It hadn't taken long for the news to spread. "It was someone I knew. He fell off the rooftop. Probably suicide," I added.

My driver shrugged his shoulders. "Sounded suspicious on WTOP." He referred to the popular news, radio, and traffic radio station in Washington.

"What isn't suspicious in D.C. during election season?" I countered.

"Good point, lady."

With that, my driver focused his attention on the harrowing merge near the Kennedy Center. Ten minutes later, he dropped me off at my condo building in Arlington, a nearby Virginia suburb of Washington.

While getting everyone's story straight, I'd neglected to let Doug know what happened. He was used to my late nights with fundraising dinners, so he probably hadn't thought anything was out of the ordinary.

After putting my key into the lock, I heard

133

a muffled bark on the other side. I cracked open the door slowly and braced myself for a full-fledged beagle mutt attack.

Clarence did not disappoint. Before I knew it, he'd wedged himself in the narrow opening, with his chunky butt wiggling with excitement.

"Get back inside, buddy. I don't need another incident this evening." Clarence liked to escape down our condo hallway, often barking to celebrate his freedom. Our neighbors, who valued the quiet atmosphere of our condo building more than Clarence's exuberance, did not appreciate this behavior.

My newlywed husband was relaxing on the couch, his nose in a book. Undoubtedly, he was devouring the last canonical work in American history. A professor at Georgetown, Doug engaged in predictable activities. When he wasn't writing or teaching, he was reading. He ran his hand through his bushy brown hair and grabbed his glasses from the coffee table.

"Later than usual, aren't you?" he asked.

I smiled and sat next to him. "The evening proved more challenging than I bargained for."

His eyebrows shot up. "Why don't you tell me about it? Would you like a drink?"

"I would, but I shouldn't." I grimaced. After the election, I was looking forward to a detox.

"Let me pour you a little something, and we'll talk," said Doug.

He disappeared into our kitchen and came back with a tall, dark bottle with a picture of a dog on it. I recognized it immediately. "That's from Barrel Oak Winery."

Doug nodded. "It's their Chocolate Lab dessert wine. Remember our trip there?"

"How could I forget?" I replied.

A few weekends ago, we'd gone to the popular destination for a nice, relaxing day in the Virginia countryside. Located an hour's drive west of Arlington, the vineyard's initials, BOW, was significant. Although not required, most people who visited Barrel Oak brought a canine companion. It was known as the most dog-friendly winery in the area.

"That poor family won't likely forget it, either," said Doug.

Clarence was a sweet but mischievous dog. He'd enjoyed his day at Barrel Oak, visiting with other pups and soaking up the fresh air. We turned our backs on him to open a bottle of wine we'd just purchased inside the tasting room. Apparently, Clarence had been waiting for the perfect opportunity to spring into action. In the span of seconds, our mutt had jumped up on a nearby picnic table and devoured a snack plate of cured meats and cheese. By the time we intercepted him, he was licking his chops in delight. Thankfully, the victims of the crime were good sports about it. After purchasing a replacement for the stunned family, we corked our wine and left Barrel Oak with our tails between our legs.

"I think I had one sip before we had to leave in disgrace," I said.

"Fortunately, it seems to have kept well since our fiasco." Doug poured me a half glass.

I took a sip. He was right. The Chambourcin port-style wine burst with earthy cocoa flavorings. A perfect Virginia vintage, which had the added benefit of supporting rescue dog organizations. Drinking for a cause seemed to make imbibing almost philanthropic.

After serving himself a generous portion, Doug joined me on the couch. "What happened?"

I took a deep breath and recounted the events of the evening. Doug had many good qualities (otherwise I wouldn't have married him), but amongst the most noteworthy was his ability to listen. Perhaps it was his training as a historian that encouraged his patient attentiveness. He liked to hear the entire story unfold and then ask questions. After a stressful evening, his placid serenity calmed the freneticism that often plundered my clear thinking. Doug was an island of rational tranquility in times of crisis.

Doug rubbed his chin, ostensibly deep in thought. "A curious circumstance. A man plunges to his death from the rooftop of a well-known restaurant. No one knows if it was self-inflicted or homicide. Quite a puzzle. It's almost like the old axiom about a tree falling in a forest."

"If it doesn't make a sound, did it fall at all?" I asked.

"Exactly. How do you know the cause of a death if no one witnessed it and there's not obvious physical evidence?"

"If a person on the rooftop killed Van, then someone did see it," I said.

"Precisely. But how do you prove it? The only credible witness is dead, I'm afraid," said Doug.

"According to the stories we've heard thus far."

"I stand corrected. Based upon the *alleged* accounts of the evening," said Doug, with appropriate emphasis.

"Have you heard of Edmond Locard?" I asked.

"Can't say I have."

I tried to mask my delight. It was truly rare for me to know something historical that Doug didn't know. I made a mental note to relish the moment.

"Locard was an early twentieth century forensic scientist in France," I explained. "He became famous for an important observation in criminal investigation."

Doug sipped his wine. "You've got my attention. Let me have it."

"Every contact leaves a trace. It's known as the exchange principle. When two objects touch each other, something is left behind."

"It's an interesting concept, I suppose," said Doug. "Why does it matter here?"

"Locard argued that there are no perfect crimes. If a person does harm to someone through physical contact, then some type of evidence of that exchange exists."

Doug furrowed his eyebrows. "Then why do some murders remain unsolved? Doesn't that refute Locard?"

"No, because even though there have been improvements in forensic science, sometimes investigators can't find the evidence." I paused to sip my drink. "But it still exists, according to the exchange principle."

"And you think Locard is pertinent to Van Parker's death?"

I sat forward on the couch. "Absolutely. If Van Parker was murdered, someone made contact with him. He didn't go over the edge of the roof willingly. So how was it done? We don't have any eyewitness accounts, so his principle could be helpful."

"Of course, if the mysterious waiter is the killer, then it might be hard to find your evidence. You don't even know who he is," said Doug.

"That's true. But murderers don't materialize out of nowhere. There would have to be a motive or an important connection to Van Parker."

Doug finished his drink and placed his glass on the coffee table. He leaned back on the couch and grabbed my hand. "I feel like we've been down this road before, but I'd be remiss if I didn't state the obvious."

I didn't pull back, even though I knew what was coming and wouldn't much like it. "Go ahead. Say it."

"If your hunch is right and Van didn't commit suicide, then the murderer was on that rooftop tonight. That narrows down the pool of suspects considerably," he said. "And might I add all of these individuals know who you are."

"That should make it easier to figure out what happened," I said defensively.

"You're missing the point, Kit," said Doug through clenched teeth. "If the killer knows you're snooping around, it's not too difficult for him or her to make you the next victim."

"I know, I know. We *have* been down this road before. I'm always careful. Detective Glass is on the case again. I won't hesitate to call her if I figure something out."

Doug gave me a skeptical look. "I'll take your word for it." He let go of my hand and put his arm around me, squeezing me tight. "There's a silver lining to all of this."

"Really? I'd definitely like to hear it," I said.

"As long as Van Parker's death remains a mystery, you get to stay here with me and Clarence. As far as I'm concerned, I hope Locard's principle *doesn't* save the day."

Doug's embrace comforted me, but I couldn't get visions of Maeve Dixon's concession speech out of my head. As much as I loved Doug and Clarence, I needed to figure out what happened to Van Parker so I could hightail it to North Carolina. The clock was ticking, and so was the vote tally for Coach Hackensack.

CHAPTER TEN

Sunrise came later these days, so it wasn't hard for me to sleep well past my normal wakeup time. I'd neglected to set the alarm, perhaps a subconscious decision after a stressful evening. When I finally opened my eyes, the morning darkness of our bedroom obscured my vision. Nonetheless, I could still hear the perfectly synchronized rhythmic snores next to me. Although I would never say it aloud, Doug and Clarence's somnolent snuffles resembled the haunting song of underwater humpback whales. How did I sleep amongst such noise? I wondered myself until an Internet search revealed that insomnia sufferers found the sounds of whales deeply relaxing and conducive to sleep. Despite the many anxieties of current and past jobs, I'd never resorted to sleep medication. Sheer exhaustion played a key role, but after my research, I realized my own private whalesong symphony helped, too.

As relaxing as the acoustics might be, it was time to get up and face the real music. Clarence, who preferred snuggling to morning exercise, showed no sign of budging. I left him tucked underneath Doug's arm. When I was showering, Doug must have awoken from his slumber and made his way to the kitchen. The smell of freshly brewed coffee greeted me as I stepped out the bathroom clad in my fuzzy pink robe. Yesterday had not gone according to plan, but today had begun with a promising start. Doug kissed me on the forehead and handed me a steaming mug as I took a seat at our dining room table.

"Is this what I think it is?" I asked.

"One double shot cappuccino, made with nothing other than the famous Dean & Deluca espresso."

I took a deep inhale. The rich boldness of the coffee greeted me. Dean & Deluca was a gourmet food store in Georgetown. Sometimes Doug surprised me with treats from the store, like chocolate babka or lobster mac and cheese. Their coffee was as delicious as the other pricey delicacies they peddled on busy M Street.

"Thank you. My day is already getting

better." I smiled after a sip.

Clarence listened patiently to our exchange and then issued a polite "woof."

"I almost forgot you," said Doug. "Here you go, Clarence." After accepting a paw for a brief shake, Doug gave Clarence a biscuit.

"Please don't tell me you bought Clarence dog treats at Dean & Deluca."

Doug adjusted his glasses. "Of course not. These are beef bourguignon biscuits from the Cheeky Puppy. I passed by the other day when I was in Dupont Circle and bought them."

I burst into laughter. "I like how you said it seriously, as if it's somehow better you bought them there."

"Well, it is a pet store, Kit. Besides, Clarence enjoys the variety. Don't you, buddy?"

Clarence knew where his bread was buttered. Although he liked the attention I bestowed, Doug was an easier mark. Besides snoozing together, Doug and Clarence were eating companions. And they both had gourmet palates.

"I suppose Clarence deserves only the best." I rubbed his floppy ears, and he growled softly in appreciation.

Doug cleared his throat. "Speaking of

superlatives, I'd like to talk to you about an opportunity that's come to my attention. It's worth a discussion."

"How intriguing," I said. "Let me fix breakfast and then you'll have my full attention."

All the talk of epicurean chow had caused my stomach to rumble. Last night's dinner seemed like ages ago. Besides, suspicious deaths were traumatic. Didn't stress burn calories? After perusing the refrigerator's meager contents, I threw four pieces of cinnamon bread into the toaster and put a stick of butter on the table.

I sat back down and took another sip of my coffee. "I'm all ears. What's this great opportunity?" Knowing Doug, it was probably a substantial advance on another historical tome. He'd already penned several successful American history books that had garnered critical claim and impressive sales. In my mind, he was one break away from dethroning David McCullough. Doug said historians didn't think in those terms. But I was confident publishers did.

Doug sat up straight in his chair. "I've had another offer of employment."

I blinked several times. "Really? Is George Washington or American University trying to steal you from Georgetown?"

"Not exactly."

Now I was puzzled. "George Mason? I'm not sure you'd like traveling all those miles every day to Fairfax. The traffic going westbound is horrible."

Doug laughed nervously. "Think a little further than that."

"Further?" I thought for a moment. "Oh no, Doug. The University of Maryland? I'm not moving outside the Beltway to College Park." I shook my head vigorously. "It's out of the question. I'm simply not comfortable in the Maryland suburbs."

"What about New York City?" he asked softly.

"New York? What do you mean?" The pitch of my voice rose several octaves.

"Columbia University would like to make me a job offer. With tenure, of course."

Doug's pronouncement knocked the wind out of me. My brain kicked into automatic overdrive. Did this mean we'd move to New York? What about my job for Representative Dixon? My thoughts quickly flashed to Meg and all our friends in the D.C. area. These converging, unsettling notions almost made me dizzy. Then I smelled the faint odor of something burning.

I jumped up. "Crap! Our breakfast!"

By the time I rescued the toast, it had

145

been burnt beyond a palatable condition. "Great," I muttered. "Now what are we going to eat?"

Doug got up from the table and put his arm around me. "I shouldn't have mentioned Columbia. You have too much on your plate these days."

"Given that I just ruined our breakfast, I actually have nothing on my plate," I said with a chuckle. "But seriously, Doug. There's no reason to hide it from me."

"Let's not talk about it anymore. We can pick it up another time. After all, Columbia isn't going anywhere." He smiled.

"You want to consider it?" I asked, even though I knew the answer.

He gave me a squeeze. "It's a good opportunity. But like I said, we don't need to make any decisions today."

I nodded numbly. "I'd better get ready for work. It's hard to say what the day will bring." *Especially given what's already happened, and it's only eight in the morning.*

"We can talk more soon." Doug's kiss brushed my cheek, and I ambled out of the kitchen. Could one day bring any more surprises? Of course, underestimation is a familiar mistake in both love and politics.

As I rode the subway to work, my mind wandered. Doug's announcement had been a bombshell. Was he tired of living in Washington? He'd said that Columbia wanted to make him an offer, but had he made it known he was interested in leaving Georgetown? If we moved to New York City, what would I do? My entire career thus far had been focused on politics and policy. Washington was the mecca for such work, but government was everywhere. Even so, I couldn't imagine working for an elected official other than a member of Congress. Who was in politics in New York? The Mayor? I didn't know anything about the Big Apple, and I certainly didn't have any solid contacts. Had Doug considered all these complications? Of course, we hadn't exactly conversed in depth on the subject. The burnt breakfast had been a convenient excuse to end the discussion and leave abruptly for work.

The subway arrived at Rosslyn station and the inevitable crush of commuters squeezing on an already crowded train reduced my personal space to nothing. The young millennial squeezed next to me was trying to read a book. I glanced at the cover. *Why Politicians Are Ruining America.* Lovely title, especially given that I worked directly for a person who was allegedly responsible for the country's demise. I sighed deeply.

Maybe Doug was onto something. We'd lived in Washington for several years now. Was it time for a change? I tried to imagine myself in Manhattan. Without thinking, I hummed the catchy theme song from "Sex and the City." There was no way I could keep up with Carrie Bradshaw. But Miranda was completely within reach. With that realization, I allowed myself a tentative smile.

CHAPTER ELEVEN

Only a few passengers got off the train at
the Capitol South stop. The exodus had
already begun. Many people had already
switched their employment status from
congressional staffer to campaign aide. By
next week, the Hill would be a ghost town.
It was a big reminder that Meg and I
needed to make a break for North Carolina
as soon as possible. Our departure hinged
on the police coming to a speedy resolution
about Van Parker's death. Unfortunately,
"D.C. Metro police" and "speed" were
rarely mentioned in the same breath.

Even the Cannon building office was
quieter than usual. We'd already sent our
press secretary and several junior staffers
south. Maeve probably left at the crack of
dawn and was more than halfway there.
With any luck, she'd be at a senior center
by noon, shaking hands and reconnecting
with voters. I was about to check her public

schedule to see where she'd visit today when Meg entered my small office.

"Detective Glass wants to chat with us," she announced.

"Good morning to you, too," I replied.

Meg rubbed the back of her neck. "Sorry. I'm a little tense."

"About last night, I presume."

"Why would Glass want to speak with us already?" she asked.

I shrugged. "Beats me." I held my breath. "Maybe she's going to say we can go to North Carolina after all. Last night, she told me she'd check in with us."

Meg snapped her fingers. "That's probably it!" Then her face fell abruptly. "I still want to go, but I'm going to miss Dash."

I narrowed my eyes. "Really, Meg?" There was no hiding the exasperation in my voice.

Meg sucked her cheeks in. "What's wrong with that? Aren't you going to miss, Doug?"

I was about to say it wasn't the same, but stopped myself. "Of course, I will. But you know how busy we'll be once we hit the campaign trail. There won't be much time for missing anyone."

"You're right. Still, I think I'll ask Dash if he'd come down for a few weekends to visit."

I shook my head. "It's up to you, but we

won't have a day off if the internal polls remain as close as they've been."

"He could campaign with us. Lobbyists can take time off their jobs to help with campaigns," she said.

Meg was right. Besides throwing money at close races, K Street also supplied a fair amount of volunteer labor the weeks leading up to an election. I wasn't thrilled about Dash tagging along, but we needed the help however we could get it.

"Fantastic," I said. "We'll put him to work if he makes the trip."

Meg's face brightened immediately. "I'll mention it the next time we talk."

Intern Brock appeared behind Meg. My office was so small, there wasn't room for him to stand inside. He waved from the doorway. "There's a police officer here to see you both," he said.

"That was fast," I said. "She must want to tell us something."

"Where do you want to meet with her?" he asked.

"Please show her to the Congresswoman's office." When Maeve wasn't in Washington, we used her office for staff meetings requiring privacy.

Brock hustled off to retrieve Detective Glass. I turned back to Meg. "Ready?"

"I don't think we have a choice," she said somberly.

We used the connecting door to enter our boss's office. Detective Glass was admiring the framed photos of Maeve Dixon. Many of them were from her days in the military. She'd deployed all over the world, including Iraq and Afghanistan, as an Army intelligence officer after her graduation from West Point.

Detective Glass must have heard us, but she kept her eyes on the wall decorations. "Representative Dixon has had an impressive career," she remarked. "And she's still quite young."

"Absolutely," said Meg enthusiastically. "That's why we like working for her."

"And we want to keep working for her," I added. "To do that, she needs to win in November."

Detective Glass turned to face us. "I wish her the best. Unfortunately, she may have to survive without you."

Meg clenched her jaw. "What do you mean, Detective?"

"Look, I know you're both busy, so I won't mince words. Van Parker's death is being ruled as suspicious," she said. "Right now, we're not sure what happened to him."

"What changed since last night?" I asked.

"Something must have happened, or you wouldn't have bothered to see us so quickly."

Detective Glass spoke slowly. "There has been a development."

Meg put her hands on her hips. "I think we have a right to know. If you're preventing us from doing our job and helping our boss, we should understand what's going on."

"I suppose you have a point," said the detective. "To be honest, it doesn't add up for me. I called the Congresswoman this morning and spoke to her when she was driving to North Carolina."

"And what did she say?" It would've been nice if Maeve had told me she talked to Detective Glass this morning. Although it was hard to blame her given how much she had on her mind these days.

"It wasn't her impression that Van was contemplating suicide," she said. "Congresswoman Dixon said he spoke enthusiastically about an upcoming piece of legislation he was going to work on. He was planning to enlist her help."

"You mean the highway reauthorization bill. That's consistent with what Van told me last night," I said.

Detective Glass flipped through her notebook. "I know. I have the notes from our chat right here. So that corroborates your story."

In an exasperated voice, Meg said, "Kit wouldn't lie. So why is that such a big revelation?"

"It supports the theory that Van Parker didn't act like a man who was contemplating an abrupt exit," said the detective. "It doesn't fit with the suicide explanation."

"Although his wife did say he hadn't been sleeping well," said Meg. "Lauren claimed he was depressed."

"Claimed is the right word," I said. "All we have is her word. Like the Detective said, Van behaved like a powerful lobbyist who was going to be around for a big fight on transportation funding next year."

Detective Glass listened to our exchange with her eyebrows raised. "All the more reason to rule this a suspicious death. Is it a suicide? Perhaps. But the police need more time to figure it out. And that means, unfortunately for the both of you . . ." She paused for a beat. "You need to remain in town until we resolve what happened to Van Parker."

Meg's expression tightened. "We're being held hostage in Washington, D.C. during the most important election of a generation. This is ridiculous."

My best friend was prone to exaggeration. Was this election pivotal to our nation's future? All elections were critical because the outcomes had serious consequences for policy decisions. Meg had the gift of hyperbole, and she wasn't giving it up.

Something didn't add up. Last night, Detective Glass knew Van Parker's demeanor didn't fit the typical profile for someone who wanted to take his life. So why was she suddenly more inclined to believe Parker had been a homicide victim this morning?

"Are you sure there isn't something else you want to tell us?" I asked. "A new piece of information besides talking to our boss this morning?" *Which didn't reveal any new information about last night.*

Detective Glass wet her lips and swallowed. I'd hit a nerve. To keep the pressure on, I stared directly at her.

"Alright. Good catch. There's another detail I might as well share with you," said Glass.

"Which is?" Meg pressed.

Detective Glass hesitated. "I probably shouldn't say this in front of a potential suspect."

"Suspect?" Meg practically shouted.

Thank goodness we were inside Maeve's office, which was surrounded by privacy walls. Otherwise, the skeleton crew of a congressional staff we still had working in the D.C. office would have thought something had gone seriously awry.

Detective Glass's chin trembled. "I'm sorry to call you that, Ms. Peters. But if we're talking about a homicide, you were in the immediate vicinity of the murder. No one can corroborate your whereabouts at the time of the crime."

"Wait a second," I said. "I can affirm that Meg was headed to the bathroom when I left. She was walking in that direction when I entered the elevator."

Glass nodded. "That's helpful. But it's not determinative, I'm afraid. You didn't see her *inside* the bathroom."

"No, I didn't," I said in a resigned tone.

"No one on the rooftop can confirm Meg's location, either," said Glass.

"I had to go to the bathroom to remove a wine stain from my dress and suddenly I'm a murder suspect," exclaimed Meg. "I wish Johnnie Cochran was still alive. He could smell injustice a mile away."

Another example of Meg's inclination to embellish. Thankfully, Maggie Glass didn't take the bait.

"Don't get too excited, Ms. Peters," said the detective. "You're a person of interest. I didn't say you were the focus of my investigation. Unfortunately, it still means you can't leave town."

"What about Kit?" asked Meg. "She has an alibi."

"You're correct. We confirmed her story with the Uber driver and the witnesses on the sidewalk at the time of Van Parker's death. Kit was definitely not on the rooftop when Van died."

"There's no reason she needs to stay in Washington," said Meg.

"The police aren't keeping me here," I said. "But the Congresswoman wants me to make sure Van Parker's death is resolved. We can't have a suspicious death hanging over the campaign."

Detective Glass nodded. "Your boss mentioned her concern to me on the phone this morning. She definitely wants you to stay put." She motioned toward me. "At least for now."

Before Detective Glass left, we needed to circle back to the detail she mentioned earlier in the conversation. "Before we started talking about suspects, weren't you going to tell us something important about Van Parker's death?"

Detective Glass chuckled. "Not much gets by you, Ms. Marshall," said the detective.

"Kit's very sharp," said Meg. "We've caught three murderers in the past year, and we'll get to the bottom of this mystery, too."

"Let's leave the police work to the professionals this time. You've gotten lucky, but we're dealing with a really nasty individual if Van Parker was murdered last night," said Detective Glass. "Someone crazy enough to push him over a railing to his death."

"No more depraved than the other killers we've encountered," I said. "But point taken. What was the update?"

"There's a suspicious mark on Van Parker's torso. The medical examiner found it last night. I don't know where it came from, but it's enough evidence to warrant a further investigation," said the detective.

In perfect unison, Meg and I responded. "What type of mark?" Then we both laughed.

"Great minds think alike," I added.

"I've probably said too much already," said Detective Glass. "I'm waiting for the chief examiner to take a closer look later today. Could be nothing but an unrelated scratch or irritation."

"It must be something important or you wouldn't have made the trip this morning to give us an update," said Meg.

Detective Glass pursed her lips into a thin line. "Have a good day. Ms. Peters, please don't leave town. When I have more information about the investigation, I'll notify you," she said curtly. Then she got up and left the office, closing the door behind her.

Meg and I looked at each other for several seconds. My best friend finally broke the silence. "We'll just have to figure out how she did it."

"Excuse me," I replied. "Who is she?" Had Meg already solved the crime? If so, I was damn impressed.

"Lauren Parker," said Meg. "If Van didn't kill himself, she did it."

"How do you know that?" I asked.

"She had motive and opportunity." Meg ticked off two fingers. "Lauren wanted her husband dead because she was having an affair with Chairman Edwards. She was on the rooftop when Van went over."

"I get the motive, although having an affair doesn't necessarily mean you want to murder your spouse," I said. "But Lauren had an online alibi at the time. She posted a selfie in front of the Washington monument. While you were in the bathroom."

Meg wrinkled her nose. "Something smells fishy. Look at it this way. I didn't do it. Dash

159

didn't do it. Who was the other guy around — the bike lobbyist?"

"Max Robinson," I said. "He wasn't on the rooftop. He'd gone downstairs to get his briefcase to show you some papers."

"So, he has an actual alibi."

"That's how it appears. Clarissa was up there, too," I added.

"That's right. She could have done it."

I spoke slowly. "Maybe, Meg. But why would Clarissa kill Van Parker? This murder could really kill her business. Pun very much intended."

Meg hesitated. "I don't know. But that doesn't mean she didn't have a reason to want him dead."

"True enough. We might not know the motive yet. But don't forget the most obvious suspect of all," I said.

Meg held her breath. She probably thought I was going to mention Dash. Quite frankly, I didn't know what to make of him. I wasn't ready to exonerate him like Meg. No need to pick a fight with her right now.

"Our mysterious waiter. Lauren and Dash both saw him on the roof at the time of the incident. No one matching his description works at the restaurant. At least that was the story last night."

"Maybe we need to find that guy. He

could be our killer. Someone could have hired him," Meg said excitedly. "Like a hit-man!"

"Certainly, murder for hire is possible," I said. "But why on the rooftop of a famous D.C. steakhouse? Aren't hits usually carried out in secluded places, like garages or the woods?"

"I don't know, Kit," said Meg. "Do I look like Tony Soprano?"

I giggled. "Not really. Bada-bing!"

Meg offered a bemused smile and smoothed her crisply ironed pleated skirt. "I'd hope I don't resemble an overweight Jersey gangster. Van Parker had a lot of enemies. It's logical to think someone wanted to bump him off."

"Quite literally, as it turned out," I said.

"I still think Lauren is our best bet. When in doubt, always take a hard look at the spouse. That's homicide one-oh-one, right?"

Meg had a point. "You are correct. And she did have a motive and possibly opportunity. However, she's missing a key ingredient, which makes it hard to think she's our killer."

Meg smoothed her blonde bob and tucked a lock of hair underneath her ear. "Which is?"

"Means," I said. "How could tiny Lauren

push Van Parker over the railing? She weighs no more than one hundred ten or one hundred fifteen pounds. She greatly resembles you, Meg. Am I right?"

Meg rolled her eyes. "I won't confirm or deny my weight, but it's a good guess."

"How could someone of her stature push a big man like Van off a building? He was double her size, at least."

"I don't know anything about physics. If he wasn't expecting it, maybe Lauren could have given him a hard shove over the edge," said Meg.

I sighed. "She would have needed a running start at linebacker speed. It seems unlikely. Van was over six feet tall and appeared to be in good shape. Definitely not a pushover."

Meg crossed her arms. "You can't completely rule her out. But there's also Clarissa and the so-called waiter."

I nodded. "Absolutely." I paused for a second and added, "Dash, too."

Meg's face tightened, and her nostrils flared. "You can take him off the suspect list."

I touched Meg's arm lightly, but she jerked away. "Try to be reasonable about this," I said softly.

"Reasonable? You're accusing my boyfriend of murder. What if I told you I thought Doug killed someone? How would you react?"

What if you knew Doug wanted us to move to New York? Meg might be the one accused of murder if she found out. Best to save that revelation for another time.

"I wouldn't believe it. But I've known Doug for years. You've only known Dash for a couple months. There's a difference," I said.

"Kit, I know Dash and believe me, he would never do this. I haven't told you this yet, but I think he might be the one."

I leaned back. "What do you mean?"

"I'm falling in love with Dash. Isn't it obvious?" asked Meg.

My mouth fell open, and I suppressed a gasp. "Are you sure?"

"Is anyone ever sure about these things? But I know I feel differently about him than the other guys I've dated."

That was a long list of previous suitors. I thought for a moment before I responded. Something bugged me about Dash, but if I was too negative about him, Meg would shut me out. I had to be careful. After all, she was my colleague and my best friend. The latter meant more to me than the former.

"That's terrific, Meg. I hope your hunch is right and he is the guy for you." I reached out again and this time she didn't pull away. "You deserve the best."

"Thank you, Kit. It feels good to hear that from you," said Meg. "I'm glad you agree Dash couldn't have killed Van."

I never said Dash was innocent.

"Let's get this sorted out as quickly as possible." I gave Meg a quick squeeze. "That would be the best for everyone involved."

"Agreed. I'd better get back to my desk and catch up on my e-mails."

"Good idea. I'll start snooping around about Van Parker," I said.

"Where will you start?" asked Meg.

"A memorable and reliable source," I said.

CHAPTER TWELVE

After pounding away on my computer for a solid hour, I picked up my iPhone and punched the button for a familiar contact. A few seconds later, a whiny male voice came on the line.

"When bodies drop out of the sky, I am never surprised to receive a call from Kit Marshall, congressional staffer and sleuth extraordinaire."

"Always a noteworthy greeting, Trevor. Thanks for picking up," I said.

"At your service, ma'am. Let me guess. Your call has something to do with the fact that top lobbyist Van Parker fell to his death last night at Congresswoman Maeve Dixon's fundraiser. Am I correct?" he asked.

"You're a mind reader."

Trevor chuckled. "Not a mind reader. Just observant. My counsel is obviously valuable to you when a suspicious death has occurred."

"That's an exaggeration, Trevor."

"Not really. I don't believe you've called me since your nuptials this past June," he said.

That couldn't be true. Or was Trevor correct? It had been a busy summer between our all-too-brief Parisian honeymoon and Maeve's reelection fight. Quite frankly, the last several months were a big blur. There hadn't been much time for casual socializing. Before my job with Maeve Dixon in the House of Representatives, Trevor and I had worked together in the Senate. The murder of our boss had brought us together to solve mysteries we stumbled across in Washington. Trevor was as smart as a whip. He was also more annoying than Anderson Cooper on steroids.

"If that's the case, I'm sorry. We've got our hands full with our challenger, Coach Hacksensack," I said.

"Apparently, you need to add Van Parker to the mix," said Trevor.

"Unfortunately, you're right. That is why I'm calling," I said sheepishly.

"I knew it. Let me guess," he said. "Van Parker didn't jump off the top floor of Charlie Palmer's because his steak was undercooked."

"No. In fact, the food was excellent."

"As always. I prefer the New York strip when I dine there. But we digress. It's safe to assume that someone assisted in Van's fall?" he asked.

"We're not entirely sure what happened. His wife Lauren swears that Van was depressed. She believes it's suicide, or at least that's what she's claiming," I said. "But Detective Glass from D.C. Metro paid us a visit this morning at the office, and she's leaning toward homicide."

"I doubt Van Parker killed himself. That explanation is as dubious as a fast-paced Senate."

Trevor and I chuckled at his joke. Known as the world's most deliberative democratic body, the Senate wasn't exactly known for its speed.

"Why don't you think Van's death was a suicide?" I asked.

"Van might have dreamed of ending other people's lives, but never his own. He was one of the most self-confident, egoistical operatives in all of Washington," said Trevor. "And he loved every blessed moment of his reign over K Street."

"You knew him well?" I asked.

"No one was friends with the man, Kit. He wasn't a guy who hung out with buddies on the weekend, drinking beer and going to Nationals games. But everyone in this town had to deal with him because he was such a powerful player."

"Do you know who wanted him dead?"

Trevor made a sound that resembled a snort. "You're asking the wrong question. Who *didn't* want to kill him might narrow the list. Not the reverse."

"Terrific. He was a real Prince Charming," I muttered.

"Don't misunderstand me, Kit. He was likable enough. An excellent schmoozer, as I recall. When I lobbied for the defense industry, our paths crossed several times. He was always professional and courteous. But I never found myself on the opposite side of his clients. If I had, it would have been a different story."

"Why do you know so much about Van if you only interacted with him on a few occasions?" Trevor wasn't a catty gossip. I was curious about the source of his information if he and Van hadn't been close acquaintances.

"Let's just say he provided good fodder for my manuscript," he said.

I'd almost forgotten about Trevor's book. After several career twists and turns, Trevor had landed a deal with a publisher to write a tell-all about life in our nation's capital.

"Are you finished writing?" I asked.

"Signed, sealed, and delivered months ago," he said proudly. "In fact, I'm waiting for the edited manuscript to arrive on my doorstep. After the election, I'll be out on a book tour. The publicity department hopes to capitalize on the excitement about politics after the campaign season ends."

"Trevor, that's quite impressive." Upon occasion, I stroked my friend's ego, which I knew he appreciated. This time, my accolades were genuine. We'd both come a long way from since our Senate days, which we spent toiling side-by-side in claustrophobic cubicles in the back of a crowded, loud office suite. "Van is in your book?" I asked.

"Anyone who is someone is in my book," said Trevor confidently. "He was a top dog on K Street. Of course, he's featured."

"Do you know any details about what Van was working on? I understand he had a litany of enemies. But I need something more concrete," I said.

The line went silent. I picked up a pen on my desk and tapped it against my "Dixon for Congress" coffee mug while waiting for Trevor to respond.

"You need to speak with one of Van's colleagues," said Trevor. "I'm almost certain I have a contact there. Let me search my database on my computer, and I'll get back to you."

"You have a database of people you know?" I tried to keep the envy out of my voice.

"Absolutely, Kit. How else could I keep everyone straight for my book?"

Trevor never ceased to amaze. He'd remade himself twice in the past year and had barely missed a beat. Washington was famous for giving ambitious people second, third, and even fourth chances. Each time Trevor resurrected himself, he'd returned with better contacts, deeper insights, and improved social skills. His stubborn resiliency reminded me that cockroaches can live without air and food for substantial amounts of time. Trevor understood that the only way to survive inside the Beltway was to adapt to the surrounding environment. Likening Trevor to a cockroach wasn't poetic, but there was a degree of truth behind the comparison.

"An e-mail introduction might work best," I suggested.

"I'm on it," said Trevor. "Anything else I should know? How is your better half?"

"Doug?" I toyed with telling Trevor about Columbia. I had a feeling he might have a valuable perspective about the decision.

"Actually, I meant Meg. But him, too, I suppose."

"I'm surprised you're asking about Meg. She's not exactly your favorite person." Meg and Trevor were like oil and water when we worked in the Senate. In the past year or so, we'd solved several murders together and the iciness between them had thawed, at least partially.

"As I recall, she was a bit out of sorts the last time we convened to catch a criminal," said Trevor.

Despite his annoying personality, Trevor was highly observant. He'd obviously remembered that last spring, the everflirtatious Meg had gone through a romantic dry spell.

"She's back on the horse, so to speak," I said. "In fact, she's dating a guy who was at our fundraiser last night."

"I see." Was I imagining, or did I detect a hint of disappointment in Trevor's voice? "Meg dating a suspect? That will throw a wrinkle in your sleuthing."

Trevor was right, and I knew it. But I let his comment go by without a response. I doubted Trevor grasped the delicate intricacies of female friendship.

"Thanks again for your help. I appreciate you sharing a contact in Van's office," I said.

"Kit, this goes without saying, but I'll mention it anyways. Be careful. Whomever killed Van Parker is bold, daring, and fueled by hatred. Not a good combination."

After assuring Trevor I wouldn't take any unnecessary risks without involving the police, I clicked off my phone. Without hearing any details about last night, Trevor seemed certain Van didn't kill himself. The likelihood we had another homicide on our hands was increasing by the minute.

My second iPhone, the one I used for campaign business, buzzed to signal a text had arrived. I dropped my government phone and grabbed the other device.

It was a message from my contact at the D Triple C, otherwise known as the Democratic Congressional Campaign Committee. Jeff Jenkins was responsible for quite a few close House races. If he was reaching out, there was a problem.

Need to chat. Have time?

It was almost noon, and my stomach was rumbling. We couldn't talk business inside a government office.

How about lunch?

Three dots indicated he was writing back.

Young Chow's at 1215.

I responded in the affirmative and headed out to the main office area where most of our office staff resided in cramped carrels. Meg sat in the largest work station, although describing it as spacious would be a stretch. She was pounding away at her keyboard when I approached.

"Meg, I'm headed out to meet Jeff from the D-Trip for lunch," I said. "Can you keep an eye on things here?"

Meg swiveled around in her office chair when she heard my voice. "Sure, although there's not much to keep an eye on. This place is deader than a doornail."

"Perhaps not the best choice of words given the situation, but I agree. Text me if something comes up."

She nodded. "Did you talk to anyone about Van's death?"

"Your favorite person, Trevor. As always, he shared helpful thoughts."

Her eyes narrowed. "Such as?"

I took a deep breath. "First, he doesn't think Van committed suicide. Second, he suggested I talk to one of Van's coworkers to find out more details about his professional life."

"It can't hurt to speak with someone who knew Van well. I don't know how Trevor could pontificate on last night's tragedy. He wasn't even there." Then she snapped her fingers in a mocking gesture. "Gee, I almost forgot. We're dealing with Trevor. All he does is pontificate."

Defending Trevor's involvement in one of our informal investigations was familiar territory. "Meg, we've been through this before. You don't like Trevor, but he knows a lot of people. And he has good insights."

Meg waved her hand dismissively. "He's a know-it-all, and he's weird."

"That's a bit harsh. Trevor has improved a lot on his social skills since we worked with him in the Senate," I protested.

"That's like saying Congress's approval ratings have improved. From thirteen to fifteen percent!"

I laughed. "Nice comparison. I'd better run. I don't want to keep Jeff waiting."

Meg twisted a lock of her blonde bob around her finger. "Why does he want to see you?"

I walked toward the door and spoke over my shoulder. "No idea. But it's rarely good news when he's involved."

After exiting the Cannon House Office Building, I headed east on Independence and Pennsylvania Avenue. Young Chow was only three blocks away. It wasn't as splashy as some of the other popular Capitol Hill eateries like We The Pizza or Sonoma. Nevertheless, it offered cheap Chinese and sushi lunch specials prepared in ten minutes or less. The anteroom of the restaurant provided an element of discretion. A table in the rear almost guaranteed privacy, a rare commodity in Washington.

Sure enough, my lunch companion had already arrived and secured seating in the far back corner. Ten years my junior, Jeff was full of energy and singularly focused on making sure our party retained control of the House after the election. Maeve Dixon's campaign was high on his list of priority races. I took a seat opposite him.

"Howdy, Jeff," I said.

A Texas native with a slight southern twang, Jeff tipped his imaginary cowboy hat in my direction. "Afternoon, Miss Kit."

"Did you already order?" I asked.

"Wouldn't dream of it. I was waitin' for you."

A young Asian woman came over to the table. "Sushi and sashimi lunch special," I said. "With egg drop soup and a diet Coke, please."

"That's a lady who knows what she wants. I like it," said Jeff. "I'll have the mango chicken, sweet and sour soup, and a regular Coke."

We both handed the plastic menus to our server. "To what do I owe this pleasure,

175

Jeff?" I asked.

He shook his finger playfully at me. "Neither of us has time for a game of twenty questions. Why don't you tell me what happened last night at Representative Dixon's fundraiser?"

Word did travel fast inside the Beltway. I gave Jeff a synopsis of last night's fiasco as our soup arrived.

He shook his head while slurping his sweet and sour, generously sprinkled with fried wonton strips. "Not good." He pulled a piece of paper out of his leather portfolio. It was filled with tables and numbers. "I reviewed our internal polling on the Dixon race before walking over here. A week ago, the race was deadlocked." He pointed to a number. "This isn't going to help. Quite frankly, she can't sustain a scandal."

My egg drop soup really hit the spot, but I ignored it. "Wait a second. I just told you Maeve wasn't anywhere near the restaurant last night when Van died." The volume of my voice rose with anxiety. "Even if we're talking murder here, she can't be a suspect."

The waitress came over to our table with our lunches. Jeff held up his hand to signal we should stop talking. When she left, he leaned across the table. "Lower the volume, Miss Kit. The last thing we need is an enterprising *Politico* reporter overhearing our conversation."

"You're right," I said in a hushed tone. "But there's no scandal here."

"Under normal circumstances, I'd agree. However, your boss is in one of the tightest House races in the country, and her opponent is trying to argue that Washington has corrupted Maeve Dixon. She's drunk the Kool Aid, so to speak."

I popped a piece of salmon in my mouth after dipping it lightly in soy sauce. "Yes, yes. We saw the television ad he's running about her international trips."

"Precisely," said Jeff. "This incident fits right into his narrative. While she's dining at some ritzy restaurant trying to raise money from lobbyists, a man dies. Who knows why? It doesn't matter. Maybe he drank too much and stumbled off the roof? The bottom line is that it happened at a Dixon fundraiser. She's to blame. A novice communications campaign staffer could write the spot with one hand tied behind his back."

I spread a generous portion of wasabi on my piece of California roll and waited for the burn. A few seconds later, my mind and my nasal passages were clearer. "Hold on. Does the Hackensack campaign know about

Van Parker? Aren't we jumping the gun, so to speak?"

Jeff skillfully shoveled a big piece of orange-colored chicken into his mouth with a chopstick. "Our opposition research guy thinks the Hackensack campaign has caught wind of it. He overheard the Coach talking about a brewing scandal in Washington at an event earlier today."

Ever since the "macaca moment" in 2006 when Virginia senator George Allen used a bizarre racial slur to describe an opposition researcher, the use of "trackers" in close campaigns had increased. The Dixon campaign had a full-time staffer who videotaped Coach Hackensack at every public event. Of course, his campaign also employed a "tracker" who recorded Maeve's speeches and comments.

"If that's the case, I'm not sure what can be done about it," I said.

Jeff clicked his chopsticks together nervously. "We need this mess cleaned up as soon as possible. If Parker was killed, then we can't have a murderer on the loose tied to Maeve Dixon."

I popped the last piece of sashimi in my mouth. "Easier said than done. We don't even know everyone who was on the rooftop at the time of Van's death." I told Jeff about the mysterious waiter who likely wasn't employed by the restaurant.

Jeff downed the last gulp of his Coke. "Terrific. Was he a hitman? Trying to explain a murder-for-hire at a Dixon fundraiser isn't going to help your boss's campaign."

"I don't know. The others on the rooftop claim they didn't see or hear anything. It's a real puzzle." I decided to leave out the fact that Meg was dating one of the potential suspects. That detail would be enough to make Jeff's head spin.

"One more thing, Miss Kit. I understand another House member was involved in last night's activities," he said.

I had to think for a moment before I knew what he was talking about. "You mean Chairman Edwards."

"Yes. When he learned about Parker's death this morning, he called our office. Of course, he's concerned about his name getting dragged through the mud."

"He left earlier, too. He can't be a suspect, either," I said.

"Someone as ambitious as Edwards doesn't leave much to chance. He's not happy about it," said Jeff.

I sighed. "Not an enemy we want right now. Especially since he chairs the transportation committee."

We both threw down our credit cards to split the bill. "Let's hope D.C. Metro has its finest on the case," said Jeff. "The sooner this matter is resolved, the better. A tight race can be tilted in either direction during the last weeks of a campaign. I don't need to remind you there's a lot riding on Dixon retaining her seat."

Such as our party's control of Congress. Jeff didn't need to spell it out for me. The stakes were tremendous and transcended above and beyond my congressional career trajectory or even Maeve's.

"I'll try to poke around and see what I can find out," I said.

We both got up from the table and walked to the front of the restaurant. "I know you've had some luck finding culprits in the past," Jeff said. "Everyone on Capitol Hill is aware of your sleuthing skills. Be careful, Kit. I wouldn't want our candidate to have to explain two homicides." He gave me a sideways grin.

"Thanks, Jeff. It's my hope this can be resolved quickly so I can join the Dixon campaign full time."

"She'll be lucky to have you in North Carolina. You probably have a few days before Coach Hackensack decides to run with it. If I get more intelligence from our guys on the ground, I'll let you know."

We shook hands, and I walked slowly back to the office. What was my next move? Perhaps I'd better visit Rory Edwards' office this afternoon. Smoothing things over seemed like a good use of time. Besides, if he was really having an affair with Lauren Parker, maybe he had some insights about her marriage. He certainly had a potential motive for murder, but it was hard to imagine how he could have killed Van Parker. He'd left with Maeve to return to the Capitol well before the incident. They were each other's rock-solid alibi.

I hadn't checked my phone since sitting down for lunch. After crossing Pennsylvania, I swiped it open to check for messages. Sure enough, Trevor had e-mailed the colleague of Van's he knew. His name was Gene Price. Had he been intrigued enough to respond? I scrolled through the more recent messages, much fewer in number now that Congress was no longer in session. Thankfully, Gene had taken the bait. I tapped on his name, so I could read his response. Apparently, Gene had refined taste. He suggested drinks at the upscale Capital Grille at four o'clock this afternoon. It was a little early to leave the office, but nothing mattered more than figuring out what happened last night. I typed a brief reply accepting his offer.

Back in the office, I scanned the Internet for any evidence that Coach Hackensack had spoken about the incident today on the campaign trail. Nothing was showing up, but accounts of Van Parker's death were beginning to mention he had attended a Dixon fundraiser. Jeff was right. It was only a matter of time before our rival started to hammer Maeve on it, especially if the police continued to view it as a suspicious death.

I picked up the phone and called the staff director of the Transportation Committee. Jeff wasn't fibbing. The chairman was in town, squeezing in a couple last minute fundraisers at the end of the week before leaving for California. He represented the bluest of blue districts in the Golden State. With no primary challenger, Rory Edwards only had token opposition to contend with in November. Instead of campaigning for his own reelection, he could focus on raising money for Democrats in tight races, like Maeve. I truly envied his plumb position. By donating generous sums to other campaigns, Edwards bolstered his status within the party and made other rank-and-file members beholden to him. His robust fundraising also strengthened his hold on the committee chairmanship. An iron triangle existed between lobbyists, campaign dollars, and committee chairs. The interdependency was next to impossible to penetrate or break.

Hence, the necessity for my visit to the Edwards' camp today. He was with his staff inside the Rayburn Building. I jotted down his office suite number and grabbed my purse. Meg was nowhere to be found, so I texted her my plan.

Rayburn was situated to the west of the two other House office buildings, the most recent addition to the triad. The building was named after Speaker Sam Rayburn, a legendary House leader. The longest serving Speaker in American history, Rayburn served as the protégé for Lyndon Baines Johnson and other successful Texas politicians. It was testimony to his noteworthy career that the House office building was named after him in 1962, only a year after his death.

The Rayburn House Office Building lived up to its namesake. RHOB, as it was known, could be described as functional, expansive, and state-of-the-art during its heyday. It now housed several committees, the House gymnasium, a large cafeteria, and a parking garage. Given these amenities, Rayburn was a favorite office location for senior, power-ful members of Congress like Edwards.

I glanced at the sticky note with Edwards' suite number: 2314 RHOB. The office nomenclature on the Hill was as puzzling as parliamentary procedure. The first number designated the office building, with all Ray-burn locations assigned "2." The second number indicated the floor. I hit the eleva-tor button for "3." The last two digits provided the location of the suite. The hallways of Rayburn were laid out in the shape of the letter "H." That often meant one wrong turn could result in a dead-end, causing late arrivals to meetings or other appointments. Luckily, the chairman had chosen a suite adjacent to the elevator. He's secured prime real estate, bonafide evidence he enjoyed a favored slot at the top of the congressional ladder of prestige, power, and influence.

I walked into the office and approached the staff assistant at the front desk. If Meg was Lauren Parker's twin minus ten years, this woman was an even younger dop-pelganger. She peered up at me with crystal blue eyes accented by makeup that ap-peared as though it had been professionally applied. Did women who looked this good get up at four o'clock in the morning to put their faces on? I really needed one of them to tell me the secret of her success. Although I couldn't fathom trading valuable sleeping time for eyes worthy of a *Cosmopolitan* cover.

"Good afternoon. My name is Kit Marshall, the chief of staff for Maeve Dixon. I'd like to speak briefly with Chairman Edwards. He's expecting me."

Lauren-in-waiting nodded curtly as her red manicured nails flew across the computer keys, producing a sound almost as annoying as dragging her claws across a freshly cleaned blackboard. I resisted covering my ears as she typed.

After staring at the screen for several seconds, Lauren Jr. finally spoke. "Do you have an appointment?" she asked in a high-pitched voice.

"Not exactly. The staff director on T and I called over for me. He said the Chairman wanted to talk."

"T and I" was the shorthand name for Transportation and Infrastructure, insider lingo for longtime Hill veterans.

I tapped my finger impatiently against the side of my iPhone. If I'd hauled ass all the way over to Rayburn for no good reason, I was going to call my contact back and give him a piece of my mind.

After several dozen more strokes across the keyboard, the twenty-something staff assistant finally deigned to address me again. "Please have a seat. Chairman Edwards will see you shortly."

In Hill time, "shortly" could mean five minutes or five hours. I hoped for the former rather than the latter. I considered quizzing the Lauren substitute further, but by the time I sat down in the waiting area, she'd begun filing her nails with an Emory board. How could I compete with a do-it-yourself manicure?

Luckily, iPhones helped pass the time. My smartphone was nothing less than a mobile office. I could check e-mail, receive instant messages, receive floor alerts, and even read memos in a pinch. Talking to people on the phone was a possibility too, but who did that these days, unless necessary?

Fortune was on my side today. I had just opened Twitter to read the latest 140-character rant from our tweet-happy POTUS when the amateur manicurist broke my concentration. "The Chairman will see you now," she announced.

I resisted the urge to issue a clever retort and instead nodded politely. She was already back to her filing, ostensibly in pursuit of a noteworthy and ambitious lofty goal. Not universal affordable health care or a better educational system, but the perfect set of nails. We all had our priorities in Washington. Who was I to judge?

The door behind the front desk opened a crack, and Rory Edwards' head popped out. He scanned left and right, his gaze eventually settling on me as I jumped up from my seat. "Ms. Marshall, I presume?"

"That's me," I said with a smile. Edwards failed to reciprocate with a cheerful countenance. With a grimace on his face that would have given Oscar the Grouch a run for his money, he opened the door and motioned for me to follow him.

He led us into his office, which appeared as standard décor for a member of Congress. Framed photos of his family were placed strategically on his desk to demonstrate his devotion to them. Of course, they were outnumbered by the litany of wall-mounted pictures showing the Chairman with an assorted array of powerful people. When we sat down, I noticed several large coffee table books featuring the wildlife and coastline of California were displayed prominently for visitors to admire. Rory Edwards knew how to play the political game. After spending less than ten seconds inside his lair, a guest would observe the

187

Holy Trinity of a well-crafted congressional persona: homage to family, insider Washington, and the home district.

Edwards ran his fingers through his thick hair. I had the same impression as when I saw him last night at the fundraiser. A decent looking man in his late fifties or early sixties, but not in contention anytime soon for the infamous "Fifty Most Beautiful People on Capitol Hill" designation.

"Well, Ms. Marshall, to what do I owe this pleasure?" The Chairman didn't bother to hide the sarcasm dripping from his question.

"I'm sure you're aware of Van Parker's untimely death last night," I said, more as a statement than an inquiry. No point in beating around the bush. I might only have five minutes with Edwards and exchanging clever retorts didn't seem a prudent use of time.

I leaned forward. "The medical examiner and police aren't sure what happened. Van may have jumped, or he might have been pushed."

The Chairman folded his hands. "And who might have committed such a crime if it wasn't suicide?"

"There were several people still at the event." I paused for a beat. "Including Lauren Parker, Van's wife. Do you know her?" I asked innocently.

Edwards' jaw slackened, but he recovered quickly to hide his reaction. "Of course, I know her. She's one of the most prominent lobbyists in the city."

I wasn't going to let him get off that easily. "I noticed you chatting with her last night. Such a tragedy she's now a widow."

Edwards fiddled with his suit jacket button, avoiding my gaze. "Yes, certainly. I'll have to send her my condolences."

Last time I checked, sympathy cards were the preferred method, not scheduling a quickie with the grieving spouse. Maybe he'd already "consoled" Lauren earlier. Nothing shocked me these days.

"When you were at the fundraiser, did you notice anything out of the ordinary? Anyone acting unusual?" I asked.

Edwards locked eyes with me for a moment. Then he burst into laughter. Not exactly the reaction I'd hoped for. "I forgot I was dealing with Capitol Hill's version of Miss Marple," he said. "The police have already spoken to me about the matter, and I told them what I'll tell you. I didn't see anything last night that I don't see every night in Washington. A bunch of rich donors and lobbyists indulging in expensive food and drink while buying access to power."

So much for *Mr. Smith Goes To Washington.* It was a good thing the Library of Congress added the movie to the national film registry for preservation because elected representatives resembling Jimmy Stewart's character were indeed a rare breed these days.

"What about Dash Dugal? Know anything about him?" I asked.

"The railroad guy? Yeah, I chatted with him briefly last night. He's an up-and-comer and worth a few minutes of my time, but he's no Van Parker. Not at his level," he said.

I might as well keep going. "Max Robinson?"

He shook his head. "Never heard of him."

"He's lobbies for cyclists," I said.

Edwards laughed again. "Charming. I don't waste my time on modes of transportation that don't require motors."

"What about a waiter, tall guy, with dark, wavy hair? Possibly Hispanic."

The Chairman sighed. "Ms. Marshall, how long have you been Dixon's chief of staff?"

"A little over six months. Since the government shutdown," I said.

"You're new to this game, so I'll forgive

you," he said. "As a chairman of a major policy committee, I'm on the line to raise millions of campaign dollars so members of Congress like your boss keep their jobs. Otherwise, I lose my chairmanship."

"I understand." Quite frankly, I didn't need a lesson in K Street politics.

"That means I go to fundraisers every day. In the morning, at lunch, and every evening. I see dozens of waiters in a given week. So, the answer is no, I do not remember a server from last night, or any other night."

This was a dead end. I stood up and offered my hand. "Thank you for your time, Chairman Edwards."

He refused my gesture to end the conversation. Instead, in a clipped voice, he said, "Please sit, Ms. Marshall. I have something I'd like to say about this matter."

Reluctantly, I took my seat again and rubbed the back of my neck. His tone didn't sound auspicious.

"As I've explained, I have devoted endless hours this past year ensuring that we maintain political control of the House. Imagine my reaction when at the last fundraiser before recess, a man plunges to his death from a restaurant rooftop," he said.

I didn't have to imagine his reaction. The flared nostrils and beads of sweat forming on his forehead gave me a clear indication.

"I get it. You're upset," I said weakly.

"That would be an understatement, Ms. Marshall," he said. "I tried to reach Maeve Dixon late this morning, but she was speaking at a Kiwanis pancake breakfast in North Carolina. I'll talk with her when she takes a break from the hustings. In the meantime, no harm in sending the message through you"

I gulped and braced myself in the high-backed chair.

"If this incident has any effect on the election, I will make sure your boss never works in politics again. She won't win a campaign for dogcatcher in her backwater North Carolina hometown once I'm through with her," he said.

He must have seen the look of horror on my face I couldn't mask because he proceeded for the jugular.

"By the way, that promise extends to you, Ms. Marshall. You should consider your career on life support until this matter is resolved."

CHAPTER THIRTEEN

I walked back to the Dixon office in a daze. Rory Edwards' stinging words repeated themselves inside my brain, like a bad viral Facebook video that was impossible to remove from your feed. The Chairman was going to eat us for lunch if Van's death caused him another iota of stress. Until my meeting with him, the motivation to solve the mystery of Van's demise had been to prevent Maeve from any potential embarrassment on the campaign trail. Edwards had upped the ante, and that meant I needed to double my resolve to figure out what really happened last night.

My butt hadn't been in my swivel chair for more than five seconds flat before Meg appeared at my doorway.

Sporting a bemused smile, she asked, "Enjoy your time with Rory Edwards?"

"As much as going to the dentist the day after Halloween," I said.

193

Meg squeezed into the empty seat adjacent to my desk. "That much fun, huh? What trouble is our favorite chairman orchestrating these days?"

As I recounted the conversation, Meg's jaw tightened. "How dare he threaten Representative Dixon." She added, "And you, too!"

"He's concerned about losing control of the House and his chairmanship. This place is about self-preservation more than anything," I said. "Members of Congress want to remain in their seats of power. The drive for reelection makes the Capitol Hill world go round."

"I find it ironic since the number one suspect has to be Lauren Parker, his paramour. Doesn't he realize if she killed Van, the police might try to finger him for the murder, too?"

"He must have figured that out," I said. "He probably wants the whole thing to disappear quickly. It's like a shadow hanging over him and the election."

Meg fidgeted in her seat. "What are you going to do?"

I wasn't expecting Meg's question. Usually she had a bevy of ideas concerning how we could proceed with an investigation. Instead, she nervously twisted the pendant attached to her long, silver necklace. No doubt about it. The circumstances surrounding Van's death had Meg out of sorts.

I reached across the edge of my desk and grabbed Meg's hand. "Don't worry. We'll figure this out. We always do, right?"

The corners of Meg's mouth turned upward. "I know. Thanks for reminding me."

"Do you know Gene Price?" I asked. "He worked with Van Parker at American Trucks First."

"I've heard of him. He was one of Van's underlings. If Van couldn't attend a meeting, then Gene stepped in."

"Well, he's a bigger dog now, I guess. He agreed to have drinks at four," I said.

"Gene is the guy that Trevor knows, I presume. Where is this happy hour taking place?" she asked.

"Where else? The Capital Grille."

"One of the favorite lobbyist bars," said Meg. "Predictable. We'd better run if we want to make it on time."

I glanced at my phone. We only had twenty minutes before the top of the hour. It would be tight, but luckily finding a cab outside on Independence was a piece of cake. We zoomed down Capitol Hill, turned right on Seventh Street past the Smithsonian Air and Space Museum, crossed the National Mall, and arrived at the designated location on Pennsylvania Avenue with minutes to spare. A mere three blocks away from Charlie Palmer's, the Capital Grille could be considered ground zero inside the lobbyist corridor of evening cocktails, fund-raisers, and endless schmoozing.

Meg and I exited our cab and stared briefly at the entrance, taking in the sheer opulence before us. The Cap Grille was as clubby and masculine as legally allowed these days within the confines of D.C. political correctness. Old school iron lanterns flanked the entrance, making sure prospective patrons knew the name of the establishment they were entering. Two weathered lion sculptures guarded the door. They weren't as regal as Patience and Fortitude, the two reclining great cats that monitored the comings and goings of the New York Public Library in Manhattan. But the Grille's mascots were no less proud. In fact, if they could talk, many journalists in Washington would give a hefty sum to ask them several probing questions about the people and conversations that passed before them, most likely after a lively meal or a long evening of drinks and merriment.

We walked directly to the lounge area, a

stately room with a gorgeous oak bar and high-backed chairs. The décor made me think we should be smoking cigarettes in a long, slim holder while sipping a dry martini. Of course, smoking had been banned for ages in D.C. restaurants, and if I tried to throw back a martini, it would be a short night, indeed. Instead, I ordered a California Chardonnay, and Meg went for her hands-down favorite, Prosecco. She couldn't get enough of the Italian bubbly. Meg claimed Prosecco was her drink of choice because it was lower in calories than other wines, but for as long as I knew her, Meg hadn't ever gained an ounce, despite her healthy appetite for good food and drink. Her skinny body somehow immediately torched every blasted gram of fat she ingested. I envied her super-hero metabolism.

"Do you want to split the truffle fries?" asked Meg.

Point proven. Unfortunately, I had the willpower of a gnat.

"Sure, why not?" I sighed heavily.

Meg raised an eyebrow. "What's wrong?"

"Nothing, really. I guess I have a lot on my mind."

My iPhone dinged. Gene, our happy hour companion, was running twenty minutes late.

The bartender served us our drinks. As soon as he placed the libations on the smooth wooden bar, Meg picked up her flute and clinked it to my glass.

"Here's to clearing up the mystery behind Van's death and getting Maeve reelected," she said.

I smiled weakly. "I wish those were my only problems."

Meg sat up straight in the leather high-backed seat. "Is there something else you're not telling me, Kit?"

I had time to tell her Doug's news before our late-arriving guest joined us. I took a deep breath and braced myself for Meg's reaction.

"I've been a little distracted today," I said as I fiddled with my two iPhones. No one in Washington could leave their devices inside purses or suit jackets. Phones were immediately placed on the table or bar, so they could be monitored for so-called important incoming messages. Big Brother wasn't watching us. Inside the Beltway, it was the other way around.

Meg fidgeted. "Out with it, Kit. Stop stalling." Her sparkling blue eyes bored into me like the summer sun scorching unsuspecting tourists on the National Mall.

"Columbia University wants to hire

Doug," I said definitively. I grabbed my glass of wine and took a big sip.

Meg repeated my words back to me as a question. "Columbia wants to hire Doug?" She tilted her head to the side for a moment. "Isn't that in New York?"

Poor Meg. The look on her face was genuine confusion. "Yes, it is. Columbia wants to offer him a position to lure him away from Georgetown."

I studied Meg as she processed the full meaning of my words. After a few seconds, she slowly shook her head back and forth.

"No," she said. "He'll have to tell them it's not possible."

My best friend's dazed expression catapulted me into action. I reached out and put my hand on her shoulder. "Meg, don't worry. Nothing has been decided yet."

Meg pulled back from my comforting gesture. "Yet? You can't tell me you're considering this?"

"I haven't even talked to Doug about it. He mentioned it this morning before I left for work." I tried to hide the exasperation from my voice.

Meg finished her glass of Prosecco and asked the bartender for another. I guess we were in for quite an interesting ride. Van's former colleague had no idea what he was walking into tonight.

"He just mentioned this little move over breakfast," said Meg. "Guess what honey? We're moving to New York!"

"I was making breakfast," I said. "And for the record, his announcement took me by complete surprise."

"That's good to know, not that it matters much," said Meg. "Let me ask you this, Kit. What are you going to do about all of this?" She motioned widely with her left arm. "You know, Washington? Are you ready to leave your career?" Then she added emphatically, "Are you ready to leave your so-called *friends*?"

"Meg, don't jump to conclusions. Of course, I'm concerned about moving away from here. My job is important to me," I said. "And you're important to me."

A tear glistened in the corner of Meg's eye. She wiped it away before it could smear her makeup. Meg might get sentimental, but she wasn't going to let emotions ruin her perfectly applied black mascara. "Careers aren't built overnight," said Meg with a slight sniffle. "Neither are best friends."

I pulled Meg into a brief side hug. "Of course not. But it's more complicated now."

Her shoulders slumped as she stared into her glass of Prosecco. Thousands of tiny bubbles raced to the top of her flute. The Capital Grille didn't mess around. The smaller the bubbles, the finer the sparkling wine. Meg had chosen a winner. I hope it softened the blow of my news.

"Because you're married," she said in a soft voice.

"Doug is my husband, so we need to make these decisions together," I said. "But that doesn't mean we're going to pick up and move to a new city on a whim. I really don't know what's at stake here. It's a tough time to fit in a conversation about relocating, given everything else that's happening."

Meg smiled. "You can't leave Maeve Dixon in the lurch, you know."

I looked at Meg squarely. "No way. We're going to make sure she beats Coach Hackensack fair and square."

Meg grinned, and we sealed the deal with our signature fist bump. As we laughed, a man approached our seats at the bar.

"Kit Marshall?" he asked tentatively.

"Gene Price?" I responded in an equally cautious tone.

"That's me," he said cheerfully.

Meg moved one chair down at the bar. "Please sit down. Thanks for joining us."

Gene beamed at Meg's invitation. By my estimation, our guest was about our age, perhaps a decade junior to his former colleague Van Parker. He was clean cut, with newly trimmed brown hair and dark square shaped glasses. Who knows if he really needed them to correct his vision? These days, it was plausible his eyesight was perfect, and he only wore the specs to increase his hipster quotient. Since it was during a congressional recess, the obligatory suit and tie wasn't necessary. Instead, he wore a pair of slim fit grey chinos, a chambray shirt, and a plaid blazer. Going by appearances, Gene Price checked off every box of the young D.C. professional. That included a double take of Meg, who more than qualified as eye candy for the sugar-obsessed males of our fair city.

Gene turned toward Meg. "I don't believe we've met before."

Meg introduced herself as Maeve Dixon's legislative director. "I've worked on a House committee and in the Senate. Before Dixon, I never focused on transportation issues, so our paths may not have crossed."

"I'm certain they haven't," said Gene. "I would have remembered."

Meg was used to guys fawning over her. She barely acknowledged Gene's overture. "Would you like a drink?"

Gene ordered a Corruption, a popular

IPA beer brewed by a local brewing company, DC Brau. Located near the National Arboretum, DC Brau was a popular place for young professionals to hang out in the evenings and on weekends, filling their take-home growlers with the various ales produced by the brewery onsite.

Our guest took a long sip of his beer and wiped the froth off his upper lip. "That really hits the spot. Trevor said you two ladies wanted to speak with me. What's up?"

Out of the corner of my eye, Meg bristled at the mention of Trevor. Before I could cut her off, she spoke up. "Let's leave Trevor out of this. He's nothing but trouble."

"Fine by me. All I know is that when Trevor calls, I listen. That book of his is going to bring this city to its knees once it's released," said Gene.

I hadn't paid much attention to Trevor's tell-all book. Would Meg and I make an appearance? I shoved the thought out of my mind for the moment but vowed to ask Trevor point blank the next time I spoke with him.

"Trevor put us in contact because Van Parker died last night at our boss's fund-raiser," I said. "We didn't know him that well, and we thought you might be able to tell us more about him."

Gene sipped his beer and rubbed his chin. "Van was a couple rungs above me at work. He was our senior lobbyist, and I only started there a year ago. Before that, I worked as a staffer on the Transportation committee in the House."

That made perfect sense. Despite the current President's emphatic vow to "drain the swamp," a revolving door in Washington persisted. Smart, ambitious professionals gained experience by working in Congress. After learning the ins and outs of a policy issue, they often became lobbyists, trading in relatively low-paying congressional jobs for much higher salaries on K Street.

We needed Gene to be a little more forthcoming, which might require a gentle push. I didn't have to communicate this observation to Meg. She knew what had to be done.

Meg inched her barstool closer to Gene's and smoothed her blonde bob. "But surely you got to know Van at work. We heard he may have been depressed lately. Was that true?"

"If Van was depressed, I didn't know about it. That guy had more energy than anyone I'd ever encountered in Washington," said Gene.

"Then why would he commit suicide?" I said, wondering out loud.

"Beats me." Gene finished his beer and ordered another. "Maybe it was temporary insanity? It looks like that's what happened. He left a note at his desk."

That was new information. "What did you say?" I asked.

"A note. When I came into work today, someone found it on his desk. I'm not sure what it said, but the police arrived and took it. They were going to give a copy to his wife, so she could read it," said Gene.

"Maybe Van got stressed out with work and decided to end it all," said Meg. "Everyone knows D.C. is a pressure cooker. Sometimes people snap."

"What was Van focused on at work?" I asked. "Was there trouble brewing?"

Gene turned his head left and right, scanning the bar. Then he motioned for both of us to shift closer to him. If Meg leaned in anymore, she was going to be sitting on his lap.

"There was a rumor going around the office that Van was going to leave America Trucks First," he said in a hushed tone.

"For a competing trade organization?" asked Meg.

Gene shook his head. "Nope. He was going to start his own lobbying firm, specializing in transportation but eventually expanding into other arenas."

I leaned back in my barstool and considered Gene's revelation. Van had plans to build his own empire. Not quite satisfied with being the top transportation lobbyist in the city, he wanted to compete with the big boys — the Podesta Group, Cassidy, BGR, Capitol Counsel, Gephardt Government Affairs. It didn't sound like a guy who was contemplating the end of his life. Quite the contrary. It seemed Van was planning the next phase of his career.

"How many people knew about Van's idea to build his own firm?" I asked.

"It wasn't a big secret," said Gene. "He'd already done a lot of the legwork, and the rumor was he'd begun cherry-picking the top consulting talent from across the city. I think he wanted to be up and running early next year to capitalize on the legislative activity of a newly elected Congress."

"And the transportation bill," I muttered.

Gene heard my comment. "That too. Van wanted to build a stellar team, so his firm would be the biggest player in the room by the time negotiations got serious on it."

"There's a lot of money in play for that legislation," said Meg.

"No kidding. The last transportation bill authorized over three hundred billion dollars in spending," said Gene. "There was also a rumor out there that Van was working on a big deal as part of this new venture. You know, that he had something up his sleeve. A company he could represent that would transform the industry."

"Van wasn't content to get the best deal for the trucking industry anymore. He had bigger ambitions," I said, almost to myself.

"Exactly," said Gene. "Imagine if Van's firm represented several important clients on the bill, including the mystery game changer. Instead of advocating for one industry, he could make big deals that actually shaped the future of transportation policy."

Meg pressed her lips into a fine line. "This sounds too much like *House of Cards* to me. What did other lobbyists think about Van's grandiose ambitions?"

Gene finished his beer and motioned for the bartender to pour him another. "What do you think? Most weren't happy about it. The top folks he recruited were ecstatic. Everyone else felt like they were being left out in the cold."

From the look on Meg's face, I guessed that Dash Dugal hadn't been one of the lucky few selected by Van to join him on this new venture. I wanted to ask Gene about Dash, but it would upset Meg because she'd think I was fingering him for Van's death. And after dropping the bombshell about the potential move to New York City, I'd better not push my luck with Meg. She was one glass of Prosecco away from a meltdown, and we didn't need to draw any attention to ourselves at the Capital Grille. I could, however, ask about another suspect.

"Do you know a bike lobbyist named Max Robinson?" I asked.

Gene laughed. "I'm glad I ordered another beer. What do you want to know about him?"

"He attended the fundraiser last night," said Meg. "He was still there when Van died."

Gene rolled his eyes. "I'm surprised his bike group, whatever it's called, agreed to spring for such a pricey dinner."

"BAM," I said. "It's Bicycle Advocacy Movement."

Gene shrugged. "It's not like that guy is a diehard for bikes."

"It didn't seem that way last night. He bent my ear about their legislative proposals," said Meg.

"That doesn't shock me," said Gene. "Max is ambitious. But let's just say he'd like to trade in bikes for something bigger.

Like trucks."

"I'm not following you," I said.

"Don't beat yourself up over it," said Gene. "The lobbyist world is pretty insular. We know each other's secrets. After all, we go to the same damn breakfasts, cocktail parties, and fundraisers. It's a lot like a private club."

I hadn't thought of it in those terms. Never having worked as a lobbyist, I wasn't intimately familiar with the culture of K Street. Maeve's close reelection and Van Parker's recent death had revealed a whole new world, and I wasn't sure I liked what I saw. Ignorance is bliss, particularly in our nation's capital.

"I'm completely lost." Meg crossed her arms. "Are you trying to say Max wants to exchange his bike for a truck? I don't think you can even do that."

I suppressed a grin. Meg was quite literal and often ignored or failed to grasp nuances.

Gene didn't seem to mind her obtuseness. He leaned toward Meg and locked gazes with her. "He wanted a job at ATF. Max applied several times for a job at my level."

"Oh," said Meg, blushing at her misinterpretation. "He seems like an earnest guy. He never received an offer?"

209

Max took the last chug of his beer. "Nope, Van Parker blocked it every time."

Now, that was an interesting tidbit. "Why would Van do that?" I asked.

Gene reached into his pocket for his wallet. Ethics laws strictly forbade us to pay for him or vice versa. Unless we were at a "widely attended event" or a political fundraiser. Then the rules changed. I didn't bother to question the logic (or lack thereof) of ethics laws.

"That's an easy question," said Gene. "Van didn't like Max. He certainly didn't consider him a talented lobbyist. So even if Max interviewed with another senior person at our organization, Van intervened and made sure Max didn't get an offer."

"That was way harsh, Tai," I said.

Gene's eyebrows squeezed together. Meg got the movie reference. She clasped her hands together in delight. "That's Cher Horowitz from *Clueless.*"

My head bobbed up and down. "You got it. The teen queen of one-liners."

Gene got off the bar stool and stood up. "Lobbyists might be closed off, but you guys are in your own world, too."

Meg and I had known each other for so long, it did occasionally seem like we spoke our own language. "Sorry about that," I said with a laugh. "Inside joke. I like movie quotes."

He waved me off. "No worries."

Then Gene turned toward Meg. "Hey, do you mind if I get your card? It's not clear how Van's duties will be reassigned, but I should be moving up at ATF. Maybe we can talk trucks sometime soon?"

He gave Meg his sexiest smile, which wasn't too shabby. Not up to Ryan Reynolds' level, but a solid effort. You couldn't fault a guy for trying. God only knows I'd seen many potential suitors swing for the fences in an attempt to vie for Meg's attention.

Meg smiled confidently and touched Gene lightly on his arm. "I'd be happy to give you my card. To talk business, of course."

Gene lowered his head. "Just business?"

"I'm afraid so," said Meg. "I'm not on the dating market these days."

"Lucky guy," muttered Gene. He stuck his hand out to me. "Pleasure meeting you. Good luck with everything. Can you tell Trevor I answered all your questions?"

The pen is mightier than the sword. Trevor's forthcoming tell-all book certainly had motivated D.C. insiders to stay on his good side.

"Certainly," I said. "You were extremely

forthcoming."

He nodded politely at Meg, threw down a twenty on the bar, and grabbed his jacket. Meg and I turned toward the bar and picked up our drinks. One drawback I'd noticed from our past mystery-solving endeavors is that we rarely got time to enjoy our drinks when interrogating suspects or following up leads. Although, if I was entirely truthful, the more accurate description was that I never finished my alcoholic beverage when sleuthing. Meg always seemed to find a way to drain her beloved Prosecco.

"What type of person decides to start an ambitious business venture and then switches gear to end his life?" I asked.

Meg tapped her long, manicured fingernail on the oak bar. "Don't know. Someone who got bad news?"

"Perhaps," I said. "A financial backer pulling out? It still hardly seems a reason to kill yourself. Van could have found a job anywhere in the city if he wanted to leave ATF."

"Good point." Meg stopped tapping her finger and pointed it at me. "Maybe we can find out the reason tonight."

"How?" I asked as I took the last draw of my wine.

Meg's eyes sparkled. "Let's go see Lauren

212

and read the supposed suicide note."

I rubbed my chin. "Not a bad idea. Do you propose stealing it?"

Meg punched me in the arm before pulling on her jacket. "You're watching too many television mysteries. If we're charming enough, I bet Lauren will show it to us."

"You're probably right. Let's find out."

After paying our bill, we left the restaurant, and Meg put her hand out to hail a taxi. I pulled it down just as a cab was about to pull over.

"What are you doing, Kit? It's not that easy to find a taxi after five o'clock when Congress is on recess. This whole town shuts down before an election."

Meg was right. I half-expected to see tumbleweeds rolling down Pennsylvania Avenue.

"We screwed up. There's a fatal flaw in our plan," I said.

"What's wrong now?" she asked. "Afraid Lauren's our killer and she might decide to make us the next victims?"

"Well, there's that." I said. "But there's a more immediate problem."

Meg put her hands on her hips. "Go ahead, Sherlock."

"We don't know where she lives," I said.

CHAPTER FOURTEEN

The so-called fatal flaw in our plan turned out to be a temporary malady. Learning Lauren and Van's place of residence was no problem for two expert Google searchers. Within five minutes, we'd located a *Washington Post* article that featured their trendy condo in the popular Style section. After reading the description in the online edition of the newspaper, I knew exactly where we needed to go.

"Atlantic Plumbing near U Street," I told our new taxi driver.

We zoomed due north on Seventh Street several miles and then headed west until we reached the U Street corridor, one of the trendiest neighborhoods in the city.

"Do you hit a lot of the night spots around here?" I asked Meg. I liked living vicariously through my single friends.

"Definitely," said Meg. "But I don't know too much about the historic importance."

"It's the home of Duke Ellington," I explained. "In the early twentieth century, it was the most prominent African-American neighborhood in the United States."

We pulled up to our destination and thanked our driver. Meg looked up and down the street. "It's ultra-modern around here these days. I wonder if it's gone a step too far."

A few years ago, a famous jazz club on U Street, Bohemian Caverns, had shuttered. It left many lifelong neighborhood residents wondering if people wanted to live in condos named after famous jazz musicians rather than listening to the music itself.

"Look no further than the new condos built at Atlantic Plumbing," I said, pointing across the street at our destination.

"That's an unusual condo building," remarked Meg.

A rectangular six-story structure with ceiling to floor windows on all sides, it looked like a Rubik's cube on steroids. "Today's our lucky day," I said. "I've always wanted to go inside one of these condos."

Meg wrinkled her forehead. "I didn't know you liked to hang out in the neighborhood."

My best friend clearly perceived herself as the hipper half of our dynamic duo. I got out more than she gave me credit for. "Doug and I occasionally come to the movies here. I watched this building transform from a vacant red brick warehouse to million-dollar residences."

"Fascinating," said Meg with a healthy dose of sarcasm. Meg was rarely amused when I mentioned Doug, since she usually competed with him for my time and attention. My latest revelation about a potential move to New York City hadn't helped.

We stood outside the building and peeked inside. "There's a concierge," I said. "We could go in and ask him to ring Lauren."

"That'll work," said Meg. "Assuming she'll see us."

"Maybe we can guarantee she'll buzz us up."

"How are you going to do that?" asked Meg. "Threaten to turn her into Detective Glass if she doesn't accept our sympathy call?"

"Not quite," I said. "Follow me."

We trotted around the corner to the other side of the building. Meg grabbed me before I could open the door to Declaration, a busy restaurant on the ground floor.

"Kit, this is no time for a second happy hour," she said.

"Don't be silly, although we might want

216

to split a drink while we wait. I'm going to order a pizza, and we're going to take it to Lauren as a peace offering. Believe me, no one can resist these pies."

The specialty pizzas, appropriately priced at $17.76, were named after signers of the Declaration of Independence. The Roger Sherman, featuring meatball and ricotta, was one of my favorites. Given Lauren's demeanor and her obvious interest in staying trim and beautiful, I ordered the less indulgent Matthew Thorton, which included mushrooms and kale as toppings.

I joined Meg at the bar. Sure enough, she'd ordered us both glasses of Prosecco. "I thought we talked about splitting a drink."

She waved her hand dismissively. "Correction, Kit. *You* talked about splitting a drink. I don't believe in sharing wine."

Since neither of us was driving this evening, my protest was an exercise in futility. Besides, another drink would embolden us when we met with Lauren, who seemed like a tough customer.

We chatted for fifteen minutes about office politics and whether our political party would survive the election intact. Moving from the majority to the minority in the Senate was a walk in the park compared to the House. If we lost control of the chamber, our jobs would switch from driving the agenda to surviving it. No one wanted to be in the minority in the House of Representatives.

After our bartender signaled our pizza was ready, we walked out the door and returned to the condo entrance. Meg inhaled deeply. "I sure hope Lauren isn't too hungry."

"Why not?" I asked. "She'll see us if she hasn't eaten yet."

"Of course," she said. "But I'm more concerned about whether she's likely to share that pizza with us."

While smart as a whip, Meg's stomach frequently drove her reasoning. "Don't worry," I said. "I'm sure you'll find a way to wrangle a piece out of her."

The concierge staffing the desk perked up when we walked inside. "You've been to Declaration, I see," he said.

I smiled. "We're here to share dinner with Lauren Parker. Could you ring her condo for us?"

The burly, middle-aged guy raised an eyebrow. "She's not expecting you? Mrs. Parker has been through a rough time."

Before I could respond, Meg piped up. "We know. We were there."

The concierge's mouth fell open. "You

saw Mr. Parker kill himself?"

I put my hand out to silence Meg before she could answer. "No, not at all. We hosted the event that night, but neither of us saw him fall."

He shook his head. "Can't understand why a man like that would want to end it all. He had a fine-looking wife and lived in this gorgeous building." He lowered his voice. "Do you know how much their condo cost when they bought it?"

"No idea," I said.

"One and half million," he said. "Wait until you see it. You'll know why."

Meg leaned in closer and whispered, "We're in the wrong business."

"No kidding." Doug and I lived comfortably, partially due to the fact he collected annually on a family trust-fund established years ago by his late grandfather, who hit it big with his Boston law firm. Digs like this were out of our league, at least for now. I hadn't explored alternatives to government service. Would New York present an opportunity to think outside the box with my career? A generous salary might come in handy if we moved to the Big Apple.

The concierge interrupted my daydream when he thrusted the phone in my hand.

"Mrs. Parker said she'd like to speak with you."

Damn. I should have thought this out more carefully. "Lauren," I stammered. "This is Kit Marshall from Congresswoman Dixon's office. I'm here with my associate Meg Peters. We wanted to check in on you and tell you once again how sorry we are about Van."

Lauren's response was pro forma. "Thank you for the kind words. I'm somehow managing to hold on in this difficult time." Nothing remarkable, yet nothing widely inappropriate, either. That Lauren was a slick one. It was hard to tell whether she had a full house or was bluffing her way through a disaster.

Time to put our cards on the table. "Lauren, we have a pizza here from Declaration. Can we bring it up to share with you?" Meg beamed at my hint of sharing.

Lauren answered, and I returned Meg's gesture with a "thumbs up" sign. I confirmed her accession with the concierge, who provided us with the correct condo number on the fourth floor.

We got inside the elevator, and Meg squealed with delight. "Great idea on the pizza, Kit. That was smart thinking."

"Let's not blow it," I said. "Remember we

need to see the supposed suicide note that Van left at his office."

The elevator dinged, and we entered a perfectly clean yet austere hallway, unpredictably consistent with the industrial chic feel of the renovated building. The décor was aggressively modern and deserved every architecture and style award it had won, but the asceticism didn't exactly scream "Honey, I'm home." Perhaps one and half million-dollar condos weren't for me, after all.

We found the right door and knocked. A moment later, Lauren Parker greeted us. She grasped a tissue in her left hand and her cell phone in the other. Her eyes appeared moist, yet her makeup and hair were flawless. It reminded me of a carefully staged crime scene. Keeping up appearances was a tricky business.

"Kit and Meg, thank you for paying me a visit. Please come in." Lauren moved out of the way. We entered a gorgeously decorated penthouse apartment with an emphasis on minimalism. The living room, adorned with a fireplace and designer couch, was dominated by the view at the end of it. Floor to ceiling windows provided a breathtaking panoramic view of the urban neighborhood.

"Your condo is beautiful," gasped Meg. It

was hard to curtail our awestruck reaction.

"Thank you. We were the original owners, of course." Lauren dabbed the corner of her eye. "Van had his eye on this building from the day it was slated for renovation."

She led us around the corner of the fireplace to the dining area of the condo. The kitchen area was small, yet all the appliances were state of the art. Quite frankly, they looked like they might have never been used.

"We can sit here and chat," she said. "Normally I avoid pizza from Declaration, but given the circumstances, I'm prepared to make an exception."

"Totally understandable," said Meg. "Why count calories at a time like this?"

Lauren nodded primly and turned behind her. "I have a terrific Chianti that would go well with the pizza. Join me in a glass?"

Even by Washington standards of alcohol consumption, this evening was getting ridiculous. Months of fundraising breakfasts, happy hours, and dinners had taken its toll on my waistline. Once this fiasco was resolved, it would go from bad to worse in North Carolina on the campaign. At this rate, I'd be wearing stretchy pants until the election.

Before I could answer, Meg signed us up

for a pour. I gave her a death stare in return. "Don't you want her to warm up to us?" she whispered. "We need to loosen her up. The woman is a ball of nerves."

That was Meg's pathetic excuse to have another glass of vino. Lauren didn't seem worse for the wear. Checking her phone with one hand, she opened the bottle of wine with her Cuisinart designer electric corkscrew with the other.

Lauren served us generous glasses and placed plates on the table. I opened the pizza box. "Help yourself, Lauren. You probably need something in your stomach."

Lauren nodded and selected the smallest slice from the pie. So much for indulgence. Meg politely let Lauren go first and then took several pieces for herself. I took a slice and waited for everyone to enjoy their first bites of dinner.

The Matthew Thorton pizza did not disappoint. It might have been the lighter of the options, but Declaration hadn't skimped on the taste. Carefully chosen garlic and herbs made the veggie pie a delicious combination. We chomped silently for several minutes before I cleared my throat.

"Have the police determined what happened to Van?" I asked.

Lauren took a sip of her wine and shook

her head. "Afraid not. But it looks like suicide."

"Why's that?" I gently kicked Meg under the table, so she understood we should play dumb.

"He left a note on his desk at work," said Lauren.

"How sad," said Meg with a slack expression. "Did he explain why he did it?"

"Not really," said Lauren. "I can show you the photocopy the police gave me."

That was easy.

She got up and returned to the table with a rectangular piece of lined notepaper with a small American flag icon in the corner. In block capital letters, it simply said: "I CAN'T DO THIS ANY LONGER. I'M SORRY." There was no signature. I studied the note for several seconds and passed it over to Meg.

"Is this Van's handwriting?" I asked. "It seems nondescript."

Lauren shrugged. "I'm not sure I've seen his handwriting in years. He texted and e-mailed, but rarely wrote anything down. He was glued to his mobile device, as you probably know." She motioned toward her iPhone, which was now plugged in on the designer granite countertop. At least she used the kitchen for something.

"Did the police find Van's phone?" I asked.

"Yes," said Lauren quickly. "There was nothing on it. No message or anything. The police told me this morning."

Lauren's patience with our inquisition about Van's death was dwindling, but I wanted to ask her one more question before we outwore our welcome.

"Have the police had any luck in locating the mysterious waiter?" I asked.

"The mysterious waiter?" Lauren repeated.

"The man you saw on the roof last night. Big guy with bushy hair?" I said.

Lauren rubbed the back of her neck. "Oh, now I remember. I'm not sure. I didn't ask when I spoke with the detective earlier today."

Meg raised her eyebrows. After several seconds, I spoke. "We shouldn't keep you any longer, Lauren. Once again, we express our condolences for your loss."

She mustered a tight smile and flipped over the top of the pizza box to close it. Meg stuck out her hand to stop it. "Do you mind if I have one more slice?" she asked sheepishly.

Like everyone else who was amazed at Meg's appetite, Lauren took a double-take, but recovered immediately. "Of course, be

225

my guest."

Meg grabbed a piece and made quick work of it. After she was finished, she said, "Dash Dugal sends his best, too."

That caught Lauren's attention. "Such a sweet man. I suppose there's no longer a need to keep up appearances as rivals now that Van is gone."

Meg's jaw clenched. She must not have appreciated Lauren's affectionate tone for her beloved Dash. Now it was really time for us to leave. I grabbed Meg's arm and guided her toward the door. "Call us if you need anything," I said as we exited.

Meg waited until we were in the elevator to explode. "What did that comment about Dash at the end mean?"

I tried to minimize it. "Who knows, Meg. They seemed friendly last night. Perhaps she felt as though she couldn't be nice to him because he and Van worked at competing lobbying firms."

I could see the bulging veins in Meg's neck. "She was trying to cause trouble because she knows I'm dating Dash."

We walked outside the building. "Don't stress out over an off-handed comment."

Meg crossed her arms. "You wouldn't appreciate it if some woman said something similar about Doug."

Meg's tone took me by surprise. My best pal never worried about competition when it came to men. Her annoyance provided a good reason to call it a night.

"I'm requesting an Uber to go home." I gave Meg a quick hug. "Promise me you'll get a good night's rest, and we can debrief in the morning."

Meg nodded. As I climbed into the car, I heard her mutter under her breath. "Promise me you won't move to New York."

Touché.

CHAPTER FIFTEEN

"Do you want to go to work with me today?"

A tail attached to a wiggly butt thumped the dining room wall. It was the most enthusiastic response concerning Congress I'd encountered in recent memory. Too bad it came from a non-voter, notably a dog.

Doug emerged from the kitchen with two cups of steaming coffee. He handed me a mug and sat down next to me on the couch. "Are you sure you want to take him with you?" he asked. "Given everything that's going on."

"It's not a problem. We still have an intern, and he likes dogs," I said. "Clarence's dog agility class starts early this evening, so the only way I can make it is to leave directly from work."

Doug sipped his coffee and scanned the headlines on his iPad. Without looking up, he said, "I hope he behaves for you."

"It's a bit risky," I agreed. "But Max Robinson should be at the class, and I want the chance to speak with him again about Van's death."

"Now the truth comes out," said Doug. "You're using Clarence as an excuse for snooping around."

"I wouldn't put it that way. More like killing two birds with one stone."

"Famous last words. How was your workout this morning?"

Still dressed in my tank top and capris, I said, "Fantastic. I really needed to punch something."

"I'm glad you aren't turning your frustration on me."

I took a gulp of my coffee. "I said something. Not someone."

"Fair enough." Doug put his tablet aside and looked at me. "Have you thought any further about New York?"

I gulped. "A bit. But the idea is still new to me. I haven't really processed what it might mean."

"Don't stress out about it. Maybe we can talk tomorrow when you're not rushing to work."

Tomorrow was Saturday. There would be no work on my schedule, but I'd be plenty occupied with trying to figure out what happened to Van Parker on that rooftop. I kept my snarky thought to myself and forced a smile.

"Sure, that sounds fine." I squeezed Doug's hand and got up. Before I could walk away, he pulled me back for a long kiss.

"Don't worry, Kit. We'll figure this out," he said.

I nodded numbly and headed to the bathroom to get ready for work.

Twenty minutes later, Clarence and I were on our way to Capitol Hill. Many people didn't realize it, but the Hill is one of the most dog-friendly workplaces in the entire city. Like everything else, rules about dogs in the office depended upon the big boss, the elected member of Congress. If he or she liked dogs, then it was perfectly acceptable to bring a pup to work. Maeve Dixon was way too busy these days to own a dog, but luckily, she'd grown up with them in North Carolina and even worked with K-9s in the military. On days in which I didn't have a million meetings to attend, Clarence was a welcome addition to our office.

After parking the car in the surface lot, we walked up the steps to the Cannon entrance. Clarence's trot always seemed more buoyant when we were headed inside a congressional building. Perhaps he knew his purpose, representing the American people and, of course, his canine brethren. The only difficulty posed by walking the Capitol Hill hallways with Clarence was that it often took us twice the amount of time to reach our intended destination due to all the people who wanted to pet him.

After several friendly greetings, we finally made it to the Dixon suite. Clarence settled in with a bone I kept at the office, and I turned on my computer to answer the e-mails which had piled up during our morning commute. Due to the recess, the usual swarm of supplicants had decreased markedly. No one wanted to bother a member of Congress who might not win reelection. It wasn't worth the time to write the e-mail.

A message popped up from Trevor. I clicked on the e-mail, with a subject line "READ NOW." Maybe Trevor had some information for me.

"Want to grab coffee at Firehook, at 10?" it read.

Trevor knew the only way to catch a busy staffer's attention was to put the subject line of the e-mail in capital letters so she'd read it immediately. It was one of the oldest tricks in the book.

I hit reply. "Sure. Was the alarmist heading really necessary?"

Twenty seconds later, an e-mail arrived from him. I opened it, although I already knew what it was going to say before I read it.

"It worked, didn't it?" he replied.

Everyone needed a Trevor in his or her life. Part nemesis, part comrade. Smarter, sassier, and more annoying than the typical friend, but also loyal and well-meaning. I had to constantly earn Trevor's respect, almost like it was always Groundhog Day. Nonetheless, I kept going back to the well because, quite frankly, it was worth it.

I sent an instant message to our intern Brock and asked him to come to my office. Less than ten seconds later, he appeared at my door.

"How can I be of service, ma'am?" he asked.

Like Meg, I wondered when I had transformed from "miss" to "ma'am?" Perhaps "ma'am" went with the chief of staff position and had nothing to do with age. I'd go with the former explanation rather than the latter.

"I'm going out for a bit. Can you watch Clarence?" At the sound of his name, my dog's ears perked up.

"Sure thing. I'll take him for a walk soon,"

he said. I gave Brock his leash and several treats.

"He likes to greet constituents who come to the office, but make sure they like dogs," I said. "We don't want to alienate any voters."

Brock straightened his shoulders and saluted. "Got it. When you get back, I can show you the photos from the fundraiser on Wednesday night."

"Did you send those to the campaign? You shouldn't be working on them at your government computer." The separation between our day job and the campaign was getting harder to maintain as we marched closer to election day, but I was determined to make sure the Dixon office remained on the ethical up-and-up.

"I worked on them last night at home," he explained. "Don't worry, boss. I understand the rules."

Although Brock was too eager at times, I'd miss him when his internship ended in December. In my humble opinion, enthusiasm trumped inexperience.

As I was leaving the office, Meg was coming in for the day. We exchanged pleasantries, but before I could walk out, she grabbed my arm.

"Wait, Kit. I had a thought about last

night," she said.

"Go ahead, but make it quick. I'm meeting Trevor for coffee."

Meg made a face. "I don't know why you waste your time with him," she said with a sigh. "If the suicide note isn't real, then who could have put it on Van's desk?"

I shrugged my shoulders. "I don't know. Who do you have in mind?"

Meg snapped her fingers. "Only one person. Lauren Parker. No one else had access to Van's office after hours."

I rubbed my chin. "I don't know. It's a good point."

Meg poked her finger gently on my chest. "She's the only one who could have killed Van. Admit it. Everyone knows she was having an affair and didn't want a messy divorce."

Meg was making some sense, but I was late to meet Trevor and didn't want to debate the finer points of her theory. "Let's talk about this when I'm back in the office. By the way, Clarence is here today."

Although not an ardent dog lover, Meg liked Clarence. "Good thing I didn't wear my black cashmere sweater," she said. Clarence's white fur made wearing dark colors a fashion nightmare.

Five minutes later, I walked inside Firehook Bakery on Pennsylvania Avenue. A local chain, Firehook was known for delicious baked goods, particularly cookies, cakes, and breads. Sure enough, Trevor was waiting for me, seated in an armchair at the rear of the restaurant. He already had a cup of coffee, so I signaled that I'd join him after ordering.

I stared at the cases of freshly baked goodies. I really wanted a seven-layer bar with my coffee. I could practically taste the graham cracker, chocolate, and butterscotch combination. Then I took a deep breath and felt the tightness around the waist of my pants. Months of fundraisers had taken their toll. Instead, I opted for the boring yet sensible low-fat fruit yogurt parfait and a large coffee.

When I reached the table, Trevor was busy reading the newspaper. He was one of the few people I knew who still insisted on reading a paper version rather than squinting on a mobile phone like the rest of us.

"What's in the news today, Trevor?" I asked lightly as I took a seat.

"Could be difficult times for your boss," he said. "The election is going to be a close one."

I sipped my coffee. "Van's death at the fundraiser doesn't help, either."

"Hackensack is starting to mention it off-handedly at campaign stops."

I blinked rapidly. "How do you know that?"

Trevor pulled out an iPad from his leather satchel. After a few swift keystrokes, he showed me a YouTube video. "I monitor all developments in close races on an hourly basis."

Sure enough, Hackensack's beefy face appeared on the screen. "While I was spending time with the fine voters of North Carolina," he drawled. "My opponent was drinking expensive wine and eating a fancy steak in Washington, D.C. to raise money from lobbyists."

Boos from the audience erupted. Hackensack put up his hand to silence them, so he could continue.

"Now I know that's part of the game in our nation's capital, but it's not part of my playbook." He paused to chuckle at his self-referenced joke. "Apparently, this party was so much fun, one of her guests fell off the roof."

Gasps from the crowd forced Coach to pause.

"That's right, friends. Your current member of Congress is involved in a suspicious death investigation. Now is that the type of person you want representing you in Washington?" asked Hackensack.

More jeers from the audience. Someone cried out, "Personal foul! It's time to bench Maeve Dixon!"

Trevor closed iPad. "Not a pretty sight, and you're stuck here in D.C. until the Van Parker case is resolved."

I dug into my yogurt cup. I should have gotten that cookie. When I was out of a job in January, I would have plenty of time to exercise and lose any unwanted pounds. I knew one thing for certain. I wouldn't be taking any phone calls from Jeff Jenkins or Chairman Edwards. Both were undoubtedly livid about Hackensack using Van's death to beat up on Maeve Dixon.

"Speaking of Van, I have some information." I updated Trevor about our happy hour conversation with Gene Price last night and the late-evening impromptu pizza dinner with Lauren Parker.

Trevor considered the details carefully after chugging his coffee. Finally, he asked, "And this intelligence leads you to suspect whom? Assuming Van did not take his own life, which frankly makes no sense if he was hell bent on starting his own lobbying firm next year."

"It's impossible to know for sure," I said.

"Lauren had motive, but it's hard to imagine how she could have pushed Van off the roof, given that he probably weighed a hundred pounds more than her. Max Robinson also had reason to kill Van, but he was retrieving his briefcase when Van died. Clarissa doesn't have a solid alibi, yet it's unclear why she'd want to kill Van at her own fundraiser." I took a deep breath before continuing. "Then there's the mysterious waiter who was seen on the rooftop at the time of death. No one has identified him yet, but it leaves open the possibility Van was murdered by a killer for hire."

Trevor tapped his finger on the table. "Kit, you're deliberately avoiding one person."

"I know, I know. You don't have to state the obvious."

Trevor adjusted his wire-framed glasses. "Why are you avoiding a careful analysis of Dash Dugal as a suspect?"

I finished the last bite of my breakfast and threw a paper napkin in disgust. "Because Meg is acting like she's in love with him, and I don't want to alienate my best friend."

"Shouldn't you be more concerned she might be dating a pathological killer?" he asked.

I sighed. "Of course, but it's a delicate time, and I don't want to piss her off any more than I already have."

I detected a faint smile on Trevor's lips. He'd always been snarky about our friendship, although I'd always suspected he was secretly jealous of it.

"And why have you annoyed her so greatly?" he asked.

"There's a possibility Doug and I might move to New York City. He has an offer from Columbia." I pointed a finger at Trevor. "Don't say a word, Mr. Bestselling Author. My boss doesn't know about it yet."

Trevor silently motioned that his lips were sealed. "I'm impressed. Columbia is the Ivy League. Doug Hollingsworth is moving up in the world."

"It's far from a done deal, Trevor. We haven't seriously discussed it. But you can understand why the situation with Meg is so delicate."

Trevor furrowed his brow. "I comprehend your predicament. That does not, however, exonerate Dash Dugal. Van Parker was his professional rival, after all."

"He was," I admitted. "But if Van was peeling off to start his own lobbying firm, he wouldn't represent the trucking industry any longer. That would take him out of direct crosshairs with Dash."

"A fair point," said Trevor. "There's only

one way we can find out more."

I waited for Trevor to continue. When he didn't, I prompted him. "Spit it out, Trevor."

"We go to the source himself," he said.

CHAPTER SIXTEEN

After confirming Brock had Clarence under control and could tend to his needs, Trevor and I sped off for K Street in my car. Normally the Metro would have been the smarter option, but since D.C. had cleared out, the usually congested route to the heart of downtown was free of traffic. We arrived at the American Railway Federation in less than fifteen minutes. Parking was a breeze, too. We found a spot right in front of the tall building where Dash worked.

As we headed inside, my non-government iPhone buzzed, and I reached for it inside my purse.

"It's a text from Clarissa Smythe," I said. "She wants to meet me for lunch at the Monocle."

"You should go," said Trevor. "Maybe she has information for you."

"You're right," I said. "And I can't forget Clarissa is a suspect. She was on the rooftop that night, too."

As we rode the elevator to the sixth floor, I asked, "Shouldn't we have called ahead to let him know we're coming?"

Trevor wrinkled his nose. "Of course not. That would ruin the element of surprise."

Did Trevor think we were going to find Dash standing at his desk, holding a key piece of evidence that proved he killed Van Parker? Although they'd never admit it, Trevor and Meg were quite similar, particularly when it came to their shared flair for the dramatic.

We walked into the office and gave the receptionist our names. A few minutes later, she told us Dash would see us. As we walked down the hallway, Trevor whispered, "I told you it would work out. Now we've caught him off guard."

But Dash Dugal didn't look off his game when we entered his office. He was dressed in a trim Italian wool suit with a dark purple dress shirt that hugged his chest. A striped designer silk necktie completed the fashionable outfit. Dash gave new meaning to the phrase "dress for success."

I spoke first. "Dash, thanks for seeing us without notice. This is my friend Trevor, who worked with me and Meg in the Senate."

Dash extended his hand to Trevor. "Of course. I've heard of you. Everyone in Washington is eagerly awaiting the publication of your book."

Trevor didn't react to Dash's comment. After sitting down, I said, "As you know, the police are investigating Van Parker's death. It may not have been a suicide."

Dash's handsome face remained placid. "The police informed me about this development. Detective Glass said she might have a few more questions for me today."

"Have you given any more thought to what happened on the rooftop? Was there something else you might have seen or observed?" I asked.

Dash shook his head. "I'm afraid not. I'll tell you what I'm going to say to the detective. She should focus her efforts on finding the waiter Lauren and I saw. If Van was murdered, he may have had something to do with it. The rest of us were occupied, as you know."

"You were searching for a replacement glass of wine for Meg, right?" I asked.

"Yes," said Dash. "And as I recall, shortly before you appeared on the scene, I had it in my hand and gave it to her."

"It's not exactly a rock-solid alibi," said Trevor.

I scrutinized Dash. Would Trevor's accusation unsettle him? His demeanor remained composed. Dash Dugal was as cool as a cucumber.

"That's neither here nor there. It's the truth," he said. "Besides, why would I want to kill Van Parker? I don't have a motive."

"Wasn't he your professional rival?" I asked. "Van led the trucking lobby and you're here at ARF. The railroad and trucking industries are like cats and dogs when it comes to fighting for scarce transportation dollars."

Dash chuckled. "Your comparison is a good one. However, the rivalry is more myth than truth. Yes, we're in competition with each other, but killing Van would have made no difference. The trucking lobby is simply going to replace Van with someone else. The fight goes on."

Trevor piped up. "But Van was legendary and had the upper hand. With him out of the way, you would have a better shot with next year's transportation bill, perhaps even the opportunity to score a more lucrative position at a larger firm. More money, more prestige."

Dash motioned around his spacious office, which had beautiful windows and a terrific view of K Street below. "Really? I think

I'm doing pretty well these days, don't you?"

We weren't getting anywhere with him, and I couldn't think of another probing question to ask. "Sorry to take up your time, Dash. I need to run. I'm having lunch with Clarissa."

"Are you going to Tosca?" asked Dash.

I shook my head.

"Blue Duck Tavern, then?"

"Sorry, my taste is a little more traditional," I said. "The Monocle by the Senate."

Dash looked disappointed. "Oh, well. Have fun. I always forget Clarissa is a fundraiser, not a lobbyist."

Only a distinction that would matter in Washington. I mustered a smile. "I'm sure I'll see you soon." He didn't know me that well. Hopefully he couldn't detect the fakery.

"Yes, perhaps tomorrow?" he asked.

I must have looked perplexed because he continued. "At the wake for Van Parker. Saturday afternoon at the Palm. Several K Street firms are hosting it."

Trevor responded quickly. "Thanks for letting us know. We'll be there."

Once we were inside the elevator, I turned to Trevor. "Dash has a point. I'm not sure he has a clear motive for wanting to kill Van

Parker. Everyone has competition in this city. It's not a strong reason to murder someone."

"Maybe so, but I feel as though we're missing something," said Trevor. "Why did he feel the need to point that out to us?"

Crossing the lobby, we almost ran into Detective Glass.

"Why am I not surprised to see you, Ms. Marshall?" she said.

I grinned sheepishly. "Great minds think alike, don't they?"

Trevor introduced himself again to the detective, who he'd met briefly during one of the previous murder investigations we'd helped solve. "Have you uncovered any additional leads on this case that you can share with us, Detective?" he asked.

"I'm not here for my health," said Glass. "There's more evidence pointing in the direction of murder."

"I knew it," I muttered. Visions of a quick exit to North Carolina were fading, possibly alongside my boss's reelection chances.

"Why do you think Van was the victim of foul play?" asked Trevor.

"There's the matter of the suspicious mark on his midsection. I told Ms. Marshall about it yesterday. We now think it might have been a stun gun," said the detective.

"A stun gun?" I said in a high-pitched voice. "I was at the fundraiser all evening. I can assure you no guest was carrying a stun gun."

"And we searched the rooftop and the personal belongings of the guests who remained," said Glass. "We didn't find a weapon. It's a puzzle, but the mark was fresh. Van Parker was stunned shortly before he died."

"Anything else? It sounds like there's more information." Trevor's pushiness occasionally helped, and this was a prime example.

"We got some preliminary toxicology screens. We won't know for sure until the full report is available, but Van Parker may have had a sedative in his system," she said.

Again, my squeaky voice appeared. "He was drugged?"

"I can't see why someone would take medicine like that willingly and then come to a fundraiser on a rooftop," said Detective Glass.

"Although Lauren Parker did say Van recently had trouble with anxiety," I said. "She also mentioned he was depressed."

Detective Glass nodded. "Van did have a prescription. We checked it out. But even if he took an extra dose the night before, it wouldn't have remained in his system at this level."

Trevor's eyes were big. "So, he was drugged, stunned, and then pushed off the roof to his death."

"That's our working theory," said Detective Glass. "We're dealing with someone who really wanted to make sure Van Parker died at your fundraiser, Ms. Marshall."

Not exactly music to my ears. Imagine that on a campaign commercial. *Vote for Maeve Dixon. Serious felonies guaranteed.*

"Thank you for being so honest with us, Detective," I said. "What about the mystery man who was seen on the rooftop at the time of the crime? A big guy with dark hair, possibly Hispanic?"

"We're chasing him down," she said. "That's why I wanted to talk more to Mr. Dugal and Lauren Parker. They both saw the individual, and we need more detail to draw a sketch. Maybe shop it around to a few high-end restaurants in the area to see if they recognize him as part of the wait-staff."

"We won't keep you from your job any longer," said Trevor. "If we uncover anything important, we'll contact you immediately."

Trevor and I turned to exit the building, but Detective Glass grabbed my arm. "I know you want this murder solved so you can leave town, but leave the legwork to us. This killer is brutal, someone who methodically plotted Van Parker's death to the very last minute. Most likely, he or she won't hesitate to take another life. Be careful, Ms. Marshall."

I nodded. Trevor and I walked onto the sidewalk on K Street. "Want to come to lunch with Clarissa?" I asked. "She's a big fish in the world of campaign fundraising. Good fodder for your book sequel."

Trevor straightened the collar on his London Fog raincoat. "I'm well aware of her, but duty calls. I have pre-release interviews with my publicist and select media outlets this afternoon."

"Good luck," I said. "I'll let you know if there are any more breaks in the case."

Trevor turned to leave, but turned around abruptly. "Kit, listen to Detective Glass. You and Meg stay safe."

Before I could respond, Trevor took off in the opposite direction. He must be growing soft in his old age. His warning may have been the most effusive show of emotion I'd ever heard from him. Either Trevor was developing a perceptible degree of emotional intelligence or the situation had become considerably dangerous. If I had to speculate, both explanations had credence.

I texted Brock for a check on Clarence. A typical millennial, he responded not with words but an image of a happy Clarence sitting next to the main receptionist desk inside our small anteroom where guests waited for an appointment with either the Congresswoman or a staff member.

Keep an eye on him, I wrote back. *He's not always an angel.*

Brock simply responded with a smiley face emoticon. I hoped that meant he'd heed my warning.

Fifteen minutes later, I backed into an available parking space on D Street, a short walk away from my destination. I hadn't dined at the Monocle since my days as a Senate staffer. Only a block away from the office building where I used to work, the Monocle was a reliable mealtime and happy hour staple. House staffers rarely spent much time there. It would be helpful to talk with Clarissa, but I also appreciated a trip down memory lane.

As soon as I entered underneath the famous green awning, the Greek maître d', Nick, greeted me with a warm handshake. "Miss Kit, I haven't seen you around here so much since Senator Langsford died. Welcome back."

"Thanks, Nick. It's good to be here. I'm meeting a friend, Clarissa Smythe. Have you seen her?"

Nick wiggled his substantial eyebrows. "She's here. No one misses Miss Clarissa, if you know what I mean." He made a motion with his hands to mimic her hourglass shape.

"Yeah, we all know what you mean," I said over my shoulder as I headed into the dining room. The white tablecloths gave it a fancier appearance than reality. While the food had improved markedly in the recent past, the impressive array of framed photographs on the walls was the real attraction. Anyone who was somebody in Washington made sure the Monocle included his or her picture, although it was verboten to ask the owners to do so. The offer was reportedly extended to loyal customers, which included John Kennedy and Richard Nixon in the early days. More recently, dedicated patrons included Senators Chris Dodd and Ted Kennedy, whose legendary bar tabs frequently exceeded their dining room expenditures.

From across the room, I spotted Clarissa waggling her red nails. Given the congressional recess, I'd thrown on the first clean pair of pants and sweater I'd located inside my messy closet. As a political fundraiser, the words "casual Friday" didn't exist in Clarissa's vocabulary. She sported a Diane von Furstenberg wrap dress and matching bone-colored heels. How she trudged all over the city in those shoes was a bigger mystery than who pushed Van Parker off the rooftop.

She stood up and gave me a half-hug.

"Good to see you, Clarissa," I said. "Hopefully under better circumstances than when we were last together."

"That's setting a low bar," she said after sipping her glass of sparkling water and lime.

We exchanged pleasantries and ordered our lunches. I yearned for the crab cake or the special rib eye angus steak and cheese. Instead, I remembered the drinks and pizza from last night and went for the smoked salmon carpaccio served over a bed of greens. Clarissa, who worked extra hard to stay svelte during campaign season, selected a Greek salad. Clarissa's good looks might rival Meg's, but my best friend's metabolism had hers beat.

As she munched on a small piece of the Monocle's famous focaccia, I scrutinized my dining companion. She had no obvious motive to kill Van Parker. Maybe the reason simply hadn't surfaced. After all, her alibi during the time of Van's death seemed flimsy.

"Did you hear from Detective Glass about Van Parker's death?" I asked.

"She's coming around this afternoon to talk with me again," she said, looking down at her empty bread plate. "The word around town is that Van was murdered."

"That's what the police believe," I said slowly. "Do you?"

"He certainly had his share of enemies. Bad news for me, of course. A suicide is unfortunate. A homicide during one of my fundraisers could put me out of business next election cycle."

Before our lunches arrived, Clarissa excused herself to use the restroom. I took advantage of the opportunity to glance at my phone. Sure enough, there was a text from Brock. This couldn't be good.

Small Clarence problem. Under control.

I sighed. Not much I could do about it now. I'd learned that as a chief of staff, I couldn't solve everyone's problems all the time. I had to delegate and say a prayer. Hopefully, no limbs or expensive purses had been damaged in the wake of Hurricane Clarence.

Clarissa returned to the table, our food

arrived, and we dug in. "Are you sure you didn't hear or see something that night? You said you talked to the restaurant manager and then checked e-mails inside," I prodded.

Clarissa wavered for a beat. It wasn't much, but I detected a hesitation.

"Were you telling the truth?" I asked.

She put down her fork, finished chewing, and took a long sip of her water before answering. "Sort of."

I clenched my jaw. "What does that mean? You were either honest or told a lie."

"You don't understand," she said defensively. "I wasn't completely forthright, but it doesn't matter."

This conversation had proven more frustrating than a White House press conference. "Clarissa, where did you go after I left the fundraiser?"

She crossed her arms. "I was exactly where I said I was, with Stuart the whole time." She paused. "We were sharing a moment of sorts."

"An intimate moment?"

Clarissa squirmed. "Yes."

Something wasn't adding up. "And why didn't you just tell the truth when I asked you the first time?"

"That's what you don't understand. I do

254

business with restaurants all over this city." She whipped her arm around. "If it got out I was involved with one of the managers, it might give me a bad reputation."

We stared at each other for several seconds. Then I got it. "Because you have this arrangement with managers at other establishments."

Clarissa nodded. She leaned closer to me and whispered, "How in the hell did you think I got Maeve Dixon booked at Charlie Palmer's on the last night of the D.C. fundraising cycle? These types of deals don't come for free."

I savored my salmon and Clarissa's words. Both were juicy and flavorful. Truthfully, I wasn't shocked at her revelation. I'd come to expect questionable morals and character flaws in our nation's capital. Was it time for me to make an exit? New York wasn't the paragon of virtue, but the shenanigans in the Big Apple typically involved business rather than government.

"Since you have," I paused for the right word, "such beneficial relationships all over the city, perhaps you can ask around if anyone meets the description of the waiter Dash and Lauren saw leaving the rooftop around the time of Van's murder."

Clarissa nodded. "Can do. Do you have a

description?"

"Nothing more concrete than what I heard before, but Detective Glass was making the rounds this morning, and she may have more details when you talk to her."

Clarissa snapped her fingers. "Before I forget, I wanted to tell you the bill for the fundraiser was a little higher than I originally anticipated. I sent the total to the campaign, of course. But I wanted to let you know, in case Maeve asked about it."

The last thing Dixon looked at was a bill from a restaurant. But her campaign manager, who kept pretty tight rein on the finances, might raise an eyebrow. "Why was it higher than you expected, Clarissa?"

"A few more bottles of wine than I thought. That wine was expensive, so it added up. Everyone drank their fair share. That's why it was a good party. At least until Van went overboard." Clarissa rolled her eyes.

"Not everyone was drinking alcohol," I said. "Max Robinson, for example."

Clarissa made a face. "Is he the bike lobbyist? I'm sure I saw him get a glass of wine at the bar."

"Really?" I said. "He made a point to tell me he didn't drink booze."

"Wouldn't be the first lie told at a fund-

256

raiser," said Clarissa.

"I don't want to quibble, but we also shouldn't be paying for wine that wasn't very good."

Clarissa straightened in her chair. "Of course not. What do you mean?"

"Dash got Meg a replacement glass of wine after her drink spilled. When she took a sip of it, she said it tasted awful. She poured it out. Believe me, Meg doesn't waste alcohol. Ever."

Clarissa scratched her head. "That's unfortunate. We didn't have any other complaints. And those bottles were at least a hundred dollars each. But don't worry. I'll text Stuart and see if there was a problem with a vintage he served. If that's the case, we'll be sure to rebate the campaign or comp you next time."

"I hope there will be a next time," I said grimly.

"Cheer up," said Clarissa. "I don't work for losers. It's what keeps me in business."

"Are you going to the wake for Van tomorrow? At the Palm?" I asked.

"Of course. I'm not a lobbyist, but they're integral to keeping my business humming along," she said. "I view it as a mandatory work gathering."

I'm sure Van would have been touched by

your kindness.

"I think I'll make an appearance," I said. "Dash said he was attending, and that means my friend Meg will also be there."

Clarissa tittered. "Should be interesting with another love triangle in the mix."

I jerked my head back. "What do you mean?"

My dining companion popped an olive in her mouth with relish. "At the gathering on Wednesday night, we had Van Parker, his wife Lauren, and her not-so-hidden lover Chairman Edwards."

"But that love triangle no longer exists. Van is dead," I said, stating the obvious.

"Yes, but there's always another tryst waiting to happen in Washington." Clarissa counted off with her fingers. "Lauren Parker, Dash Dugal, and your friend Meg."

I cleared my throat. "Dash and Lauren are having an affair?"

Clarissa tilted her head from side to side. "I don't know about that. I've heard Dash is hot to trot for the grieving widow."

"Since when? Is this a new development?" Perhaps Dash knew Lauren had likely inherited a mint and wanted to take a short path to Easy Street.

"Nah," said Clarissa as she grabbed the check. "He's been into her for a while. She's

258

always had her sights set on bigger fish, like Van and Chairman Edwards."

I whipped out my credit card and placed it next to hers. "Sorry, lady. Ethics rules don't allow you to pay for my lunch." Even though our conversation had almost nothing to do with politics, appearances were everything.

Clarissa sighed. "How I wish for the days before Jack Abramoff ruined it for the rest of us."

Before our waiter returned and we signed our receipts, I needed to clarify what Clarissa had just said about Dash. "If Dash is in love with Lauren, then why is he going out with Meg?"

Clarissa gave me a knowing glance. "Well, she looks just like Lauren."

How icky. Was this something I needed to share with Meg? There was no good way to broach the subject. I put it out of my mind.

We said our good-byes after Clarissa promised to give me an update tomorrow about her conversation with Detective Glass. In a world where information was currency, Clarissa certainly could buy anyone in town. If she wasn't hell bent on sleeping with every high-end restaurant manager in town, I would have suggested Trevor should ask her out. She'd give him a run for his money on the gossip circuit. On second thought, maybe it was best to keep them separated. The notion of the two of them teaming up was frightening, even by Washington standards.

I crossed the street and was about to open the door to my car when I noticed a piece of paper was stuck to the windshield, most likely an annoying advertisement inviting me to an all-you-can-drink mimosa happy hour on Capitol Hill this weekend. Really, didn't anyone pay attention to environmental standards these days? I zapped my car with my remote key and grabbed the flyer. After climbing into the Prius, I was about toss it aside when I noticed the small typeface. It wasn't an ad. Instead, it was a note. I flipped it over. In printed letters, it read:

Stop sticking your nose where it doesn't belong, or you'll be next.

CHAPTER SEVENTEEN

I should have been trembling during the short drive back to the House of Representatives. Instead, the adrenaline made me feel emboldened. There was no question that something nefarious had happened on the rooftop and the responsible party was getting nervous. The murderer had methodically followed me to determine the location of my car and then issued a threatening missive. That meant the culprit was worried about the conversations I'd been having. The threat could only mean one thing. I was getting closer to figuring out who killed Van Parker.

After returning my car to the surface lot, I stuffed the note inside my purse. I hadn't paid any attention to who might have been following me today. Dash knew where I was having lunch, but Detective Glass was headed inside to interview him when we left. It would have been hard to give her the slip. Clarissa had been waiting for me when I arrived at the restaurant, but she did excuse herself to use the bathroom. Had she used the opportunity to place the threatening note on my windshield? I had no idea about Lauren Parker or Max Robinson's whereabouts earlier today, yet it was entirely plausible either could have tailed me.

Five minutes later, I opened the door to the congressional office. Quite frankly, I had more trepidation about Clarence's shenanigans than the hostile note I'd just received. My priorities needed a serious reevaluation.

Our small waiting area didn't show any signs of World War III. The staff assistant, who manned the front desk, sat quietly at his workstation with his headset. A call had just come in, and he rang out in a friendly voice, "Representative Maeve Dixon's office, how can I help you?"

Not wanting to interrupt the phone conversation (constituents who called our office were likely voters), I zipped past him and entered our office area. Clarence was sitting next to Brock's cubicle. When he spotted me, he ran to me, his tail wagging vigorously. There was a familiar guilty look on his face.

I crouched down to rub his satiny ears.

"Give me the bad news. What did he do?"

Brock swiveled in his chair to face me. "It wasn't that terrible. Honest." He crossed his heart to emphasize his veracity.

Meg appeared from behind a cubicle wall. She shook her finger. "Clarence was a naughty boy. But we managed to mitigate the damage."

"Is someone going to tell me what happened?" I asked, not bothering to hide the exasperated tone.

"Clarence became exuberant when a family visited the office," said Brock. "Let's just say his welcome was memorable."

I pivoted to Meg, who wouldn't whitewash the damage for me. She continued the story. "A mother came in with a toddler. She said her son loved dogs, so we let Clarence go over to him. Unfortunately, the little tyke hadn't finished his ice cream from the cafeteria."

"Uh oh." I knew where this was headed. Clarence loved three things in life: pizza, ice cream, and me. In that precise order.

"He circled him and then went in for the kill," said Brock. "In five seconds flat, Clarence had consumed his prey."

"Sounds about right," I said. "Actually, I'm surprised it took five seconds. Clarence must be mellowing out."

"Of course, we apologized. I gave her money for a replacement ice cream. I sent them to Good Stuff for a gourmet milkshake," said Meg. Good Stuff Eatery was a block down the street and well worth the walk. The gourmet chef who owned the establishment specialized in delicious burgers and handmade shakes.

"He'll forget he ever had an ice cream from the Longworth Cafeteria," said Brock.

I knew the answer to the question but had to ask. "Constituent?"

Meg nodded. "Of course. From Clinton."

"There's one vote out the window."

"Not necessarily," said Brock. "Those milkshakes at Good Stuff are amazing!"

I shook my head. "Let's focus on the bigger picture. Any word from the campaign today?" We were allowed minimal contact to coordinate schedules and other inquiries.

"They received the photos I sent last night," said Brock.

"Good, although I don't know if they can use any of them because of what happened," I said.

"Probably not," said Meg. "But Brock uploaded them to the online drive so once things settle down, the campaign press team can go back and see if any of them are usable."

"Understood. Any numbers from the campaign?" I asked. Public polls weren't usually done at the congressional district level. That meant our own knowledge concerning how Maeve was doing came from an internal pollster, who was employed out of campaign coffers at a heavy price. Analytics didn't come cheap in politics, but you get what you pay for.

"It's not great," said Meg. "She's down a few points from last week."

My face grew hot with anger. "How can that be? What are they doing to staunch the bleed?"

"I didn't get into it with them," said Meg. "But I think Hackensack has really gone on the offensive against her, and she's been out of sorts since returning back to the state."

"What do you mean?" I asked.

"She's just not in the flow," said Meg, using her fingers to indicate quotations. "Candidates struggle sometimes to find their voice. Don't worry, Kit. She'll get her groove back. And the couple of points are still well within the margin of error."

Meg had worked in politics longer than me, and I trusted her judgment. But I knew why Maeve had lost her "flow" or whatever we wanted to call it. She was worried about what happened at her fundraiser. It was distracting, and prevented her from focusing on the real enemy, Coach Hackensack. We'd get Maeve Dixon back when the killer was in custody. It was as plain as the nose on my face — or Clarence's. I was reminded of his presence when he rubbed his muzzle against my hand. Clarence didn't like too much human-to-human talk.

I rubbed his cheek, and he licked my fingers in return. "Meg, can I see you in my office? I need to tell you about some, um, recent developments."

Meg nodded curtly. In a clipped voice, she said, "Yes, I'll be there in a moment. I'd also like to speak with you."

I grabbed Clarence by the collar and guided him into my office. If the ice cream episode was any indication about his state of mind, maybe it would be best to skip the agility session tonight. On the other hand, it might be my only chance to speak to Max Robinson alone. I glanced at Clarence, who had settled down next to my desk with a sweet expression on his face.

"Are you going to be a good boy this evening?" I asked.

Meg appeared at my door. "Clarence is a wonder dog, but last time I checked, he still doesn't speak English."

I waved her inside. "I know, I know.

Someday, I still think he's going to open his mouth and answer me."

"Let me know when that happens, Kit," said Meg as she twirled her finger in a circular motion next to her head.

"You'll know I've had a bonafide breakdown if I claim that Clarence is speaking to me," I said.

"You said it, not me," said Meg. "Shall I go first or you?"

I extended my right hand in front of me in a friendly gesture. "By all means, the Gentlelady from the District of Columbia has the floor."

"Dash came by at lunchtime. He said you and Trevor went to see him this morning at his office."

Uh-oh. I knew where this was headed. "We did. I would have told you, but I didn't have a chance."

"Really, Kit? This isn't 1999. You could have texted me."

"You're right. But after we left his office, I headed right back over the Hill to have lunch with Clarissa. And then this happened." I threw the note from my windshield on the desk.

Meg picked it up and studied it. "Someone is threatening you about Van Parker. It's official. We're dealing with a homicide."

"Beyond a shadow of a doubt." Then I told Meg about the conversation with Detective Glass about the stun gun and sedative.

I had to mention the obvious. "Dash knew I was having lunch at the Monocle. He could have put that note on my car."

"It does appear we have a murder on our hands," said Meg slowly. "But Dash couldn't have done this, Kit. He doesn't own a stun gun. For goodness sake, he told me he's never even fired a weapon in his life! We should focus on the other suspects and figure out the identity of our mystery waiter."

There's a first time for everything. I kept my thoughts to myself, at least for now. I picked up and waved the note. "This proves we're onto something important. We just need to figure out what it is. The sooner, the better. I don't like those numbers coming out of the campaign."

"I agree," said Meg. "What's the plan?"

"There's agility practice tonight for Clarence," I said. "Max Robinson told me his dog was ready for a time trial, which is on the schedule. I planned to go and see if I can find out anything juicy."

"Good idea," said Meg. "I hope Clarence behaves."

"Doubtful. But that's the price we might have to pay to find our killer."

The remainder of the afternoon passed uneventfully. Working on Capitol Hill was either feast or famine. When Congress was in session, there wasn't enough hours in the day to get all our work done. With an election looming and the outcome uncertain, our jobs had slowed to a snail's pace. Finally, it was five o'clock and time to leave for Clarence's class.

"Have a good weekend everyone!" I called out. I stopped at Meg's cubicle. "Are you going to the Palm for Van's memorial?"

"I want to go, but Dash has another appointment beforehand. He'll arrive late," she said.

"I can pick you up if you want a ride," I said.

Her face brightened. "Perfect. Taking the subway on the weekend is a bummer." Metro had cut back service, and trains ran infrequently on Saturday and Sunday, making it difficult for District dwellers who relied on public transportation to arrive on time for weekend appointments.

"We can touch base tomorrow for a time," I said. "Wish us luck!"

Meg crouched down to pet Clarence. "We need your doggie sleuthing skills in full force tonight."

Clarence stared back at her with his big brown eyes and then gave her hand a lick.

"I think that means he understands. Or he wanted a taste of those barbecue potato chips you just ate." I pointed to the empty bag on her desk.

Minutes later, we were headed south on the I-395 freeway. The home of hip restaurants, expansive parks, and several award-winning theaters, Shirlington was an up-and-coming Arlington neighborhood. It also had the reputation as one of the most dog-friendly suburban communities in the greater Washington, D.C. area. Hence the location for WOOFS, a premiere dog training facility. I'd gotten the idea for Clarence to try an agility class after watching an Animal Planet special about it. The trainer had explained that agility was perfect for high-energy dogs who liked challenges. Clarence certainly enjoyed figuring out how to steal unguarded food, shoes, or remote controls. Doug and I thought agility training might give Clarence a newfound focus for his inquisitive exuberance. Thus far, he'd done well in the lessons, as long as I kept the treats coming. With the amount he ate during a class, I doubted the additional exercise was helping Clarence shed the extra pounds of puppy fat he was carrying around.

After a quick walk around the parking lot for a bathroom break, we strolled into WOOFS. Shelby, one of our favorite trainers, greeted us at the door.

"Welcome, Kit and Clarence. I didn't know if you'd make it this week for the practice trial," she said in a friendly voice.

"Congress adjourned, which means shorter days at work for me," I said. "New hair color?" Shelby had spiked short hair which changed colors more frequently than a traffic light in DuPont Circle.

Shelby ran her fingers through her newly dyed fuchsia locks. "Yeah, I got tired of green. I figured it was time to go for something bolder."

"You managed to do it," I said. "Do you know if Max Robinson is here?"

"Sure is. He and Bruiser arrived a few minutes ago." She pointed toward the rear of the building. "They're warming up on the weave poles."

"Great. See you inside," I said. Clarence gave a half bark, half growl.

Stop talking and let's get to the obstacles so I can earn my treats, lady.

I pulled Clarence's leash in the direction of the large facility, which was divided into stations. This evening, dogs would be given the first opportunity to run through the course sequentially. Until now, we'd only practiced one obstacle at a time. Tonight was the real test to see if a dog could keep focus while moving through the entire course. I had my doubts about Clarence's ability to sustain interest for that long, but perhaps the treats, which were allowed in practice trials, would keep him moving along. Quite frankly, Clarence's agility training was secondary to interrogating Max.

I spotted him standing in the corner with a large Boxer. Now I remembered Bruiser, whose imposing stature implied he was appropriately named. I waved my hand as I walked up to them. "Max, it's Kit Marshall. Good to see you."

Max was watching Bruiser weave through the poles. Once he was finished, he gave him a reward and turned to face us. "Hopefully under better circumstances this evening."

"Certainly," I said. "How's Bruiser doing?"

Max pushed up his glasses. "Pretty well. He's ready to run the course tonight. We need a base time so we can set targets for improvement each week."

"Clarence isn't nearly as ambitious," I said. "If he finishes without incident, I'll be ecstatic."

Max didn't laugh. "I suppose we all have our appropriate goals in life."

This guy had a sense of humor comparable to Attila the Hun. Time to switch gears and get down to business. Before I could, Clarence pulled at the leash. He wanted a chance to run through the poles to earn a treat.

"Okay, buddy. It's your turn." I unhooked his leash and walked alongside him as Clarence expertly weaved his chunky butt through the standing pipes. At the end, he sat down and looked up at me, his tail wagging against the floor. I dove into my pouch and produced a treat, which he gobbled up in less than a second.

Max raised an eyebrow. "He's certainly eager."

"Yes, he'd win a treat-eating contest with no problem. By the way, have the police contacted you about Van Parker's death?" Not the smoothest transition, but I wanted to move this conversation along. Like Clarence, my patience was wearing thin.

"Detective Glass stopped by earlier today. I guess Van had some help with his fall."

It wasn't a joking matter, but I held my tongue. "That's an understatement. The police think he was drugged and hit with a stun gun."

Max released Bruiser again, who weaved through the poles like he was headed for Westminster. After finishing, he sat obediently and waited for his treat. Instead, Max simply patted him on the head.

"No reward?" I asked.

"Bruiser appreciates my affection even more than food," said Max smugly.

"Clarence has different priorities," I said. "Back to Van Parker. Can you remember anything else about that night?"

"Nothing I haven't already shared with the detective. Van had a lot of enemies. The list of people who wanted him dead might run the length of tonight's agility trial." He pointed around the large exercise room.

Clarence fidgeted and growled softly. He wanted another chance to earn a treat. I let him go and when he finished the drill, I bent down and gave him two treats.

In a low voice, I said, "Behave, please. I'm trying to interrogate a suspect." Clarence's ears perked up. He'd helped solve several other mysteries, and I imagined he considered himself a canine Watson.

I turned to face Max. "Would you be one of the names on that long list?"

Smirking, Max moved closer. "And why would you think so?"

Never a good sign when a suspect answered a question with a question. "I heard through the grapevine Van blocked you from getting a job at ATF. Maybe you needed to clear the deck to move up. Sounds like a pretty good Washington, D.C. motive. People have killed for less in this town."

"You're forgetting an important detail, Ms. Marshall. I wasn't on the rooftop when Van died. I was on the elevator, coming back to the gathering after retrieving my briefcase from the coat check downstairs." He wrinkled his nose. "In fact, I was doing my job. Your legislative director wanted to see the latest bike lanes proposal. It was inside my bag, so I went downstairs to retrieve it."

Max's point was solid. No doubt he had the motive to want Van dead, but there was no way he could have been in two places at once. Clarissa's paramour Stuart had seen him get on the elevator. Max had a legitimate alibi.

He lined Bruiser up for another practice run through the weave poles. Before Max unleashed him, I asked, "You don't drink alcohol, right?"

Max didn't miss a beat. He released Bruiser and walked to the end of the obstacle. Without facing me, he answered, "Nope.

Don't care for it."

"I thought you said that before. Funny thing is, I had lunch with Clarissa Smythe today. She remembered seeing you with a wineglass in your hand at the fundraiser. There may even be evidence to support it." That last part stretched the truth, although who knows what might show up on the photographs Brock took that night.

I stood up straight and tightened my grip on Clarence's leash. In response, he sat at attention, seeming to notice the increased tension between the two of us.

Max secured Bruiser on his leash and whipped around. "Consider your source. Clarissa might have been three sheets to the wind herself. Or maybe she took one of Van's Xanax. I'm surprised she had the opportunity to observe my choice of drink. She's usually in a dark corner, thanking the restaurant owner for how well he treated her guests that night."

Despite his status as a relatively minor player in the lobbying universe, Max was fully appraised of K Street shenanigans. I was about to mention he hadn't answered my accusation about why he'd been holding a glass of wine, but my train of thought was interrupted by Clarence's bark of impatience. I unleashed him, and he wiggled through the first several poles. Then Max, standing next to the course with Bruiser, reached into his fanny pack for a treat. But it was no ordinary biscuit. In dog agility terminology, Max had selected a "high value reward." A coach gave a dog such recognition after a job well done. Bruiser, who had executed the weaves flawlessly, certainly deserved it. Nonetheless, I predicted the poor Boxer would never get his special reward.

I saw the chunk of hot dog the same time as Clarence. Unfortunately, that meant I had absolutely zero chance of intercepting my audacious beagle mutt. Instead of continuing his prescribed path through the poles, Clarence exited the course and leapt to his right, snagging the piece of frankfurter right out of Max's hand. Bruiser wasn't about to let Clarence steal his thunder or, in this case, his hot dog. He jumped on top of Clarence, and they rolled on the ground, knocking down the weave course and creating a path of destruction in their wake.

It took Max several seconds to respond to the melee unfolding around him. Then he sprang into action, running toward me while waving his hands in the air.

"Has your dog lost its mind? Don't just stand there. Do something!" He bellowed.

Obviously, Max wasn't up on the latest episodes of the "Dog Whisperer." If he was, he would have known yelling and screaming only escalates the situation. Despite the fact they'd just wiped out the agility poles, there was no aggressive growling or teeth showing. Instead, it was a good old doggie play fight, pure and simple.

I put my hand out to stop Max from advancing. "Settle down. They're just rough-housing. It's harmless."

As if on cue, Bruiser broke free from Clarence and rolled over, exposing his tummy. I bent down and scratched him. "See, he wants a belly rub."

Max's face reddened. "Bruiser, get up." Immediately the dog stood at Max's side.

"No harm, no foul," I said. "Sorry that Clarence stole Bruiser's treat. He's got a healthy appetite."

Max peered at me disapprovingly. He removed his glasses and cleaned them with a tissue. "This has been highly embarrassing," he said with a haughty sniff. "I hope Bruiser will be allowed to participate this evening."

I saw Shelby the trainer fast approaching. "Don't get your panties in a knot. I'll tell her Clarence was the responsible party," I said.

278

Max stayed silent as I explained how a tasty wiener had led to Clarence's boisterous explosion. Shelby pursed her lips tightly together, undoubtedly suppressing a giggle as I recounted the story. She must have known Max didn't find the debacle too amusing.

"Clarence is guilty. Don't penalize Bruiser for Clarence's antics. I think we've probably had enough agility training for the evening. Right, Clarence?" I threw my hands up in the air in exasperation.

I must have spoken too soon. Clarence ran through the knocked over poles, weaving as best as he could through the destruction. When he finished, he sat down and barked.

"Good boy!" I yelled. "Max, can you spare a piece of hot dog?"

CHAPTER EIGHTEEN

Twenty minutes later, I fished through my purse to find the key to our condo. Before I could locate it, the door opened. "How'd you know I was here?" I asked.

"For goodness sake, Kit. Between you rummaging through your bag and Clarence's clinking dog tags, I could hear you both coming a mile away." Doug got out of the way, so we could enter.

"Subtlety was never my strong point," I said sheepishly.

"How did Clarence's practice trial go? Did he complete the course?" asked Doug.

I shook my head. "We didn't really make it that far." I quickly explained my conversation with Max and Clarence's bogart of the hot dog.

Doug collapsed into the couch and motioned for Clarence to join him, which he did. "Our dreams of Clarence making the dog agility Olympics have been dashed, I suppose." He petted Clarence on the head, who didn't seem fazed by the frank admission of his failure.

"It was a short-lived career. Maybe we'll try again if Max decides to attend another class," I said. "The worst part was that I never got to press Max about why Clarissa saw him with a glass of wine at the fundraising party. Before Clarence's bad behavior, he was acting squirrelly. Something is up with him."

"Isn't he the one person on the rooftop with a solid alibi?" Doug picked up an opened bottle of white wine, filled an empty glass, and handed it to me.

I took a sip and smiled. "This is excellent. From our recent trip to Loudoun County?" In recent years, a thriving wine industry had grown up less than an hour's drive west of Washington, D.C. The fall weather meant mulled wine, apple cider, and pumpkin picking at our favorite locations. Too bad I'd be spending my time knocking on doors and urging random strangers to vote for Maeve Dixon.

Please vote for my boss so I can keep my job. The preferred campaign slogan for thousands of congressional staffers.

Doug nodded. "A blend from that small farm vineyard we found off Route 7."

281

"Ah, I remember now." Then I looked at Doug directly. "Not too many vineyards in New York City."

Doug smiled. "Not in the city, no. But plenty upstate in the Finger Lakes. Speaking of New York, should we resume our discussion about Columbia?"

I grabbed Doug's hand. "I promise we'll talk about it. I'm exhausted from this week. Can we talk this weekend?"

Doug's shoulders slumped. After looking at me, he spoke slowly. "Sure. There's no immediate rush."

"Thank you," I said as I sipped my wine. "I really needed a drink."

Doug raised his eyebrows. "The stress can't be due to Clarence. He's caused bigger scenes than stealing a hot dog."

"True," I said, recalling the episode early this year when he single-handedly ruined a dog celebration on Capitol Hill. "I've got other non-canine worries."

I told Doug about our conversation with Dash Dugal, the revelation about the stun gun and toxicology report, and my lunch with Clarissa. Then I paused.

Doug knew me all too well. "And?"

I stammered. "Then I came back to my office, and Meg was annoyed with me because I visited Dash and didn't tell her about it."

Doug pursed his lips. "And?"

"What? Isn't that enough?" I placed my glass on the coffee table. "I mean, Meg was really upset with me. Do you know what it's like when your best friend is angry with you?"

Doug adjusted his glasses. "Yes, it can be likened to a major national security crisis, particularly in this household. I still think there's something you're not telling me."

Damn, he was good. I couldn't get away with anything these days. It seemed like only yesterday I was able to keep Doug in the dark when sleuthing. But lately, he'd become a regular gumshoe. Or maybe my typical smokescreens had become more transparent. After all, Doug was a brainiac. I'd have to improve my game in the future or admit that honesty was *usually* the best policy.

"Something else did happen today," I said, tapping my fingers nervously.

Doug's iPad buzzed. Probably another one of his news alerts. While glancing at it, he said, "Spit it out, Kit. I'd like to order food for dinner before all the restaurants close and we're relegated to delivery pizza from some conglomerate chain specializing in preservatives and additives even the

Scripps National Spelling bee champion can't pronounce."

Doug was officially in a funky mood. No doubt my rebuff of his desired Columbia talk had him in a snit. Right now, I was consumed in murder and my boss's reelection. Talk of the Big Apple would have to wait.

"Someone put this note on my car when I was having lunch at the Monocle today." I fished through my purse and produced it.

Doug immediately stopped fiddling with his iPad. He grabbed the piece of paper and read it. "You didn't call me when you received a threatening letter?"

"It's hardly a letter, Doug," I said. "It's a sentence."

"A definitive and clear sentence. In fact, I'd call it a directive. Stop snooping or you'll get tossed off a high rooftop."

"It appears that's the message." I took another gulp of my wine and helped myself to another pour. This conversation had turned south quicker than a Hill staffer headed for the Outer Banks in August.

"Who could have put this on your car?" he asked.

"Trevor and I met with Dash earlier that morning, so he might have had motive to scare me off. Clarissa had opportunity because she excused herself during lunch to use the restroom." I paused for a breath. "And who knows about Max or Lauren. Either one of them could have been tailing me to see what leads I was following."

"It's not like your car is hard to identify," said Doug wryly.

"I know," I said. "My license plate gives it away." My father had called me Kit Kat as a nickname growing up. A few years ago, I thought it would be perfect for a vanity plate. Doug had protested at first, but then admitted it was easy to remember. Perhaps a little too easy, in this instance.

"Did you call the police to tell Detective Glass about it?" he asked.

I averted my eyes downward. "No," I said quietly.

Doug's face softened. "Kit, I'm worried. You find yourself again in the crosshairs of a nasty killer. You need to notify the cops," he said. "Don't you think this is an omen? That maybe we should think about moving somewhere else?"

I got his drift, but Doug's logic was flawed. "We're going to leave Washington for Manhattan? It's not like you've got a job offer at the University of Iowa."

"Of course, there's plenty of violence in New York, but there's less politics. I'm afraid that's the deadly component." He added, "At least for you."

"I'll have to think about it. But right now, I'm more concerned about figuring out who killed Van. It's only a matter of time before Coach Hackensack explicitly ties Maeve Dixon to the murder and makes it a major part of his campaign. In a close election, that type of unsavory connection could be deadly." Then I added, "Pun intended."

Doug managed a tight smile. "I can see there's no point in dissuading you from the investigation. Given this threatening poison pen note you've received, I insist you involve me in your sleuthing until this is solved, and notify Detective Glass."

I smiled. "Okay, you got it. Tomorrow is Van's wake for the K Street crowd. It's at the Palm. Do you want to go with me?"

Doug grimaced. "Lobbyists. With all the backstabbing that goes on in this town, it's amazing there's aren't more murders to solve on K Street."

"An astute observation. Perhaps we should go over everything one more time." I gave Doug a complete recap of the suspects, their whereabouts and alibis, and potential motives.

Doug poured himself the remainder of the white wine and crinkled his forehead. "I

286

hate to say it, Kit, but you have a real puzzle on your hands. It doesn't seem like any of your suspects could have killed Van Parker."

"That's a problem," I admitted. "Lauren was taking a selfie of herself in front of the Washington Monument. She even posted it on Instagram so there's a timestamp. Max left the rooftop to retrieve his briefcase downstairs. Clarissa read her e-mail and squeezed in time for a quickie with Stuart, the restaurant manager."

Doug made a face. "She gives new meaning to the art of multi-tasking."

"That's a nice way of putting it," I said. "And then there's Dash Dugal."

"I imagine Meg doesn't like the fact you consider him a suspect," said Doug.

"We've managed to avoid a major altercation thus far, but it could be unavoidable."

"Dash was looking for a glass of wine for Meg?" he asked.

"Yes, while she was in the bathroom. He said the bar was shut down outside, so he came inside to where we ate dinner and found an open bottle. Clarissa remembers seeing him by the table with a glass of wine in his hand after she finished messing around with Stuart," I explained.

"If Dash did it, then would have anyone seen him?" he asked.

"Yes, because Lauren said that after she took her photo and posted it, she walked toward the edge of the rooftop where Van was killed. That's when she heard the screaming from below."

Doug nodded. "If Dash had done it, then he would have been headed right in Lauren's direction."

"Exactly. But he wasn't. He was inside the dining area, looking for a glass of wine for Meg."

Doug tapped his fingers on the coffee table. "Either someone is not telling the truth or the key to this case is the mysterious waiter."

"Unfortunately, I don't know how to locate him. The police have had no luck, and they certainly have more resources at their disposal than me," I said. "Looking for a waiter matching that vague description in Washington, D.C. is no different than trying to find a needle in a haystack."

"You'd probably have more success finding an honest person on K Street," said Doug. "That could be pretty tough."

"No kidding. You can see why I'm at my wits' end here. Besides having a killer running loose, I'm worried the news of Van's death and Maeve's connection is going to play right into the hands of the Hackensack campaign. She's already not connecting with voters. I know my boss. She's worried about what happened and can't focus on the campaign. Her poll numbers are dropping."

Doug moved closer and put his arm around me. "Kit, you need to relax. Some things are outside of your control. The police will figure out who killed Van or they won't. Either way, I'm sure you'll be on your way to North Carolina soon."

I appreciated Doug's attempt to comfort me, but his words didn't have their intended effect. By the time I got to the campaign, Maeve Dixon might be ten points down. That type of deficit would be impossible to overcome. Political instinct told me it was now or never.

I managed a smile. "We'll see. Maybe I'll catch a break soon."

"That's the spirit." Doug moved his arm and patted my thigh. "I don't know about you, but I'm starving. How about I order some dinner?"

Neither Doug nor I were world-famous chefs. However, we had acquired an impressive array of menus from local restaurants who delivered to our condo building. We conveniently kept our stack of takeout options neatly arranged in a three-ring binder underneath the end table next to our couch. When Clarence saw Doug reach for it, he wagged his tail in excited anticipation. Our pup was so well trained; he knew that reaching for the sacred folder meant that food was on its way.

After brief negotiations, we settled on a pie from Pete's New Haven Style Pizza, half "Long Wharf" with clams and garlic and half "Cutler's" with pepperoni and sausage. Doug used Clarence as a convenient excuse to justify the latter. If the truth were told, Doug usually ended up eating more slices of pepperoni than Clarence.

Our order placed, Doug retreated to his office to squeeze in precious minutes of writing and research before dinner. I decided to make good on my promise and call Detective Glass. She didn't pick up, so I left a message on her voicemail explaining what happened. The adrenaline rush from earlier today had worn off, and I was thankful Doug had insisted that I notify the police about the threatening note. I hadn't realized how tense I was after finding it. After all, there was a crazed killer on the loose. I wanted to identify the person responsible, but without becoming the next victim.

Satisfied that I'd informed the proper authorities, I turned on the television and found an old mystery movie I'd seen several times. A direct result of my years on the Hill, I rarely found it satisfying to focus on a single task. At work, C-SPAN was always on, and we were expected to keep our eyes on the debate or a committee hearing while we drafted talking points, answered e-mails, or even wrote legislation. Curling up on the couch and watching a movie wasn't enough stimulation for my frenetic brain, especially given current woes.

I grabbed Doug's iPad and logged onto the Dixon campaign's private intranet. This website existed only for internal staff and allowed everyone who volunteered or worked on the campaign to have access to Maeve's schedule, upcoming events, and other campaign resources. Sure enough, Brock's photos from the fundraiser appeared. I scrolled through them quickly. Even if Van's murder was solved, there was no way the Dixon campaign could use anything from that evening. Everyone was all smiles in the shots, ostensibly unaware of what would transpire. But all the sunny visages weren't genuine. Someone knew what was going to happen later that evening.

There was a shot of Dash Dugal, looking as handsome as ever. Meg was in the corner of the photo, staring at her beau with an almost adoring gaze. Max Robinson wasn't the most photogenic of the bunch, yet even he managed a reluctant smile for the camera in one of Brock's shots. Clarissa had been caught in a pose with Lauren Parker, their hair lightly blowing in the wind with the fading sun and the Washington Monument in the distance.

If one of these people had decided to kill Van Parker that evening on the rooftop, it wasn't apparent from examining the photographs. On the surface, it looked like any other autumn fundraiser in Washington, D.C. Had I missed something? For the first time since Van's death, I felt a familiar nagging tug. Experience demonstrated this annoying sensation presented itself when I'd overlooked an important detail. I scanned through the photographs again to see if anything popped out. Nothing did.

On impulse, I grabbed my non-congressional iPhone and fired off an e-mail to Detective Glass.

Our intern Brock photographed the fundraiser for the Dixon campaign. I examined them tonight and didn't see anything out of the ordinary. Brock will send you the photos so you can take a look.

Then I signed my name and copied Brock on the message. Hopefully he'd check his e-mail soon and e-mail Glass the photos. It couldn't hurt to have another set of eyes on the shots. My sixth sense was rarely wrong, but it could take a few days to realize what I'd missed. On this case, we didn't have the luxury of time.

The pizza arrived, and we dug in. Doug joined me on the couch, and we half-watched the mystery classic while we caught up on gossip about our friends, family, and acquaintances. The combination of the stressful day, threatening note, wine, and a substantial portion of pizza took its toll. I drifted off to sleep and woke as the closing credits to the movie scrolled across the television screen. I ambled toward the bedroom, still half asleep. Nonetheless, the nagging feeling I'd missed an important clue remained.

CHAPTER NINETEEN

I was about to hit the button on our espresso machine when Doug grabbed my hand to stop me. "Want to go out for breakfast? Perhaps a stroll down the street to Northside Social?"

I had nothing planned until Van Parker's wake later this afternoon. Doug rarely patronized coffee shops, finding them a convenient excuse for people pretending to work.

I cleared my throat. "I'm up for it. Have you changed your mind about cafes?"

Doug's face turned a light shade of red. "No, of course not. But it's a nice morning, and I thought you'd enjoy the walk. We can take Clarence, of course."

At the mention of his name, Clarence tilted his head to the side. "Don't get too excited," I said to him. "You've already eaten breakfast. No bagels for you."

On cue, his ears drooped. Clarence was

blissfully unaware that dogs were descended from carnivores. Such ignorance gave him license to devour pasta, all types of breads, and of course, pizza.

Fifteen minutes later, we selected an outdoor table at the popular eatery. Doug went inside to place our order. The popular hangout included a sprawling sidewalk cafe, indoor couches and seating, and a second-floor wine bar. Located near a Metro stop at the intersection of two busy streets, Northside Social wasn't hurting for customers. We'd been lucky to find an available seat.

My phone buzzed. It was a text from Meg.

When can you pick me up for the wake?

She had mentioned yesterday that she wouldn't be going with Dash.

Doug is coming. See you at 1?

A minute passed, and then three dots appeared. Meg was typing a response. She was probably already annoyed because Dash wasn't accompanying her. Adding a dose of Doug and his Columbia news might send her over the edge. I braced myself for a snarky reply.

Come early. HH before wake at my apt.

It was only ten o'clock in the morning and the day had been filled with surprises. Meg wanted to hang out before heading to the wake. *HH* was her familiar abbreviation for "Happy Hour." Meg's apartment resembled Martha Stewart's minimum security federal prison cell. It was tiny and decorated with a modern, tasteful style. Given the tight quarters, she rarely invited guests over. She must really want a chance to have a go at Doug about moving to New York City. Should I take the bait? After considering my options, I typed a short reply.

C U then.

After working together to solve our latest murder at the famous Continental Club, Meg and Doug's relationship had improved. They'd never become best buds, but they'd recently reached a Nixonian level of comfortable detente. Hopefully the Columbia news wouldn't send us barreling into armed conflict.

Doug returned with my coffee and bowl of piping hot steel-cut Irish oatmeal with apple compote. The cinnamon aroma reached my nose before he could place the tray on the table. Doug had opted for a country ham and egg breakfast sandwich. Clarence carefully evaluated the choices and sat down next to Doug. Pork trumped fruit and oats any day.

We dug into our food in silence. After several minutes of munching, I spoke. There was a reason Doug had suggested breakfast out. He wanted to discuss New York.

"So, tell me why you're so enamored with Columbia," I said.

Doug's eyebrows raised in feigned surprise. He didn't say anything.

"Come on, Doug. We both know that's why you wanted to go out for breakfast. It's not our normal Saturday routine." Clarence sensed the impatience in my voice. He growled softly, gently reminding Doug he was waiting for a bite of ham.

Doug finished chewing and wiped his mouth. He spoke slowly. "Of course, it's a great opportunity to teach at Columbia. But there are other reasons."

"Which are?" I crossed my arms in front of my chest. "Let me guess. The price of D.C. real estate isn't high enough for you, so you want to move to New York."

Doug pursed his lips into a thin line. "Very funny, Kit." He stared into space for several seconds before continuing. "I'm getting restless. The job at Columbia would enable me to run a research center on early American history."

Now we were getting somewhere, although I was still confused. Doug had always seemed perfectly content with his work. "You want to do something other than teaching, researching, and writing books?"

He traced the rim of his coffee cup. "Maybe. Don't get me wrong, I still love the academic discipline of American history. But this position would give me the opportunity to run conferences, apply for research grants, and work with museum exhibits."

"But I thought you liked reading and writing in your office. You always seem so happy when you're doing it," I said.

Doug had really thrown me a curve ball. For as long as we'd known each other, he'd exuded certainty about his purpose in life. Doug seemed to enjoy locking himself in his office, pouring over his notes and sources to write his latest masterpiece. In fact, I'd envied his firm sense of direction, especially when I struggled to find a similar professional grounding.

Doug must have sensed my puzzlement. He shared the last piece of his sandwich with Clarence and smiled. "I am happy, Kit. But that doesn't mean it's not time for a change."

He had a point. This was a lot to process, particularly when I had murder and politics on my mind. I didn't want to put Doug off, but I needed more time to consider everything.

I chose my words carefully. "I appreciate everything you've said. Hopefully we don't have to rush into a decision soon."

"Absolutely not. I'd been wanting to talk to you about it, so you'd understand why the opportunity is appealing to me. I thought you might be surprised."

"Just because you've been on a path doesn't mean you have to stay on it the rest of your career," I said. "Sometimes it's good to try your hand at other things."

Doug laughed. "Like solving murders?"

"You said it, not me. Speaking of solving murders, Meg invited us over before the wake this afternoon. She's coming with us."

Doug narrowed his eyes. "Not with her boyfriend? Is there trouble in paradise?"

"I didn't dare ask for details. She's been defensive about him," I said.

"Could he have killed Van Parker?" asked Doug.

"He had opportunity, but not a real motive," I said. "Van was the top transportation lobbyist and was going to strike out on his own soon. But that happens all the time in Washington. There's no obvious reason for Dash to want Van dead."

"That's a big problem." Doug stood up with Clarence in tow.

"You're right. No motive, no murder," I

said with a sigh.

When we returned to our condo, it was almost time to get ready for our afternoon engagements, especially since Meg wanted us to hang out at her place beforehand. What was the appropriate attire for a lobbyist's wake? Not casual, for sure.

I opened my closet doors and scanned the contents. What screamed somber, fashionable, and understated simultaneously? Not much. Yes, my Capitol Hill attire, which consisted mostly of black pantsuits and colorful yet conservative blouses, served me well daily, but what could I wear to a wake memorializing one of the most famous lobbyists in Washington, D.C.? Talk about a fashion crisis. I wished Tim Gunn was on speed dial.

After a quick survey, I decided on a forest green dress and matching jacket. This wasn't the time for anything festive or fun. I fished out my strand of authentic pearls, which I only wore to commemorate the most somber occasions. Along with a pair of my small stud diamond earrings, I looked ready to mingle with the savviest Beltway crowd. This afternoon, we would be inside the belly of the beast. All the important K Street players would make an appearance at Van Parker's memorial service. If I'd had the time and energy, I would have scheduled a blowout for my hair. All chairs at the local dry bar were undoubtedly occupied in honor of Van Parker, each high-profile woman dutifully sipping a libation while casually lamenting his demise. Van would have approved.

I walked out of our bedroom and found Doug sitting on the couch, looking perfectly coiffed in his dark grey suit. Men never had a problem getting ready for these events. The standard uniform had already been chosen for them. As long as they owned enough classically cut suits, the average professional man could easily ride out several generations of fashion innovation. Women, even in Washington, weren't so lucky. We constantly had to keep abreast of recent trend or suffer the same horrible publicity fate as Marcia Clark during the O.J. Simpson trial.

"Ready to hit the road?" Doug asked.

"Absolutely. We're going to Meg's apartment first. Remember?"

"How could I forget?" he asked.

Twenty minutes later, Doug cruised the streets of the up-and-coming Shaw neighborhood of the District of Columbia. Meg had moved here a year ago, eager to relocate to the latest trendy neighborhood of our fair city. Shaw was named after a Union general during the Civil War who accepted command of the first-black regiment. Killed in battle in South Carolina, Shaw's strong advocation for African Americans inspired many people of color to enlist on the side of the North. Historians viewed his sacrifice as a pivotal moment in the Civil War.

Finally, we found a parking spot near Seventh Street and Q. I texted Meg and a few minutes later, we headed inside her apartment building. Before we knocked, my best bud opened the door and greeted us with a wide smile. "Greetings, Virginians!"

Meg liked to emphasize she lived east of the Potomac. For some unbeknownst reason, she viewed her residential experience as infinitely superior to ours, even though our residences were a mere eight miles apart. Geography influenced lifestyle choices more than anyone in D.C. cared to admit.

We followed Meg into her cozy yet stylish one bedroom enclave. She guided us to her dining room table, situated tightly between her short hallway and kitchen. Meg had outdone herself. She had crackers, pita bread, hummus, and a veggie tray laid out on her Ikea contemporary glass top table. Doug eyed the mid-day feast. The king of

302

afternoon snacks, my husband had already burned through his breakfast sandwich feast at Northside Social. He was ready for the second round.

Before we knew it, Meg had poured us generous glasses of Prosecco. After making ourselves hearty plates, we sat on Meg's mid-century eggshell love seat and settled in. Doug munched away happily, eager to partake in the afternoon festivities. I grabbed a piece of broccoli and dunked it in hummus.

"Delicious," I murmured between chews.

Meg wore a long black formfitting tank dress with a shimmery silver sheath and large hoop earrings. Compared to Meg, I looked like Mary Poppins. I might as well scream *supercallifragilisticexpialidocious* and call it a day.

I sipped the bubbly and cleared my throat. "Why aren't you going with Dash to the wake?"

Meg waved her hand indiscriminately. "He's going with his K Street colleagues from ARF," she said with a sigh. "It can be difficult dating someone who is in such demand."

Doug raised his eyebrows but said nothing. He was used to Meg's penchant for high drama. Sometimes he took the bait, but with the savory bits before him, he must have decided to keep his mouth shut so he could continue to feed it. However, there was a murder to solve, so I threw caution to the wind.

"Dash must be relieved to have Van out of the way," I said slowly. "The trucking lobby is his number one competitor."

Meg pursed her lips together so tightly, she might have flattened a penny between them. "There was no love lost between Dash and Van. That's not a secret. You know how this world works, Kit. In a week's time, ATF will replace Van Parker. The beat will go on."

"That's true, Meg," said Doug. "But Van was no regular lobbyist. According to Kit, Van was highly skilled and at the top of his game. Surely his disappearance from the K Street scene is a boon for Dash."

Meg's mouth turned downward in a cute pout. "This seems like a fishing expedition. Why are both of you ganging up on Dash?'

I spoke up. "We're not, Meg. We are concerned for your safety, though. Until we find Van's killer, you need to stay out of danger."

Meg snorted. "That's the pot calling the kettle black. Isn't that right, Doug?"

Doug had just stuffed a large rye cracker

in his mouth. "Mnnhmm."

Meg turned away from him. "I have no idea what you're saying."

"He's agreeing with you," I said.

"Well, there's a first time for everything," said Meg defiantly.

I put one hand on top of the other, forming the letter T. "Timeout. And don't say a word about Coach Hackensack." Meg's glass was empty and mine was nearly so. I stood and picked up both. "I'll get us a refill. Doug is driving, so we might as well enjoy ourselves."

"No kidding," Meg murmured. "Hard to enjoy a happy hour together if you're living in *New York*."

Doug remained silent as I walked five steps away into Meg's tiny kitchen. My best friend didn't keep her shoes inside her oven like Carrie Bradshaw, but I doubted this room got much use. Meg consumed most of her meals at happy hours or on dates. If she ate at home, someone else had done the cooking.

As I put my hand on the fridge to open it, I stopped abruptly. A handwritten note caught my eye. I removed the "GrubHub" magnet attaching it to the refrigerator front door, so I could read the script.

My darling Meg. You brighten my day. I can't

imagine what I'd do without you! With love, Dash.

I had to hand it to Dash. In this era of text messages and Snapchats, he had taken the time to write a love note. Something bothered me about it. I fingered the piece of paper. Doug and Meg were engaged in a conversation and I heard the word "Columbia" mentioned. I didn't have a lot of time to figure out why the note made me squirm. On a whim, I grabbed my phone out of my suit jacket pocket and took a photo of it. Then I placed it in exactly the same position as I found it and grabbed the half-full bottle of Prosecco from the fridge.

"What's taking you so long?" asked Meg.

"Just a minute," I announced in a sing-song.

I returned to the living room and handed Meg her refill. She plastered a fake smile on her face. "Doug was just telling me about this fabulous opportunity he's received in New York."

"Nothing has been decided," I said quickly. "Between Van's death and the election, I can't see straight, let alone make a decision about moving."

Doug cleared his throat. I hadn't meant it to sound so negative, but it was the truth. It was impossible to focus on the future with so many uncertainties in the present.

Meg acknowledged my words with a slight nod. Then she looked at her phone. "We should leave soon. Dash said something about remarks at two o'clock."

We had plenty of time before then, but arriving early would give us time to mix and mingle with the crowd. "Let's go," I said. "Trevor will meet us there."

As Meg donned a light jacket, she remarked, "Well, we wouldn't want to keep Mr. Hotshot Writer waiting, now would we?"

I ignored Meg's comment. Although Trevor had his pluses and minuses, he did provide another set of eyes and ears. More importantly, he had the uncanny ability to unearth Washington, D.C.'s most guarded secrets. Hopefully, Trevor wouldn't let me down this time.

Twenty minutes later, we approached Dupont Circle and stopped in front of the Palm Restaurant, a lobbyist mainstay. Two Italian immigrants opened the first Palm Restaurant in 1926. When they registered the business in New York City, the clerk misunderstood their heavy accents. They meant to name the restaurant "Parma" after their hometown in Italy, but instead, the clerk heard "Palm." They kept the name and eventually brought the restaurant chain to D.C. in 1972, after George H.W. Bush, the United Nations ambassador at the time, urged them to expand to the nation's capital. Since then, the Palm has served as a signature fine dining experience in Washington, a mainstay for political power players looking for good food and drink while brokering the latest deal. It made perfect sense for the Palm to host Van's wake. With his stature on K Street, no doubt he'd been a frequent patron.

A valet took the car from us, and we walked inside the restaurant, which was already buzzing. The Palm operated perennially at a dull roar; Van's wake was no exception. A sea of dark business suits, black dresses, and conservative pants suits greeted us. I spotted Lauren Parker across the room with her hot pink iPhone pressed to her ear. Was it socially acceptable to take a phone call during your husband's wake? Miss Manners, a fellow Washingtonian, would not approve.

Meg surveyed the room as we gave our coats to the checkroom attendant. "We're definitely in the right place."

"So, this is what a lobbyist's funeral looks like," said Doug wryly. "I always wondered."

I shot him a disapproving look as we made

our way past the glass enclosed patio inside the main dining room. The entire restaurant had been reserved for the occasion, a testimony to Van's stature inside the Beltway. A waiter presented us with glasses of sparkling water and wine. I took a water, and Meg went for the wine. At least she was consistent.

I spotted Trevor halfway across the room. He'd just stuffed an appetizer inside his mouth. "Come on, let's go talk to our esteemed former colleague." I grabbed Meg's hand and guided her across the room. Doug started to follow us but then stopped to inspect the hors d'oeuvres. At least my husband was consistent, too.

Trevor had finished chewing by the time we reached him. He nodded politely. "Kit and Meg. What a delightful surprise."

Meg rolled her eyes. "Cut the crap, Trevor."

Trevor peered at Meg through his horn-rimmed glasses with a look of mild distaste. "Fine, *Megan.* I was going to suggest you try the beef carpaccio. It's excellent."

Meg wrinkled her nose, but as soon as the waiter passed by us with a full tray, she grabbed one. I could tell by the look on her face she concurred with Trevor's assessment. Her silence about the tastiness reflected her unwillingness to concede any ground to Trevor.

"Lots of caricatures on the walls here," remarked Meg.

We turned around to survey the artwork, which covered almost every inch of the room. It was easy to spot the usual suspects, such as Barack Obama, Donald Trump, Joe Biden, and George W. Bush. In addition to famous politicians and journalists, there were a lot of unfamiliar faces, too.

"Who are all these people?" I asked, not addressing anyone in particular.

Trevor piped up. "Heavy hitters in Washington. Or perhaps I should say heavy spenders."

"How much?" asked Meg.

Trevor grabbed a broiled crab cake as it passed by. "Last time I checked, the Palm offered a coveted spot on the wall once an individual's tab reached the fifteen-thousand-dollar mark."

I let out a soft whistle. "That's a lot of steaks and lobster."

"No kidding," said Meg. "I'm in the wrong business."

Trevor gestured over Meg's right shoulder. "Van's likeness was memorialized several years ago."

Sure enough, Van's portrait had been

included on the side wall of the dining room, a few feet above one of the booths lining the perimeter. His smiling face showed a man in his prime, with a full head of hair, a strong jaw, and a thick neck. Van Parker had been a formidable man in every sense of the word.

Trevor followed my gaze. "Any updates on figuring out who was responsible for Van's death?"

"No breakthroughs, but I must be on the right track." I described the note placed on my car yesterday outside the Monocle.

Trevor shook his head slowly. "This isn't adding up," he murmured.

"Keep your eye out for a man with a dark complexion and bushy hair," I said. "We still haven't been able to locate the waiter who was on the rooftop that night."

Trevor squinted and adjusted his glasses. "Sometimes missing data can be valuable in itself," he said softly.

"What are you muttering, Trevor? I can barely understand you," I said.

He shook his head. "Nothing that matters, at least right now."

Doug joined us and shook Trevor's hand. "Congratulations on the book. I hear it's going to make waves in Washington."

"The bigger question is whether it's going

to sell," said Trevor. "Quite frankly, not much else matters in the publishing industry these days."

Before Doug could respond, a waiter approached us and offered to refill our glasses. A sip of wine remained in her glass, but Meg offered it anyway.

"Really, Meg? Was that the same wine you had before? You didn't even check," said Doug teasingly.

"Everyone knows you can blend wines. Well, most of the time," said Meg, with an air of confidence enjoyed only by someone who had vast experience in the subject.

"I've never heard such a thing. I must have missed that lesson in Advanced Vinoculture," said Trevor in a mocking voice.

Meg rolled her eyes. I felt a tap on my shoulder, and I spun around. It was Gene Price, Van's former coworker who'd joined for drinks two days ago.

"Have a second to chat?" he asked.

"Absolutely," I said. He pulled me away from the group.

Doug caught the drift. "Let's go find the rest of the appetizers. The calamari and crab cakes are excellent at the Palm," he said. "Or at least I've heard."

After the three of them headed off in the opposite direction, I turned to Gene.

"What's up?"

"I thought you might like to know I found out what Van had been working on. Remember I told you he had a big surprise up his sleeve? Something that would be a game changer?" said Gene.

I nodded. "That was the reason for his departure from American Trucks First."

Gene turned his head from side to side to inspect who was standing near us. Then he moved closer to me and lowered his voice. "Driverless rigs."

I narrowed my eyes. "That's what Van was working on?" I wasn't following.

Gene nodded vigorously. "Do you understand how revolutionary that will be for the trucking industry? It changes the entire model of transporting goods and completely blows apart the labor force!"

Now that Gene spelled it out, I began to comprehend the political significance. "Van couldn't do that while working for ATF."

"No way," said Gene. "What he planned to do would dismantle the structure of the entire industry. It would put drivers out of work."

"Trucks are big money," I said.

Gene grabbed my arm, his face animated. "Not just trucks! It would affect the entire economy. Greater efficiency, more reliability, faster delivery times. Think about it."

While I didn't share Gene's enthusiasm for transportation policy, I got the gist. But I still had a question or two. "Van's dead. But driverless trucks aren't. Won't someone else lead the effort?"

Gene rubbed his chin. "Maybe. Van had a plan for selling the proposal to Congress and drastically reforming the transportation bill. He'd been working on it for over a year. No one else can put it together in time for the next highway authorization bill."

"Who else knew he was working on this?" I asked.

"Before he died? Nada. No one at ATF, for sure." Gene thought for a moment. "I guess Lauren would have known."

"Sure. But that's not a motive to want Van dead. She would have struck it rich, along with him, if all went according to plan," I said.

"Definitely. It was a risky move. But, Van Parker was the guy who could pull it off," said Gene.

I touched Gene's arm lightly. "Thanks for letting me know. It could be an important piece of the puzzle."

"You don't put together those types of deals in Washington without ruffling some feathers," said Gene.

The understatement of the year. I smiled at Gene and looked around to locate my friends. The speeches about Van were bound to start soon, and I wanted to find them before it became impossible to move around the crowded room.

The sea of men and women dressed in black suits and dresses inside the large dining room resembled an upscale Goth convention, minus the pale faces and dramatic eye shadow. Then I spotted Meg's silver coverup. Something didn't look right. She was rubbing her eyes. Were there tears streaming down Meg's face?

I hustled across the room. Sure enough, thin, vertical streaks marred Meg's perfectly applied makeup. When I reached her, she was blotting her cheeks with an old tissue she'd found in her purse.

I moved close to her and whispered, "Meg, what's wrong?"

She shook her head vigorously. "I don't want to talk about it now. Not here in public."

"I'll find a place for us to chat privately."

I dashed across the room and almost ran into Trevor. "What did you do to Meg? I left her with you and now she's crying."

Trevor took two steps back. "Settle down,

Kit. I didn't do anything. It's what she saw."

"What could have upset her so quickly? It must have been a humdinger. Meg isn't a crier."

Trevor pursed his lips. "She spotted a waiter with a full tray of calamari. We followed him and walked past a private dining room. Meg must have heard his voice."

"Whose voice?" Although I didn't really have to ask the question to know the answer.

"Dash, of course. Only he wasn't alone." Trevor blinked his eyes several times. "Maybe Meg should tell you the rest."

"Good idea," I said.

Meg was huddled in the corner of the enclosed outdoor terrace, trying to hide her tears. I guided her by the arm to a secluded corner. "Meg, Trevor told me you saw something upsetting with Dash. What was it?"

She took a big breath to steady herself. "He was with Lauren Parker," she said, her voice cracking.

I waited for her to elaborate. When she didn't, I prodded gently. "And?"

"She was against the wall and Dash was . . ." Meg couldn't bear to finish the sentence as she wiped streaming tears from her cheeks.

"Kissing her?" Playing twenty questions

about Meg's cheating boyfriend wasn't my idea of a fun time. On the other hand, I needed to get a handle on the situation. Obviously, Clarissa's omen about Dash and Lauren had some truth to it.

Meg nodded. "And his hand was on her big butt."

For some reason, that last detail was too much. I burst into laughter. Not a giggle, but a full-blown guffaw. Meg's semi-bloodshot eyes widened, and her mouth formed a perfect oval of surprise.

Nice work, Kit. What a great way to treat your best friend.

I braced myself for Meg's response, mentally preparing myself for a tongue-lashing. Instead, the corners of her mouth turned up slightly.

I took her cue and ran with it. "Her butt is sizable," I said.

Meg tittered, her eyes sparkling with life. "That's Dash's problem, not mine."

I put my arm around her and gave her a sideways hug. "He's not worth the tears, Meg."

She wiped her cheeks. "Everything is changing. You're married now. Hell, you may move to another state. I'm stuck in the same rut. I think I just wanted Dash to be the guy who changed my life."

317

I turned to face my best friend and placed my hands gently on her shoulders. "Meg, the only person who has the power to change your life is you."

With a numb look on her face, she nodded mechanically. "I know."

"Let's get back to the wake. The speeches are starting," I said.

Everyone had gathered inside the dining room. The tables had been removed so that the only seats were the small booths that outlined the periphery of the restaurant. A colleague of Van's from ATF began the program, explaining this would be a "lighthearted affair." He encouraged everyone in attendance to share his or her "favorite Van Parker memory" to honor him.

We found spots on the edge of the gathered crowd. My iPhone buzzed. Thank goodness, I'd silenced it or the theme song from "Knight Rider" would have interrupted the first mourner. I glanced at the text. It was from Doug, who I'd somehow lost in the melee.

You heard about Dash and Lauren?
Yes. Where are you?
Across the room.
I'd better stay w/ Meg.

There was a pause, and then the dots appeared. Doug was writing a reply.

318

Dash has a motive?

I stared at my phone's screen. Doug was right. I'd been so concerned about Meg, I hadn't quite processed what she'd mistakenly uncovered. Clarissa had hinted that Dash had a crush on Lauren Parker. I'd discounted it as nothing more than idle gossip. But what if Clarissa was right and Dash had been in love with Lauren the whole time?

The satisfaction of placing the last piece of the puzzle in its proper position overwhelmed me. The stark realization that I knew how Van had died caused me to waver. Meg noticed my unsteadiness.

"Did you have too much to drink?" she asked. "Maybe you should sit down."

I moved closer and whispered. "Did you ask Max Robinson to see the latest bike lanes proposal from the Bicycle Advocacy Movement?"

Meg looked like I'd just asked if Barney's had sold its clothing line to Target. "Absolutely not. Why would I? Max is a gadfly, and I'd never encourage him. We're supporters of cyclists, but there's no need for Maeve Dixon to go the extra mile for that cause."

I nodded. "I think I am going to take a seat for a few minutes. Excuse me."

I found an empty seat in the corner of the room. Before I had a chance to think, Trevor joined me across the table.

"You look perplexed," he said.

"I need to clear my head and think for a moment," I answered. "Can you get me a club soda and a few napkins?"

Trevor raised an eyebrow but didn't ask any more questions. A minute later, he returned with both items.

"Might you care to enlighten me about what's happening?" he asked.

"That's a fair question," I said. "But I've not quite worked it out yet. I'd rather not say."

Trevor watched as I furiously scribbled several sketchy diagrams and notes on the napkins he'd provided and sipped my drink. Ten minutes later, I stared at my messy scrawl.

"Yes, I think this explains it," I said.

Trevor craned his neck, so he could decipher what I'd written. Before he could read my chicken scratch, I gathered the napkins and placed them inside my purse.

"Sorry, Trevor," I said. "I'm only ready to share my theory with one person."

"Your husband?" he asked, a heavy dose of skepticism in his voice.

"No, although that's not a bad guess.

Before I tell Doug, I want to talk to Detective Glass."

"So she can arrest the murderer?" asked Trevor.

"I wish it was that easy. I'm afraid we're going to have to step it up a notch to catch the culprit," I said. "If I'm right, a web of lies and shady conspiracies are covering up the truth."

A grinning Trevor smoothed his Brooks Brothers suit jacket. "I'm not surprised. After all, we are dealing with a K Street killing. It's only appropriate."

Meg and Doug noticed that Trevor and I had scored seats. With no indication, the litany of vocal mourners might abate anytime soon, they sought refuge at our table. Her makeup reapplied, Meg had recovered. Perhaps not fully, but enough to mask the disappointment she'd internalized.

Doug sat next to me. "This may go on for a while."

"He was one of the best known people in Washington," said Meg. "Everyone wants to offer their two cents. Do you think the speeches might give us a clue about the killer?"

"If they do, I guess I won't hear it," announced Detective Glass as she approached our table.

Doug offered his seat to her. Instead, she grabbed an empty chair from a nearby table and joined us. "To what do we owe this pleasure?" asked Doug.

The detective shrugged. "I don't know. Kit texted me a minute ago and said we needed to chat. I figured I'd better respond quickly since the killer threatened her yesterday."

Doug's forehead wrinkled. "Kit texted you?"

Trevor spoke up. "I think your wife might have an idea concerning whodunit."

Doug flinched. "You solved the case and you didn't tell me?" he asked in a hurt voice.

I squeezed his hand. "Not on purpose. And I'd say it's more a theory now. We might need to work a little harder to put this murder to rest."

"Don't keep us in suspense," said Meg. "Spill the beans, Kit."

"I was going to keep this between me and Detective Glass," I admitted. "But now that you're all here, I might as well lay it out for everyone. The police might need our help."

"It can't be any crazier than the last time our paths crossed," said Glass.

"Au contraire, Detective," I said. "Wait until you hear what I think happened."

CHAPTER TWENTY

An hour later, the plan was set. Conveniently, the tributes for Van Parker were ending. As we rose from our seats, I gave the final instructions. "We'll reassemble in an hour at the designated location, assuming everything proceeds appropriately with our special invitations."

We each had specific assignments. Meg made a beeline for Dash as Trevor sought to locate Max and Lauren. Doug retrieved the car from the valet, so we could make a speedy exit once the plan was in motion. I scanned the crowd for Clarissa, who would hopefully provide critical assistance.

It wasn't too difficult to locate her. In a sea of funereal colors, Clarissa sported a long-sleeved crimson dress. It complemented her wavy chestnut hair and curvy figure. She was sipping a glass of bubbly, chatting with a forty-something handsome man clad in a dark green tailored-fit checked wool suit. He might have stepped off the pages of British *GQ*.

"Clarissa, so glad I found you," I said breathlessly.

"Kit Marshall, allow me to introduce the general manager of the Palm, Kevin James." She gestured to her attractive companion, who offered his hand.

"My condolences for your loss, Ms. Marshall," he said politely.

Clarissa was obviously up to her old tricks, which was her business. Far be it for me to question how a woman made her way in the rough and tumble world of Washington. Clarissa might be pushing some ethical boundaries, but she wasn't breaking any laws.

"Kit was at Charlie Palmer's when poor Van went over the edge." Clarissa then lowered her voice. "She thinks it might have been murder rather than suicide. Isn't that right?"

"I'm not sure of anything these days, Clarissa, but I do need to speak to you about an important matter. I'm afraid it can't wait." I shot her acquaintance an apologetic look.

Clarissa turned toward Kevin and put her hand on his shoulder. "I'll come find you, later. After all, I need to thank you for putting this shindig together on such short notice and closing your restaurant for it," she purred.

I bet he'll get some gratitude — and not a pat on the back.

Then Clarissa faced me. "Let's walk into the atrium." She grabbed my hand and pulled me to the front of the restaurant, apart from the crowd. Apparently, the somber phase of the afternoon event had ended. It was now a full-blown party, filled with alcoholic drinks, good food, and deal-making. Trevor was undoubtedly soaking in the atmosphere for his next book. As journalist Mark Leibovich famously observed in the opening pages of his tell-all bestseller *This Town,* D.C. funerals were filled with caddy observations, insider jockeying, and political intrigue. If we were able to pull off our scheme, Van's wake would be no exception.

We walked inside the sunny atrium, currently unpopulated with the increasingly rowdy crowd. Everyone wanted to be part of the buzzing conversation taking place in the main dining room. No one seemed to pay any attention to two women huddled in the corner of the restaurant, who were conveniently chatting about who killed the person they were supposedly mourning.

These days, such pesky details seemed to matter less in Washington. It was more about "get it done." Only a few ambitious reporters and bloggers still bothered to ask probing questions concerning the details. Consequently, they were often treated as pests, worthy of extermination if they proved too bothersome.

"Can you phone Stuart and call in a favor?" I asked.

"Stuart?" She stared at me with a blank look.

"The manager at Charlie Palmer's. You know, your special friend."

"Oh, that Stuart," said Clarissa. "Really, Kit. You should be more precise."

Did Clarissa have affairs with multiple men named Stuart? It was on the tip of my tongue to ask, but given time constraints, I resisted. "I need access to the restaurant's rooftop later this afternoon. Can you arrange it?"

Clarissa rubbed the back of her neck. "I can request it. But it's Saturday. I'm sure he's booked it for a pricey event, likely a wedding."

"Tell him not to worry. This won't take long, and we won't touch anything. But we do need the rooftop cleared of all waitstaff and caterers."

Clarissa sighed deeply. "You're not making this any easier."

"If you'd like, I can have the D.C. homicide detective in charge of the investigation call him with a formal request," I said.

Clarissa's eyes widened, and she raised her hands to signal that wouldn't be necessary. "Please. The last thing I need is Detective Glass bothering Stuart again. He's barely recovered from what happened on Wednesday night."

Clarissa whipped her phone out and furiously jabbed out a long text message. After finishing, she said, "Stuart will get back to me shortly. Given his job, he's never far from his phone."

"Thanks, Clarissa." I swiveled my head around. Meg had found Dash and had steered him to a dark corner. Hopefully she was persuading him to participate in our staged scheme.

"Do you mind telling me why you need access to the rooftop?" Clarissa asked.

I looked around again to make sure no one was eavesdropping on our conversation. I moved closer to Clarissa and whispered the general outline of our plan inside her ear.

After I was done, a smile spread across her face. "Good work, Kit. I hope everything turns out the way you've strategized."

"It's a crapshoot," I admitted. "But it might be the only way to find out if my theory is right."

Clarissa's phone dinged. She reached for it and read the text message. "That was Stuart. He's not thrilled about it since he does have a wedding reception planned for the rooftop this evening. However, he'd rather not antagonize Detective Glass. What time will your private party arrive?"

"I'm heading over there immediately with Doug, Meg, and Trevor. Everyone else should show up about a half hour later."

Clarissa nodded. "I'll tell Stuart to expect you soon." She gave me a quick hug. "Please stay safe."

"Don't worry. I'm always careful, especially when I'm dealing with murderers," I said.

Clarissa smoothed her auburn hair. "We can't have anything happen to you, Kit. I want to host more fundraisers for Congresswoman Dixon, and it just wouldn't be the same without you!"

Only in Washington was catching a murderer second-fiddle to the reelection of a member of Congress and subsequent fundraisers. This city encouraged strange priorities. I let Clarissa's parting comment stand without a reply, instead waving good-bye as I waded back into the crowd.

Meg was leaning up against one of the bars in the corner. She'd switched from wine to a club soda. Not a bad choice, considering we had to keep our wits about us. If everything went as planned, we could enjoy refreshments later as a well-deserved reward. But I wasn't counting my chickens (in this case, lobbyists) before they were hatched.

"Is the condor ready for takeoff?" I asked, smiling at my best friend.

Meg stared into the distance with a clouded gaze. She looked surprised when she heard my voice. In a confused voice, she said, "What do you mean?"

I punched her gently in the arm. "I'm trying to lighten the mood. You know, using a coded message."

"A coded message?" She frowned.

Meg often suffered from a slavish devotion to literalness. For the most part, it served her well on Capitol Hill, enabling her to cut through the annoying political cant. Upon occasion, such as right now, her prosaic demeanor proved challenging.

"Never mind," I said, giving up. "How did it go with Dash?"

Her face immediately brightened. "Really

well. He'll meet us on the rooftop at the designated time."

"Did you tell him what's up?" I asked.

She shook her head vigorously. "I told him I needed to speak with him about our relationship, and it was one of the most romantic spots in the city. You know, setting the ambiance." She made a face. "Blah, blah, blah."

With a heavy dose of sarcasm, I said, "Look on the bright side. Maybe after all this is done, you'll get recruited to write the next big screen rom-com."

Meg squealed in delight. "I'd love that! It's one of my favorite movie genres on Netflix."

I didn't have the heart to tell Meg I was yanking her chain. Meg certainly had her choice of paramours, but I wouldn't use the word "romantic" to describe her, at least in the classic fairy tale sense.

"We'd better get over to Charlie Palmer's pronto. Where's Doug and Trevor?" I asked.

"Doug went to get the car. Trevor has already spoken with Max and was going after Lauren," she said.

"We need both there," I said. "I really hope Trevor comes through for us."

"I wouldn't worry, Kit." Meg touched my shoulder. "Trevor is one of the most annoyingly persistent people I know in Washington. If he can't get them to come, I don't know who can."

"Good point. Besides, wasn't he planning to promise that he'd include them in his next book?" I asked.

Meg nodded. "Not just include, but feature. That should motivate them." She added, "Especially Lauren Parker."

I glanced around. "After all, the grieving widow can't stay too long at her husband's wake, especially once it becomes a full-blown party."

As if on cue, Trevor appeared next to Meg. Our friend had the uncanny ability to materialize out of nowhere. We'd never been able to figure out how he did it. I considered it one of Trevor's many odd, intriguing quirks.

"Mission accomplished, I presume?" I asked.

Trevor pulled out a handkerchief from his pocket and wiped his wire-framed glasses. "Of course, Ms. Marshall. Would you expect anything less?"

"Not from you, Trevor," I said. "Should we head for the exit? Doug should be waiting to give us a ride."

On cue, Doug had the Prius waiting across the street. After we got into the car and fastened our seatbelts, he revved the engine. "Ready to solve a murder?" he asked mischievously.

Meg smoothed her blonde bob, tucking a few stray strands of hair neatly behind her ears. "Doug, you've come a long way. Not too long ago, you made it a point to stop Kit and me from sleuthing. Now you're driving us directly into the eye of the storm, so to speak."

Doug smiled as he made a left-hand turn onto Constitution Avenue. "I suppose you have a point. History has taught me some important lessons."

"About solving mysteries?" I asked.

"Nope," said Doug. "Much broader than crime solving."

"I'll bite," said Trevor. "What has history taught you that's so revelatory, Professor Hollingsworth?"

"If you can't beat them, join them," said Doug. "For example, the Hessian soldiers who fought with the British during the Revolutionary War. Many of them remained in the United States. When they didn't win the war, they decided to become Americans instead." Doug grinned.

"When you couldn't defeat us, you decided to join the fun?" I asked.

"Better than being left at home," said

Doug as he squeezed my hand. "Besides, I'd rather keep an eye on you in person."

"Now the truth comes out," said Trevor. "But I'll admit it, Hollingsworth. Your devotion is admirable."

Meg leaned forward and stared intently at Trevor. "That's an emotionally sophisticated observation. Especially coming from you."

Trevor fidgeted in his seat as a flush of red covered his cheeks. "I'm not an automaton," he mumbled.

This was a fascinating exchange which I would have liked to pursue under almost any other circumstances. Doug had just pulled up alongside Charlie Palmer's.

"No time to find a parking space," I said.

"I heartily agree," Doug said as he tossed the keys to the valet.

"Do you have a reservation for this evening?" asked the parking attendant.

"Not a typical one," I said. "Stuart is expecting us."

We marched inside the restaurant, and I scanned the bar area for a familiar face. Sure enough, Stuart rounded the corner. If his gig as a restaurant manager didn't pan out, he could always try to compete for an Olympic speed walking medal. He'd be a shoo-in.

Stuart gave me an air hug. "The Maeve

Dixon crowd returns. I hope you're able to put this nasty Van Parker business behind you."

"That's exactly what we're aiming for," I said. "Thanks again for giving us access to your rooftop. We're not certain if our plan is going to work. If it does, it won't take very long to find out."

Stuart crossed his arms. "You know I'm always happy to help the police. After all, we can't run a business where people are getting tossed off the side of the building. We have a ritzy wedding this evening on the rooftop." He lowered his voice and leaned closer to us. "I can't say who our client is, but I'll tell you it has something to do with an important court. And I don't mean the Washington Wizards."

We nodded our heads solemnly. "We certainly don't want to get in the way of the festivities tonight, Stuart," I said. "Is Detective Glass already here?"

"She arrived several minutes ago, and I sent her upstairs. If you follow me, I'll punch the elevator for the top floor," he said.

An enormous white tent occupied a substantial portion of the rooftop. It was decorated elaborately on the exterior, complete with garland and lights. The couple's initials were projected onto the top of the structure. I didn't even want to speculate who they were and how they were related to the "important court" Stuart had referenced earlier.

Meg whistled softly. "Fancy stuff. Mind if we take a look?"

Stuart motioned for us to follow him. Inside the tent was a set of twinkling chandeliers, ornately decorated tables, blush drapery, and a panoply of large flower arrangements. Carefully accented plush carpeting made the temporary structure seem like the interior of a mansion ballroom. At the edge of the tent, a lavish wedding cake rested on a suspended swing.

I pointed to the cake. "Stuart, I've never seen anything like this."

"It's the latest trend," he explained as he gave the swing a tiny push. "All the brides want chandelier cakes these days. It used to be very niche, but now it's mainstream."

Doug whispered, "Not like our wedding, huh?"

"Thankfully not," I said. "A little too fancy for me."

Meg must have overheard our conversation. "A little? That's the understatement of the year."

Trevor seemed unusually interested in the

setup. "Impressive," he remarked. "I imagine my wedding will have a similar footprint."

"Planning on tying the knot anytime soon, Trevor?" I asked. "Who's the lucky lady?"

"No one now," Trevor said quickly. "Of course, that could change in an instant. One never knows when a chance for love will present itself."

If we didn't have a murder to solve, I would have peppered Trevor with more questions. For some reason, he was in a revealing mood. Was Trevor a closet romantic? He'd always seemed like an island unto himself. Maybe the days of Trevor's impenetrable solitude were coming to an end.

"This is lovely," I said. "But we're here to solve a murder."

As if on cue, Detective Glass emerged from the rooftop interior. "I see the gang has arrived," she said.

"We have," I answered. "Even though only Meg and I are necessary for the setup."

Doug spoke up. "You can put Trevor and me wherever you think is best."

"You'll stay inside and out of sight with me. Once everyone is in place on the rooftop, then you'll man both exit points," the Detective said, sighing heavily. "This plot is so far-fetched, I didn't want to call in

336

backup. How would I even explain it? On the other hand, I don't want any of our so-called guests to make a run for it by heading for the elevator or stairs."

She handed me a small digital voice recorder. "We're going to have to do this the old-fashioned way. No time or resources to wire either of you. Press record when they arrive, and you start talking. Don't worry. It will pick up everything that's said."

"Shouldn't we have a code word or something?" asked Meg.

"A code word?" asked Detective Glass.

"You know, if something goes terribly wrong," explained Meg. "To let you know we need backup."

Detective Glass responded slowly. "You do realize I won't be able to hear everything. I'll be inside the building."

Meg blinked rapidly. "Still, I think it would be a good idea."

I rushed to agree with her. I didn't want Meg to have second thoughts about our plan. "How about DIXON?" I asked helpfully.

"Too easy," said Meg. "We might mention our boss's name in conversation, and then it would be confusing. It needs to be an unusual word, but easy enough to drop in conversation."

For several moments, no one spoke. "How about PROSECCO?" asked Trevor. He turned to Meg. "Surely you could figure out how to use that word in almost any conversation."

Meg beamed. "That's perfect. I won't forget it."

I silently mouthed "Thank you" to Trevor. He'd picked the perfect code word for my best pal and subtly put her at ease. I couldn't blame her for the nervousness. It wasn't every day that you returned to the scene of a ghastly homicide to set a trap for the purported perpetrator.

Detective Glass went over the plan with us one last time. I glanced at my phone for a time check. "Showtime," I said.

Doug gave me a kiss on my forehead. "Good luck. Don't take any chances."

I bowed my head. "I know."

Our three observers retreated to the inside room adjacent to the outdoor rooftop area. Trevor glanced back before walking through the door. Was he also anxious about our ruse?

"Ready for this?" I asked Meg.

She checked her makeup and reapplied her lipstick, which was my best friend's equivalent of putting on her game face.

"Definitely."

We heard the elevator ding. Someone had arrived. The party was about to start.

CHAPTER TWENTY-ONE

Meg and I stood on the edge of the large tent to maintain a sightline with Detective Glass, Doug, and Trevor. As we turned toward the building to discover the identity of our first guest, Dash's distinctive voice beat us to the punch.

"Well, well. This is a surprise. I thought this was a private talk about our relationship," he said. "Obviously, I was misinformed."

I hadn't gotten a closeup of Meg's soon-to-be ex-boyfriend at the wake. He certainly put the "Dash" in "dashing." He wore a fitted grey cardigan underneath a stylish black wool blazer. His camel chinos were slim-fitting yet not cringe-worthy. A silky red handkerchief in his right breast pocket completed the look. With his strong jaw, perfect teeth, and wavy black hair, I understood Meg's deep physical attraction to him.

Nonetheless, all I saw was a cold-blooded killer.

"You weren't misinformed. I do want to talk about our relationship," said Meg. "To get a more accurate perspective, I asked Kit and a few others to join the conversation." Meg avoided Dash's direct gaze, but her voice didn't waver.

"Accurate perspective?" asked Dash. He smiled tightly. "How romantic."

"I'm not so sure we'll be talking about rose petals and satin sheets," said Meg.

Dash wrinkled his brow and remained silent. The elevator announced the arrival of another guest. Lauren Parker strode confidently across the rooftop to join us. She was wearing a black dress with three-quarter length sleeves. Her couture showed off the best elements of her figure, including her substantial derriere. If Lauren didn't watch it, her prison nickname might be become Kim Kardashian.

"Now I see what's going on," said Dash. "You're going to accuse me of having an affair with Lauren. I know you saw us at the wake, but you've got it all wrong."

I'd held my tongue for long enough. "You're right about one thing, Dash," I said. "We got it all wrong. But not anymore."

Lauren wagged her finger. "Don't make

assumptions you can't back up. Dash was consoling me. That doesn't mean anything. There's nothing between us."

I glanced at Dash. His chin trembled. "Do you agree with Lauren's characterization of your relationship, Dash?" I asked.

His shoulders slumped, but he said nothing in response.

We were interrupted by a final ding of the elevator. "Don't bother answering my question now," I said. "We might as well wait until our last visitor has arrived."

Max Robinson's mouth fell open when he saw the four of us gathered near the edge of the tent. A detectable tremble in his voice, Max asked, "Where's Trevor?"

"Not going to make it." I casually examined my nails. I really did need a manicure when this ordeal was over.

"I was supposed to meet him here to talk about his sequel. He said he's going to write a book about the unsung heroes of Washington," he stammered. "You know, the little guys."

"Doesn't sound like the Trevor I know," said Meg. "What do you think, Kit?"

"Nope," I said. "Trevor is interested in big fish, not guppies."

Max swallowed hard. "Then why am I here with these two?" He motioned toward

Dash and Lauren.

"A very good question, Max. I'm glad you asked it," I said.

Meg gave me a wary look. *You're enjoying this too much, Kit.*

She was right, of course. I did enjoy seeing the three musketeers squirm, mostly because they deserved it. Hopefully a harsher punishment than my sanctimonious attitude would be administered soon.

"We have good news and bad news," I said.

Lauren put her hand on her hip and played with her long silver bangle necklace. "Stop beating around the bush. Just tell us what you have to share."

"The good news is that we know who killed your husband," said Meg.

Lauren's face twitched. "That's funny. I didn't know you'd left Congress to work for the D.C. police."

"As long as Van's murder remains unsolved, there's a cloud hanging over our boss's reelection campaign. Not to mention that Kit and I are stuck here until the investigation is closed," said Meg. "We should already be in North Carolina."

"That's the good news," I said. "The bad news is we're planning to tell the police

343

about how the three of you killed Van Parker."

I scrutinized Dash. His face remained placid, his jaw set firmly. He didn't scowl, smile, or flinch. So that's how he was going to play it. *Game on.*

On the other hand, Max Robinson looked as though we'd just told him bikes had been banned within the continental United States. His gaze shifted around the room, apparently afraid to make direct eye contact with us.

Lauren Parker rolled her eyes while waving her hand dismissively. "Don't be absurd," she said. "How did you ever reach such a ridiculous conclusion?"

"It had me puzzled for a while," I said. "But then I caught an old movie on television and things started falling into place."

"A movie? That's your evidence?" sneered Lauren.

"Nope, but it pointed me in the right direction," I said. "It was a classic. Can you guess which one?"

By the look on Dash's face, he knew where I was headed. But he kept his mouth shut.

I sighed. "Not a film buff in the crowd today, huh? Well, I guess I'll have to tell you. *Murder on the Orient Express.* The original, by the way. Not the remake."

"I don't read mysteries like this one." Meg pointed in my direction. "Her nose is always in a book. But even I know the plot of Agatha Christie's masterpiece."

"Lauren Bacall, Ingrid Bergman, Sean Connery, Anthony Perkins, Vanessa Redgrave, Albert Finney," I said. "A star-studded cast, yet that's not what caught my attention. Hercule Poirot figures out there's inconsistencies in everyone's stories. No one person could have killed the victim on the Orient Express. So, Poirot determines all the suspects are guilty."

Dash spoke slowly. "No offense, Kit. You're no Hercule Poirot."

I was waiting for that one. *"Exactement!"* I said with my best French accent. "I will never be as clever as Poirot. Unfortunately for all of you, I'm not as virtuous, either. We can get to that later in our discussion."

The corner of Dash's mouth twitched. It wasn't a big reveal. It was the first crack of his otherwise unflappable demeanor.

"Where's the evidence to support this so-called theory?" asked Lauren.

"It actually started with you, Lauren," I said. "Quite frankly, I was perfectly content with accepting Van had committed suicide. Unfortunately, that didn't make a lot of sense, especially when I discovered he was planning to form his own lobbying firm to pave the way for the next generation of trucking. People who kill themselves usually don't have such ambitious plans."

"As the evidence for homicide grew, we assumed the mysterious waiter had killed him and then disappeared," said Meg.

"That's how the movie helped me realize we'd been duped," I said. "Creating the waiter was a perfect foil. It kept the police chasing someone who didn't exist. Not much different than the woman in the scarlet kimono the suspects in the Orient Express invent to baffle and misdirect Poirot."

"This is pure conjecture," said Max. "And it has nothing to do with me."

"I'll get back to you later, Max. But you're right. The evidence didn't begin to mount until I started scrutinizing the details," I said. "The first clue was courtesy of our intern and amateur photographer, Brock. He took a lot of photos for our boss's campaign website the night of the fundraiser, including one with the Washington Monument in the distance. The sun was fading in the background. That didn't mean much to me until I remembered your alibi for Van's death. You said you were taking a

346

photo and then you posted it online. In fact, you rifled through your purse to find the phone you used and showed it to me."

Lauren put her hand on her hip. "That's right. Van was too wasted to take a photo of me. I took one of myself and uploaded it."

"The problem is that in your photo, the sun is still in the corner of the shot. By the time we'd finished dinner, the sun had already set," I explained. "You took that photo earlier than you claimed. Then you posted it online to create an alibi for yourself, probably right before Van was killed."

"What are you? An amateur meteorologist?" she sneered.

"Nope. But I've lived in D.C. long enough to know the sun sets quickly in the fall. It doesn't linger like the summer months. Brock's photos reminded me that something didn't fit with your timeline," I said.

"That doesn't mean squat," said Dash. "People put photos online long after they take them. It's not a crime."

"True," said Meg. "But Lauren claimed otherwise. It points to an inconsistency in her story. Plus, there's more."

"There was a detail I'd noticed on the night of the fundraiser that bugged me," I said. "It didn't dawn on me until we shared that pizza at your condo."

"It wouldn't surprise me if you planned a listening device of some kind inside my place," said Lauren. "I can't believe I invited you into my home."

"Nope," said Meg. "We're not that sophisticated with technology. It's a good idea for a future mystery, though." Meg smiled mischievously. *She's enjoying this as much as me.*

"You were juggling two phones at the cocktail reception," I said. "I remember because I was impressed you didn't spill your glass of wine. It's difficult to handle two phones at once."

"Last time I checked, it's not a crime to have two phones," said Lauren. "It's common in Washington."

"It is," I agreed. "But it's only typical for those who work for the government. We need to keep our federal business separate from our personal or campaign communications. Why would you need two phones as a lobbyist? Wouldn't it confuse clients?"

"In fact, we don't think you own two phones," said Meg. "When we went to your condo that evening, only one phone was charging on your countertop. The other one had mysteriously disappeared."

"It didn't bother me too much until we learned from the police about how Van died," I said. "Detective Glass believes Van was drugged, hit with a stun gun on his midsection, and then thrown over the side of the building. That left me thinking. Where did the stun gun go? The killer didn't throw it over the edge. If someone had done that, surely the police or a bystander would have found it."

"No one had a weapon on the rooftop that we could recall," said Meg. "The police secured the area and searched everyone in a matter of minutes. A stun gun would have been located, even if it was hidden."

"That made me think the culprit left the restaurant that night with the weapon. Naturally, I suspected Max since he'd retrieved his bag from the coatroom. But the timing was impossible. He'd returned to the rooftop after Van had gone over the edge," I said. Dash and Lauren frowned. I took their silence as license to continue my explanation. "That's when I started to think creatively. Maybe the stun gun didn't look like a gun. A few years ago, I read about a TSA agent who discovered a stun gun disguised as a cell phone at National Airport. I went online and sure enough, it wasn't difficult to find what I was looking for. In fact, the latest model looks like an iPhone and delivers an eighty-thousand volt shock."

"That's enough to immobilize someone, but not kill them. Stun guns with a high voltage can penetrate heavy clothing. That means Van would have still felt the shock even though he was wearing a suit jacket," said Meg. "And when the dirty deed was done, Lauren could simply put the so-called phone inside her purse."

"You're saying I zapped my husband and shoved him over the edge?" Lauren's jaw remained set, although I noticed her eyes flitted toward the exit.

"Absolutely not!" I exclaimed. "Van Parker was a big guy. He was at least six feet tall and weighed well over two hundred pounds. Lauren, you're as petite as they come. I bet you wear a size four."

Lauren couldn't resist taking the bait. "Size two, actually."

"Of course, I apologize," I said. "Those of us in the double digits can't really tell the difference. Regardless, my point still stands. Even with Van immobilized by a stun gun, it would have been impossible for Lauren to push Van over the railing. The laws of physics don't lie."

"What are you implying?" Dash assumed a wide stance with his arms crossed. Nothing communicated confrontation better than good, old-fashioned body language. Dash was screaming for a fight.

"That someone bigger than Lauren pushed Van off this roof," I said simply. "And that conclusion led me to you."

"Because I'm closer to Van's size, it means I killed him?" said Dash, his question dripping with daring accusation.

"Not necessarily," I admitted. "For a long time, I didn't have anything to tie you to the crime. It was working out perfectly for you. Meg wanted to protect you, and out of deference for my friend, I backed off."

"It sounds like your word against his," said Max. "This is a waste of time."

"Don't try to pedal away too soon," warned Meg. "We'll get to you later."

Max's face reddened but offered no reply.

"This afternoon, I went to Meg's apartment to pick her up for Van's memorial service. You shouldn't have ditched Meg for Lauren so soon, Dash. That was a big mistake," I said.

"Kit is a great best friend," said Meg. "But she's also damn nosy."

"That's right," I admitted. "I saw the love note you wrote to Meg, which she'd placed on her fridge. I took a photo of it because I couldn't quite figure out what seemed familiar." No need to add that the sappiness of it made me slightly nauseous at the time.

"Are you a handwriting analyst now, too?" Dash shifted his weight from one foot to the other. Our guests were getting restless, and we'd promised Stuart our intervention wouldn't cause any problems for this evening's wedding reception. We needed to move this forward.

"Hardly," I said. "But I doubt you gave a second thought to that note you wrote Meg. I imagine it was just another ploy for you to string her along, ensuring you would secure an invitation to Congresswoman Dixon's big fundraiser."

"Sounds like sour grapes to me," said Lauren. "You're jealous that your best friend has a hunky boyfriend."

Meg tittered. "Kit's married. She's got no interest in Dash or anyone other than her boring professor husband." She grimaced. Clever of her to give Doug a back-handed jab.

"In addition to being nosy, I'm also observant. And I noticed the note you wrote Meg had a little American flag in the corner. Then I remembered where I'd seen it before. Van Parker's supposed suicide note. Lauren showed us a photocopy when we stopped by her condo," I said.

"Kit and I have a theory about what happened. Lauren had planned this murder a while ago. The Dixon fundraiser provided the perfect opportunity when Van decided to attend. She had every detail worked out in her head until she found out that a Capitol Hill amateur sleuth had a motive to figure out what happened to Van," said Meg.

"We think you got nervous when you overheard my conversation with Detective Glass after Van's death," I said. "You told Dash to write a suicide note, which he did using the small pad of paper he kept in his suit jacket. Then you planted it on Van's desk that night before going home."

"I'm sure he's gotten rid of the remaining evidence by now," said Meg. "But he conveniently forgot he'd used it to write that silly love note to me weeks earlier. He certainly didn't know I'd saved it and placed it on my refrigerator." Meg simpered. "When Dash visited my apartment, we never spent any time in the kitchen."

"And don't forget we also have a copy of it on my phone," I added, waving the photo of it in the air. "Not to mention in the cloud, too. Don't even think about trying to steal my device. It won't matter."

Dash glanced at Lauren, whose expression could have frozen Key West in July. She nodded her head slightly in response.

Dash cleared his throat. "What do you want?"

"Ah, the magic words," said Meg. "I thought you'd never ask. Frankly, I didn't want to be used as a doormat in your crazy plot to murder your rival and crush's husband. It's too late for that." There was a bitterness to Meg's voice I hadn't detected before. She was going to need some serious therapy to get over this episode.

Max edged toward the exit. "I think it's time for me to leave," he stammered. "You have business to discuss."

"Don't move another step, Max," Meg barked. "We're running out of time, but that doesn't mean we've forgotten your role in this mess. You drugged Van Parker, and we all know it."

"I did no such thing." Max's eyes blinked rapidly. This guy couldn't bluff his way out of a card game with preschoolers.

"Yes, you did," I said coolly. "We have the photographic evidence to prove it. We just don't have time right now to get into the details."

"Evidence?" Max took such a big gulp, I'm surprised he didn't choke.

"Holding that wineglass, dropping a pill into it, and handing it to Van. Pretty obvious, especially for someone who professed not to drink alcohol," said Meg.

"I might have gotten Van a drink from the bar," stammered Max. "That doesn't prove anything."

"It's a thin excuse, Max. Why would you get Van a drink? You detested him. More importantly, when we were at dog agility training, you mentioned Xanax to me. How did you know Van had taken Xanax?" I asked.

"I must have heard it from the Detective," he said, in a meek voice. "Or a lucky guess?"

"Wrong answer!" exclaimed Meg. "No wonder Van was never impressed. You can't keep details straight if your life depended on it. Detective Glass never mentioned *which* drug was in Van's system. But you'd know that detail because you were the one who gave it to him."

Max said nothing, but he stopped moving toward the door. We had his attention. He wasn't going anywhere.

"Getting back to Dash's question," I said. "Before we were interrupted, I believe your ex-boyfriend asked what we wanted."

Meg rubbed her chin and drummed her fingers across the side of her face. "Perhaps an all-expenses paid trip to Paris? First class, of course."

We'd had no time to rehearse the details of this conversation. Give Meg a stage and she had no problem finding the spotlight.

"I don't think so," I said slowly. "I prefer Paris in the springtime. Instead, I think regular cash payments might work better."

"There's three of you who will require our silence. Payments alternating every third month of an amount under the ten-thousand-dollar limit that requires IRS reporting," said Meg. "After all, we wouldn't want to be greedy."

I nodded in agreement. "If the payments keep coming, we won't tell the police about everything we put together. But if you decide to stop paying, just be aware we have Detective Glass on speed dial." I paused for a beat. "Locard's principle is on our side."

"What are you babbling about?" asked Lauren, her face tightening.

"Dr. Edmond Locard, a famous forensic scientist. He determined that every contact leaves a trace. When a crime is committed, the perpetrator cannot help but transmit physical evidence. He or she will always leave something behind."

"The police have no such evidence," said Dash, the smugness oozing from his voice. "If they did, we'd know about it."

"It's only a matter of concentrating the

search in the right place. Perhaps the transfer of minute skin cell fragments onto Van's jacket when you pushed him over the railing," I said. "If we go to the police with what we have, it will give them cause to investigate until they find something. Detective Glass is like a pit bull. She won't let go until she discovers the physical evidence to substantiate the crime."

Dash and Lauren exchanged glances but said nothing. Dash stared at his feet, and Lauren's complexion grew pale.

Meg filled the silence. "By the way, don't get any funny ideas. We'll have the entire story drafted for the *Washington Post* in case anything happens to either of us. Or both of us."

I'd almost forgotten we weren't *really* conning the three of them out of a small fortune. I thrust my shoulders back with brazen confidence. "What do you think? Do we have a deal? It's a small price to guarantee that you'll continue to get away with murder."

"That's going to be a difficult arrangement to sustain," said Dash. "How long is this going to last?"

Meg answered before I could. "We'll revisit it on a yearly basis. But there's no statute of limitations on homicide. Our silence will be equally as valuable a decade from now as it is today."

Dash shook his head. "I'm afraid that's unacceptable. Lauren and I," he paused briefly. "Assuming she'll have me, of course." He smiled an unctuous grin that made my stomach turn. "We need to move forward in our lives, and that requires resources. We can't be burdened by blackmail."

"You don't have a choice," said Meg, her hands planted firmly on her hips. "Unless you want to go to prison for a very long time."

"Oh, that's not going to happen, darling." His arrogant laugh filled the air as he stepped closer to us. "You see, there's a flaw in your plan."

I took several short breaths. Detective Glass, Doug, and Trevor couldn't hear our conversation. But they could observe body language. Was it me or had our talk taken a menacing turn? If it had, Meg didn't seem to notice, or perhaps she didn't care. There was a gleam in her eye and a playful grin on her face.

"Really? Care to enlighten me?" asked Meg.

"I suppose I will, since you've not been so quick on the uptake otherwise. You may have some scheme to include a missive to the newspapers if something were to happen to you or Capitol Hill's Sherlock Holmes." He jerked a finger in my direction. Was it wrong that I was flattered someone thought of me as Capitol Hill's Sherlock Holmes? Elated, I straightened my posture and stuck my chin out.

"We sure do," said Meg. "We have plenty of contacts in the media. Don't underestimate us."

"I'm sure you know a litany of Hill flacks who would gladly do your bidding. I seriously doubt you had any time to set up a comprehensive arrangement before this evening's meeting," said Dash.

Meg hesitated. "That's not true," she stammered.

"Liar," said Lauren with a scowl on her face. "After all, it takes one to know one."

We were losing control of the situation. Using my most assertive voice, I said, "We most certainly have come up with a backup plan. Believe me, you don't want to test it."

Dash shook his head. "You must think we're dolts. Only a few minutes ago, you admitted to figuring everything out a few hours earlier. There wasn't any time for copying evidence and stashing it somewhere for the next Bob Woodward to find it."

The next ten seconds were a blur. Lauren reached into her purse and pulled out a phone. Only I strongly suspected it wasn't actually a phone. It was her trusty stun gun, which had zapped Van before Dash tossed him over the railing.

I was reasonably confident I could take Lauren down with a strong roundhouse kick. But then she surprised me and passed the stunner to Dash. My heart sank. There was no way I could tackle him.

Dash decided to go for Meg first, either because he'd grown to hate his ex-lover or because her willowy stature made her an easy target. He thrust the gun in her direction, pressing the button to emit a frightening buzzing noise and an impressive lightning bolt of electricity. Meg eluded him, moving closer to the tent. I desperately looked toward the rooftop exit. The door opened, and I spotted the shiny reflection of Detective Glass's pistol.

But Dash didn't see Glass or anyone else. He was focused on Meg, who was now standing directly in front of the swing holding the wedding cake.

"Meg, be careful!" I screamed. "PROSECCO! We have a PROSECCO situation here!"

My words fell on deaf ears because Meg

knew exactly what she was doing. She waited until Dash made a final lunge to zap her. After he did, she promptly stepped aside. Instead of Dash connecting with his intended target, he stumbled and landed face first on top of the swing. Unfortunately, our villain did claim another innocent victim that day, namely a pricey wedding cake. But at least it wasn't my best friend.

CHAPTER TWENTY-TWO

Several hours later, we sat downstairs at a beautifully adorned table inside Charlie Palmer's picturesque dining room. Our waiter popped open a bottle of Cristal. After pouring several glasses, he handed Doug the bottle, which my husband examined closely.

"Tsar Alexander II of Russia asked the winemaker, Louis Roederer, to reserve the best house wine for him each year. To distinguish the wine from the others, Roederer used clear, flat-bottomed lead crystal bottles. Hence the name," he said.

Meg took a long sip. "Nice story. But what really matters is how it tastes." She smacked her lips in approval.

I expected a witty quip from Trevor, deriding her capricious comment. Instead, he laughed. "I'm afraid I have to side with Meg on this one."

"Wonders never cease!" Raising my glass,

I offered a brief toast. "To solving the K Street killing."

"I'll definitely drink to that," said a familiar voice from behind us. We turned around as our favorite political fundraiser approached the table.

"Clarissa!" I exclaimed. "Please join us."

She motioned for the waiter to add a chair from an empty table. "Thank you. Of course, Stuart texted me with the news."

"Which news?" asked Doug. "Catching the killers or destroying a wedding cake in the process?"

"Both, of course." Clarissa leaned in closer and lowered her voice. "Apparently the bride was FUR-I-OUS." She drew out each syllable. "But then Detective Glass chatted with her and explained the situation. You know, appealed to her civic sense. She calmed down and listened to reason."

"Really? That was awfully nice of her," said Meg. "After all, Dash ended up wearing more of her wedding cake than was edible."

"Well, it wasn't only her goodwill. Stuart made a speedy phone call to Georgetown Cupcake. You know, the famous bakery from that popular cable TV show. Given the situation, the owner agreed to make an emergency delivery. Everyone at the wedding will indulge in red velvet or chocolate ganache treats tonight," Clarissa said. "Believe me, those cupcakes are better than a run-of-the-mill wedding cake."

"I'm glad everything wasn't ruined," I said. "Even with the unfortunate accident, we still managed to catch the responsible culprits."

After Dash extricated himself from the mountain of buttercream frosting, our trusty accomplices arrived at the scene. Detective Glass slapped handcuffs on Dash and Lauren and ordered Max to stay put. Just to make sure no one tried to make a break for it, Meg held the stun gun at attention until the cavalry arrived.

After the police took our statements, we were ready to leave. Stuart intercepted us and offered the prime table downstairs for a *gratis* dinner. The restaurant had been under a cloud of suspicion after Van's death, and now Stuart could claim he'd helped apprehend the guilty party. Free publicity is always the best publicity.

Trevor lifted his champagne flute and pointed it toward me. "I rarely bestow compliments, as you know." He paused for a moment. "But Kit, I have to hand this one to you. How did you figure it out?"

"It was a series of circumstantial clues. It

dawned on me that a single person couldn't have killed Van Parker. From the beginning, I was pretty sure Lauren was mixed up in it. She had a good motive, after all. Her affair with Chairman Edwards implied she might want out of the marriage, but divorce would have been a nightmare. She might have lost a good chunk of money. How could have she pushed Van over the railing? There was no possible way she could have done it alone. She didn't have the strength to do it, even if Van had been stunned."

Meg shook her head. "I know I stuck up for Dash and that might have caused you to overlook him initially." She stared into her wineglass. "I don't have the best track record with men."

I put my hand over hers. "Don't beat yourself up over it."

She smiled and helped herself to an oyster on the half shell. "I won't," she said with more resolve than I expected.

"What clue was the nail in the coffin?" asked Doug.

"I had a well-formed hunch before Van's memorial service," I admitted. "Especially when I saw the note on Meg's refrigerator and I remembered where I saw it before. I thought Dash was shady, yet without a motive, it didn't make any sense. Van Parker was his competitor and more successful, but that's hardly a reason to kill someone."

"Then his motive became all too apparent," said Trevor.

"Exactly," I said. "Clarissa had mentioned something about Dash having a crush on Lauren. I didn't pay much attention to it at the time. It didn't seem to make sense. When Meg saw Dash and Lauren together, I realized Dash might have used Meg as a way to set Van up."

Meg's face grew red. "You think I was part of the plot?"

"I'm afraid so. Dash had to find a member of Congress who would host a lot of fundraisers. So that meant someone who was in a particularly close race. He also needed to find a staffer who was single and a good match," I said. "You fit the bill perfectly. After that, it was only a matter of time before he could invite himself to a Dixon fundraiser which Van was also attending. Then Lauren used her ties with Clarissa to get added to the list, too."

"A tangled web we weave when we practice to deceive," said Doug.

"I think this plot had been in the works for a while," I said.

"Wasn't Dash looking for a replacement glass of wine when I was in the bathroom?"

asked Meg.

"That bugged me," I said. "Then I remembered you remarked the wine Dash handed you tasted funny. I mentioned it to Clarissa because I didn't want the Dixon campaign charged for bad wine. She insisted there were no complaints from any other attendees at the dinner. It wasn't until Van's wake that I figured it out. Dash had taken two partially filled red wineglasses from our dinner table and poured them together, so you'd have a drink. It gave him an alibi for the minutes you were in the restroom cleaning up. Plenty of time to push Van over and then have a cocktail ready for you. Who knows what he mixed together? Something that didn't taste very good as a blend."

Trevor muttered, "Probably a Pinot Noir and a Merlot." He shuddered in distaste.

Meg's eyes widened. "I bet he made me spill that wine on purpose."

"Of course," said Trevor. "It was a clever diversion to get you off the rooftop, so he would be alone with Van and Lauren."

"Just like our supposed waiter who raced down the stairs," I said. "Lauren and Dash both claimed to spot him. At first, the fact that their stories corroborated each other gave it credibility. That's where the movie was helpful."

"The Orient Express?" asked Doug.

"Absolutely. In the story, Poirot is thrown off by the fact that several suspects saw a mysterious woman in a red kimono on the train," I explained. "It leads him to believe that someone wore a disguise while committing the murder. It turns out to be nothing other than a diversion."

Trevor rubbed his chin. "As I recall, it sent the good detective on a bit of a wild goose chase until he was able to spot the ruse."

"Absolutely. Lauren and Dash created an old fashioned red herring," I said. "The description of our waiter was both vague and plausible. Remember that Lauren remarked he was a big guy. She included that detail, so we'd think our mystery man could have pushed Van off the roof. I started to doubt the story when Clarissa and Stuart couldn't corroborate it."

Our dinner entrees arrived, and we dove in. Trevor waved his fork. "This is probably the last decent meal you'll have for six weeks. Campaigns aren't known for fine cuisine."

"We'll head to North Carolina on Monday," I said. "Hopefully we're not too late to salvage our boss's race."

"At least you prevented Van's murder from ruining Maeve's chances," said Clarissa. "She would have been a goner if Coach Hackensack successfully tied her to an unexplained death."

"What about that threatening note that you found on your car after having lunch at the Monocle?" asked Doug.

"Quite frankly, I thought Clarissa might have excused herself from lunch and put it on my car. But then she confessed she was having a private moment with Stuart when Van was killed," I explained. "I realized Clarissa had a legitimate alibi for the murder. My guess is that Dash got nervous after Trevor and I paid him a visit. He couldn't have followed me because he had an imminent appointment with Detective Glass. He could have looked out the window, identified my car, and told Lauren where to go. I'd mentioned I was having lunch at the Monocle."

"I have one last question about the murder," said Trevor. "What about Max Robinson?"

I sighed as I put down my fork filled with salmon and crabmeat. "I'm not entirely sure about Max's role, but I suspect he knew Lauren and Van were up to no good."

"He was responsible for drugging Van earlier in the evening, right?" asked Meg.

I nodded in between bites. "Dash and

369

Lauren stayed away from Van during the cocktail reception. I think Lauren persuaded Max to drop a Xanax in Van's glass of wine, which she provided to him. Remember, Van already had a prescription."

"Do you think Max knew what Lauren and Dash had planned?" asked Doug.

"I'm not sure," I said slowly. "Max seemed clueless. Meg mentioned she never asked him for a fact sheet about building bike lanes in the Congresswoman's district. That made me think Max knew what was going to happen and decided to leave the rooftop so he'd have a solid alibi. Retrieving his briefcase was a good excuse."

"Why would Max agree to slip something into Van's drink at a fundraiser?" asked Clarissa.

"He hated Van Parker because he refused to give him a job. Van bad-mouthed him all over town, which might have hurt his chances for other positions. Lauren knew about Max's history with Van. She exploited it, probably by convincing Max if he did it, Van would embarrass himself at the event," I said. "I also think Lauren and Dash planned to pin Van's death on Max if the suicide explanation didn't hold."

"Lauren and Dash really wanted to get

rid of Van to weave such a crazy plot," said Doug.

"Undoubtedly. Lauren wanted out of her marriage and led Dash along the primrose path. He believed they'd be together after the dust settled. Quite frankly, I doubt it. I'm inclined to believe Lauren used Dash for the murder, but didn't intend to stay with him," I said.

Meg slumped in her chair. "I'm going to take a break from dating for a while."

I suppressed a gasp. Meg had been through her share of ups and downs with men. But she'd never foresworn them altogether.

Doug narrowed his eyes. "Isn't that a little extreme?"

Meg raised her chin and threw her shoulders back. "Maybe it is. I don't care. It's time for a change."

I stared at my best friend. For as long as I've known her, Meg had always had a guy on her arm or a plan to reel in her next victim. Her good looks and success made it easy for her to find romantic companionship. Meg renouncing men was like Garfield swearing off lasagna. It just didn't seem possible.

With an amused look on his face, Trevor said, "You'll be too busy in North Carolina to worry about dating."

"Absolutely. Murder solved. Now onto more important matters, like getting our boss reelected to Congress," said Meg. In acknowledgement, we raised our glasses and drained the last sips. I couldn't help but repeat the lyrics from an old Doors song my parents liked to play in the background: *The future's uncertain, and the end is always near.*

Meg was turning over a new leaf. Doug had an exciting job offer in New York. Was our time together in Washington coming to an end? As usual, I had more questions than answers. But this time, there were no clues to uncover or killers to catch. Even the best sleuth can't provide a tidy solution to every conundrum. Some problems simply need to resolve themselves.

CHAPTER TWENTY-THREE

Nothing was objectively mind-blowing about the décor of a big chain hotel ballroom in coastal North Carolina. Nonetheless, the scene unfolding before my eyes may have been the loveliest thing I'd seen in months.

Red, white, and blue streamers fluttered from the light wind of the air conditioner, still required during a seventy-degree day in early November. The makeshift stage in the rear of the ballroom was littered with balloons and confetti. Maeve Dixon slowly navigated her way across the dais, careful not to ruin her big moment by tripping over a stray decoration.

A military veteran, my boss always appeared as neat as a pin. But tonight, she glowed in the spotlight. She grabbed the microphone out of its stand and yelled, "Thank you, North Carolina!" One thing was certain. Maeve Dixon was returning to

Congress for another term. I wasn't quite sure if I'd join her.

Meg threw her arms around me and hugged tightly. "Congratulations, Kit. You did it!"

"Correction. *We did it.*" I smiled at my best friend, who sported a "Dixon for Congress" T-shirt, a pair of skinny Levis, tennis shoes, and minimal makeup. Meg's attire reflected her new approach to life for the past six weeks: more relaxed, less focused on the opposite sex, and amazingly enough, not as obsessed with her looks or appearance.

Our trusty intern Brock approached. "Photo for the campaign website?"

"Absolutely," we both said at the same time. We grinned, and he snapped away.

"Thanks again for your hard work," I said. "Without your photos at the fundraiser, I'm not sure there would have been a Maeve Dixon campaign."

Brock tipped his baseball hat. "After I finish law school in three years, you can hire me as a staffer for Representative Dixon."

I shook Brock's hand. "I'm glad you learned something during your stay in Washington."

My gaze shifted across the crowded room. I elbowed Meg. "Is that Trevor? Why did he come to North Carolina?"

Meg shrugged. "I don't know. He e-mailed me a few days ago and asked if he could come to the victory party. I told him if he was sure Dixon was going to win, he should make the trip."

"Let's find out why he's here," I said as I tugged Meg in his direction. I might have gotten in my fair share of scrapes, but "Trevor" was typically synonymous with "trouble" as far as I was concerned.

"Trevor, I'm surprised you're here." Subtlety wasn't one of my virtues.

"Nice to see you, too, Ms. Marshall." Trevor popped a fried mushroom into his mouth. Even winning campaigns didn't spring for fancy refreshments.

Meg tilted her head. "Aren't you supposed to be headed out on a book tour?"

Trevor chuckled. "Despite your ditzy demeanor, you have a very good memory."

"That's right," I said. "Why aren't you visiting every bicoastal bookstore known to mankind?"

"Unfortunately, election fatigue has proven problematic," said Trevor. "There's less enthusiasm for my book than antici-pated. Consequently, the book tour has been canceled."

Meg's face softened. "I'm sorry, Trevor. I

know you worked hard on it." Meg's compassion threw me for a loop. Maybe her transformation went deeper than changes in wardrobe and cosmetics.

Trevor slumped a bit. "It's a tad disappointing," he admitted. Then his expression brightened considerably. "I have good news to share, though."

"Go ahead, we're all ears," I said.

"I've decided to accept a senior advisor position with the Chief Administrative Officer in the House of Representatives," he said. "We're going to be congressional colleagues again!"

Meg and I were speechless for several seconds. Finally, I managed to speak. "What a surprise, Trevor. That will really be . . ." I searched for the right word.

"A new challenge?" said Meg.

"Yes, it certainly will be," said Trevor. "Every Capitol Hill insider knows the CAO runs the show in the House. Technology, finances, contracting, human resources. I'll have my hand in all operations."

"We look forward to working with you," said Meg. "Well, at least I will."

"I almost forgot. Kit, you might be moving to New York. When will you know?" asked Trevor.

As if on cue, the front door opened, and

Doug entered, followed by a leashed Clarence. "Excuse me," I said. "Gotta go!"

I broke into a trot across the ballroom. Doug grinned and waved. When Clarence caught sight of me, his tail wagged furiously, and he issued several excited barks.

"Surprise!" said Doug. He gave me a big kiss. "And congratulations, of course."

"I thought you weren't coming to pick me up until tomorrow," I stammered.

"That was the plan. Then I woke up this morning and had a good feeling about the election today. I figured I'd drive down a day early and join the celebration. Besides, Clarence missed you." He winked.

I kneeled close to the ground, so Clarence could give me a few licks on the cheek. He sat down politely and offered me his paw. That was Clarence-speak for "give me a treat."

I motioned toward the table of appetizers lining the wall. "I think there's some pepperoni on a platter over there. I'll get him a snack." Clarence's history with pepperoni was legendary, and it was better to share a few slices rather than leaving him to his own devilish machinations. I started to walk in the direction of the food.

Doug gently grabbed my arm and pulled me back. "Wait a second. I'd like to talk to you." My husband straightened his glasses.

"What's wrong?" I asked automatically.

"Kit, you always think there's something amiss," he said, chuckling. "I have to admit, you're mostly right."

"I'm always anxious," I mumbled, glancing at my feet.

He lifted my chin, so he could look in my eyes. "You are. Your level of concern is what makes you good at your job." Then he added, "Both jobs. Congress and sleuthing."

I smiled. "Job security for a worrywart, I guess."

Doug grabbed both of my hands. "I've been doing a lot of thinking since you've been away, about relocating."

"I promised we'd discuss it after the election, and we will. Can it wait until tomorrow?" Was it too self-centered to ask Doug to wait a few more hours? I wanted to relish Dixon's win, especially if it was my last political victory before moving to the Big Apple.

"I know you want to join your friends and boss. This won't take long," said Doug.

I nodded. Had he already found us an apartment in New York? Or perhaps he'd negotiated a job for me at the university.

"Go ahead." I braced myself for his news.

"I turned down the job at Columbia."

Still holding his hands, I blinked rapidly. Had I heard him correctly? "You did what?"

Doug smiled. "You heard what I said, Kit."

"Why did you do it without talking to me?" I asked.

"It would have been prestigious to be an Ivy League professor. It's glamorous, and there's a lot of resources at Columbia for my work. It's pretty much the same gig that I have in Washington. Moving would mean you'd have to give up your job." He squeezed my hands tighter. "And you're great at what you do."

For once, I was at a loss for words.

Doug continued, "To be totally honest, I'm bored at work these days. The routine is getting to me, but I solved that problem."

Clarence gave a low growl. He'd heard the word "pepperoni" a few minutes ago, and his patience was waning.

"What do you mean?" I asked.

He let go of my hands and held his arms out widely. "Give a big hug to the newest American history senior fellow at the Library of Congress!"

For the second time, I was speechless. Instead, I fell into Doug's arms. Clarence, never to be left out, joined our group hug.

"That's right across the street from where I work," I sputtered.

Doug ran his fingers through his thick hair. "You got it. Ready or not, I'm coming to Capitol Hill. When the next murderous adventure happens, I'll be right there."

I planted a big kiss on Doug's lips. Elated with the day's events and the prospect of returning to Congress, I didn't pay attention to the foresight of his words. I should have.

ABOUT THE AUTHOR

Colleen J. Shogan has been a fan of mysteries since the age of six. A political scientist by training, Colleen is a senior executive at the Library of Congress and teaches American politics at Georgetown University. A proud member of Sisters in Crime, Colleen won a Next Generation Indie Award for her first novel, *Stabbing in the Senate.* She lives in Arlington, Virginia, with her husband Rob Raffety and their beagle mutt, Conan.